His Mistress's Voice

Also by G. C. Scott
available from Carroll & Graf:

The Passive Voice

His Mistress's Voice

G. C. SCOTT

CARROLL & GRAF PUBLISHERS, INC.
NEW YORK

Carroll & Graf Publishers, Inc.
260 Fifth Avenue
New York, NY 10001

ISBN 1-56865-366-2

Manufactured in the United States of America

Chapter One

Luckily, there are many sorts of virginity to lose, so one can enjoy the sense of loss more than once. On the Saturday when Tom saw Beth for the first time he didn't know he was going to enjoy the loss once more. He thought he was only doing what he had done many times before. Nothing more to learn; nothing more to lose. It was a Saturday in September. Autumn had set in. The cool days were perceptibly shorter, the evenings drawing in. Tom saw the woman with the red hair before she saw him. Autumn was Tom's favourite season. The clear crisp air and the high blue skies that seem to occur more often in that season (though that may be an illusion) made him feel as if he could accomplish seven impossible things before breakfast. So when he saw her he knew she was going to be his next lover.

She didn't know that yet, of course. It was his task to let her know of their mutual good fortune. Not that he thought of himself as God's gift. It was just that there seemed to be a certain inevitability in catching sight of her through the shifting crowds. They parted, and there she was, her red hair appearing to crown her with the clear fire of the day. He felt an inner lurch when he saw this glorious creature – or so he told her later. She joked that it was lust at first sight.

1

Beth (for that was her name, as he learned later) didn't notice him staring at her. She was standing beside a stall that sold second-hand jewellery, waiting for the stall holder to finish with another customer and come to her. She held an enamelled butterfly, set with iridescent stones that caught fire in the sunlight. He thought the brooch a good choice, complementing her own vividness. He moved closer, wanting to speak but not knowing how to begin. One of the signs of our separateness is the inability to approach a stranger and open a conversation. 'Do you come here often?' was all he could think of. That was much too banal, inviting a monosyllabic reply and a quick escape.

The man behind the counter was almost finished with the other customer. Soon he would turn to serve her. On impulse Tom said softly, 'I think it's a lovely piece, but you shouldn't pay the first price he asks. You're supposed to bargain at markets like this.'

Not softly enough. The stall holder heard him and gave them both a malevolent glance. Tom welcomed the look. It made them conspirators against him. She looked at this stranger with a puzzled frown. 'Bargain? But there's already a price tag on it.' Then she brightened. 'Of course, darling. But you're so much better at it. I remember how you got the man to sell us the leather handbag in Greece. But I feel so foolish when I do it. Could you . . .?'

Surprised by the success of the opening, Tom nevertheless recovered quickly. He took the pin from her and examined it more closely. The price tag said twelve pounds. He did a swift calculation and offered eight. The stall holder countered with ten, proving that he was open to haggling. They settled on nine. Tom handed the pin to her and, moving swiftly, paid

2

the man. As they turned away she made a move to open her purse. Before she could get the money out to repay him he said, 'Please don't. Let it be a gift from a recent admirer. Besides, the pin is *you*.' It was the best compliment he could come up with at short notice.

She reached a decision of her own. 'All right, but only if you'll let me buy lunch. Pick a place nearby and let it be my treat.'

This is turning out to be my lucky day, Tom thought as they set out in search of a watering hole. Over lunch they introduced themselves and exchanged brief biographies. Tom noticed that Beth didn't waste time explaining that she didn't make a habit of being picked up by strangers, as so many other women would have done. He liked her ready acceptance of the situation and her willingness to let things develop from there. They both laughed over the way they had fallen into their roles at the market. Sometime during the lunch they made the decision to adjourn to Beth's place. There was no sense of forcing things on his part, nor of reluctance on hers. Their rapport made the next step seem inevitable.

They took the bus to Beth's place, and the easy mood of fun stayed with them for the ride. She lived in a block of flats, but on the ground floor at the front of the building. She had a good view of the street and the flow of traffic and pedestrians. As the door closed behind them, before Tom even had a chance to look around and remark on the decoration, Beth turned up her lips to be kissed. They reached the bedroom by something akin to teleportation. He couldn't remember walking there. One moment they were in the front hall; the next they were in her bedroom and she was adjusting the blinds to darken the room.

'Take off your clothes and lie down on the bed,' she told him.

Tom kicked off his shoes and got out of his jeans and shirt. As he stood in his underpants to hang his clothes over a chair, he noticed that she was still fully dressed. She gestured once again for him to lie down. When he did, she sang 'Let Me Entertain You' in a mocking tone. Her voice was untrained but quite good. She smiled when she saw that his cock was standing up to attention.

Beth began to undulate slowly to the rhythm of her song, smiling into his eyes as she slipped out of her dress. She let it trail from one hand as she did a slow pirouette for his benefit. Like many men, Tom fantasised about women in red or black lace underwear. Beth's was dark blue: a lacy push-up bra that presented her full breasts to the world and let him see her nipples through the sheer fabric; matching half-slip and pants; stockings and suspenders. He saw all this as she did a slow striptease, moving from shadow into the bars of light that came through the blinds. She seemed to leap out of the gloom with a fiery suddenness before disappearing again into the darkness. The play of light and shade on her body made her more mysterious and elusive. He could smell her fragrance whenever she came close to the bed.

She twisted her arms behind her in that way men have never learned, and unsnapped her bra. As it fell to the floor she cupped her breasts, holding them up for him to see. She stroked and pinched the nipples until they stood out stiffly. Tom's excitement grew as the dance went on. His cock felt big enough to burst. Beth came closer and dangled her breasts near his mouth. Tom reached up to pull her down alongside him, but she eluded him and stepped back.

4

'There's no hurry,' she admonished him. 'Relax and enjoy the show.' Whenever she stirred, a waft of her perfume enveloped his head in a cloud of delicious scent. Tom's senses swam dizzily. Beth knelt suddenly beside the bed and drew his face to her breasts, inviting him to lick and nuzzle them. No second invitation was needed, and she sighed with pleasure as his lips and tongue circled her nipples, his teeth nipping gently at the taut flesh. She swayed forward to offer herself to him. His hands rose to join his busy mouth. It seemed that Beth was about to lose control, but she drew back once more, pushing his hands away. She stood up and made a small *moue* of annoyance.

'I told you there's no hurry. Lie still.' She moved to her jewellery box on the bureau and picked out a pair of handcuffs. She came back to the bed and told Tom, 'Put your hands through the bars of the headboard above your head.' She looked both stern and mocking at once. Although surprised, Tom did as she directed. Beth drew his hands together and locked the handcuffs onto his wrists.

'We can get on with things now,' she remarked as she stepped back to admire the effect and to be admired in her turn. 'You may look as much as you like, but you can't touch just yet.' Once more that mocking tone.

Beth sat down on the bench before her vanity mirror. From where he lay Tom could see both a front and a rear view of this strange and disturbing woman he had picked up on impulse. He thought that maybe the pick-up had been the other way round. A new experience for him. Usually it was he who had to make the approach, and he found the role reversal strangely exciting.

5

Beth stretched like a cat, arching her back and lifting her breasts invitingly. Tom felt an accompanying rise in his cock as he looked at the woman who was just out of reach. Beth smiled when she saw his reaction, as if she enjoyed being responsible for his arousal. When she crossed her legs, Tom heard the sibilant whisper of nylon against nylon. Beth seemed to be settling herself comfortably, and Tom wondered how long he'd have to wait. Or if she intended to consummate the encounter at all. And when did she intend to let him go? He thought briefly of what he would do when she let him go if she had only teased him for hours. And the idea of hour-long teasing by this remarkable woman was exciting in itself.

Beth toyed with her nipples and he watched as she made them harden again. 'Like what you see?'

'Come here,' he said.

She shook her head, no. 'Watch and enjoy.' Beth slipped her pants slowly down her legs and kicked them aside. She turned to face Tom on the bed and spread her legs for him to admire. Her pubic hair was a darker shade than he'd expected. It was thick and curly but didn't conceal her labia, which showed as a slash of delicate pink between her thighs. She used her fingers to spread her lips and Tom caught a glimpse of the clitoris. He felt his cock harden again.

Beth noticed too. 'I see I've got your attention,' she remarked. She stood up and strode about the room, turning so that he could see her from all angles. At one point she turned her back to him and spread her legs. Then she bent over and grasped her ankles. Her long hair swept the floor and he could see a tiny twist of dark curly hair where her long legs divided. Her upside-down smile was wide. She seemed to be enjoying his reaction and his helplessness.

Beth straightened up and made a move to come over to the bed, but at that moment the telephone rang. She left the room to answer it, and Tom heard her speaking to someone about repairs to her car: 'Today? You think you can begin today?' There was a touch of annoyance in her voice when she said this. 'But you told me you couldn't possibly do the work until tomorrow.' There was a pause, and she continued, 'Well, I'll have to get it down to you then. I can't wait until next week.' She put the phone down and came back into the bedroom. She bent over Tom and offered her breasts to him. He resumed work on them with his lips, tongue and teeth and was gratified to see her prompt response. The nipples grew taut and the areolae crinkled as he worked on them. Beth's hands shook slightly in excitement as she cupped herself for him, and her breath grew shallow and rapid. She closed her eyes as he aroused her.

Abruptly she shifted onto the bed, kneeling astride him with her face poised above his erection. She spread her thighs on either side of his head and lowered herself until his mouth met her cunt. When she felt his tongue on her sex she leaned forward to take him into her mouth. She ran her tongue around the head of his cock and he stiffened in pleasure. His tongue found her clitoris and he licked eagerly away at it, now and then nipping it gently between his teeth as it became engorged. She bit back a groan as he worked over her cunt. Apparently she was holding back so as not to find her release too soon. She applied herself to his cock as he applied himself to pleasuring her. It may have been her way of taking her mind off what was happening between her own legs, but she was only capable of so much resistance. He could feel her warmth, and there was no hiding how wet she had become.

There was another abrupt shift and Tom felt the cold air on his cock as she turned around to position herself over it. She took it in her hand and guided him into herself, and the renewal of warmth around that most sensitive part of himself almost made him lose control. It required all his will to tear his thoughts away from the warm slickness that engulfed him. He thought of going to work, taking a walk – anything but what was uppermost in his mind. But try as he might, Tom was only too aware of the handcuffs and the musky smell of the body that was moving to its own rhythm atop him. Beth was now grinding her breasts against his chest, and her hips were describing a tight circle as she swooped and dived on the spike of flesh embedded in her. With a strangled cry Beth came. Tom felt her clamp down on him. He clamped down on himself just in time. He wanted to give her as many orgasms as he could before he reached the point of no return himself. The smooth brushing of her nylon-sheathed thighs against his flanks didn't help his self-control.

One of his – indeed many men's – fantasies involved making wild abandoned love to a beautiful woman in stockings and suspenders, and this was exactly what he was doing. Ordinarily he would have been using his hands to caress those legs and savour the feel of the smooth nylon beneath his fingers. That Beth had handcuffed him so that he couldn't touch her made him even more aware of her erotic appeal. He wanted to reach up and touch everything – every part of her. This was the first time he had been unable to touch his partner, and that made him want to touch her all the more. Was Beth aware of the effect she had created by making him her prisoner? He didn't know then, but later, when they had become lovers, she told him she had used the handcuffs quite deliberately to tantalise him with her body.

She shifted once more above him, stretching her legs down along his so that their whole length of nylon-sheathed flesh was rubbing on him as she came again. She groaned deep in her throat and squeezed her legs together convulsively around him. She slid her arms around his neck and pulled him fiercely against her as she came again and again. Tom lost count of her orgasms. When he could hold himself no longer he lost all interest in counting. Beth rode him as he spent himself inside her. His growl and her groan of completion blended nicely. Beth lay atop him for a long time, the sweat drying on their bodies as their breathing slowed. Eventually she stood up and he could see the dark patches where the sweat had soaked through her sheer blue stockings. She looked almost indecently sated as she stared down at him in sleepy contentment. 'Don't you think there's something deliciously decadent about making love in the afternoon?' she asked.

The question didn't seem to require an answer. Once again he felt the urge to stroke her and rouse her to her earlier passion but the handcuffs ensured that he was still playing by her rules.

She went to fetch a towel from the bathroom and came back drying herself in all of the places he wanted to touch himself. Beth seemed to be well aware of his desire. She took her time, letting him see all of her as she dried her legs and her crotch. The smell of her still filled his nostrils. She turned around so that she faced him fully and stretched her arms above her head, lifting her magnificent breasts with the nipples looking all crushed and flat after their lovemaking. Her eyes were half-closed as she looked at Tom lying on the disordered bed. She finished drying between her legs and moved over to the bed. Idly she reached out to touch Tom's now flaccid cock. He felt a stirring almost like an electric shock as she dried him off, using the towel one-handed and holding him with the other.

'I'm not complaining, mind you, but you don't have to do that,' he heard himself saying. 'I'll do it myself if you'll just unlock these,' nodding toward the handcuffs.

'I'm not ready to let you go yet. I have to go out for a bit. The car has to go into the garage and I'd like to find you still here when I get back.'

'You needn't worry about that. I was hoping you'd suggest something like that anyway.'

'Still, I think I'll keep you as you are,' Beth replied as she began to take off her damp stockings. 'The thought of you waiting here for me will be pleasantly stimulating. Don't you think so?'

Tom didn't answer her question. He wasn't sure he knew the answer. This situation was entirely new to him, and he couldn't say just what he felt. He watched as she chose a dry pair of stockings from the bureau and put them on. When she had clipped the suspenders to her stockings, Beth picked up the damp sweaty pair and a scarf. With these she approached the bed. 'Open wide.'

Tom did as she asked. It never occurred to him to demur. She then gagged him with the stockings and tied them in place with the scarf. He could taste her perfume faintly, and the salty tang of her sweat more strongly, in his mouth.

He watched while Beth finished dressing. As she left, she said casually, 'I'll be back as soon as I can. You'll be all right here. No one will be coming in.

10

And I'll have a special treat for you when I get back. Try to get some rest.' And she was gone. Tom heard the door close, and the rattle of her keys as she locked it behind her. Then her footsteps receded along the hall and silence filled the room. Tom couldn't do anything else, so he tried to take Beth's advice. He dozed and woke several times. There were footsteps coming and going from time to time, and the late afternoon turned into early evening. Still no Beth. Tom began to see the down side of the situation he'd let himself get into. When she had handcuffed him, Tom had felt a new excitement. And the sex afterwards had been great, made all the more enjoyable by his inability to influence the action. Having to leave all the initiatives to the woman had been a great turn-on. But now he was just a bit worried about the consequences.

The room darkened as night fell. Tom began to wonder if he'd have to try to break the bars of the headboard to get loose. He wondered if they'd break. The thought crossed his mind that maybe Beth was not coming back. He had met her only this afternoon. He didn't even know if this was her flat, although she appeared to know where everything was. Suppose a stranger came back and found him? Briefly he toyed with the idea of another woman like Beth coming in. Suppose no one came and found him? Tom tugged experimentally at the headboard of the bed. It was solid.

Footsteps came down the hall, the rapid tattoo of high heels. They stopped outside the door. There was the sound of a key in the lock and the footsteps entered the flat. The light in the front room was turned on, but Tom couldn't see who was there. And whoever it was said nothing. There were sounds of someone moving about in the front room and kitchen, but if it was Beth she was prolonging the suspense by staying out of sight.

Tom thought that if she prolonged the suspense much more there would be a messy accident. Thoughts of the toilet were beginning to occupy him almost as much as thoughts of yet another sexual encounter with the startling Beth. As if reading his mind, Beth herself chose that moment to make her entrance. She said cheerily, 'Glad you decided to stay. Everything all right?' Tom grunted. She continued, 'I imagine you'll be wanting to get to the loo about now. I had intended to get back sooner but there was an awful crowd at the shops.' So she had been casually shopping while he waited for her to come back to release him! Tom felt a momentary flash of annoyance at her cavalier treatment, but it faded when he remembered the earlier encounter. And besides, he realised at that moment, he was really enjoying the novel situation. It was a relief for once not to have to make all of the moves. If things went wrong, there was nothing he could do about it. But things showed no sign of going wrong so long as he got to the loo soon.

'I got us something for tea. I thought you'd be hungry by now,' Beth continued as she removed his gag. She bent to fondle his erect cock. 'Is that for me? How thoughtful!'

Before he could reply, Tom worked his tongue around to wet his dry mouth. When he could speak he said, 'That one is for the toilet, but I promise to work up another one just for you as soon as I've taken care of the other business. Not that it will take all that much effort,' he continued gallantly while Beth moved to unlock the handcuffs.

She stepped back and put them on the bureau.

12

Tom rolled out of the bed and stretched stiffly. Then he made his way into the bathroom. The relief was wonderful. He poked his head around the door when he was done. Beth was putting the bed to rights. 'Okay if I have a shower?'

'Good idea,' she replied. 'In fact I'll join you in a minute. I can point out the towels – and some of the other features of the place.'

'Are you one of them?'

'I could be one if you'd like,' she replied.

'I'd like. Get out of those clothes and get in here.' Tom stepped into the shower stall and adjusted the water temperature. While he was soaping himself Beth came in and got undressed. Again Tom watched closely.

She got into the shower and took the cloth from him. 'Turn around. You can ogle me later.' She began to do his back.

'Wouldn't it be nicer if I faced you and let you reach around? That way we could rub the interesting bits together.'

By way of reply Beth reached around him and used her soapy hand to caress his cock. That got his attention. His cock came to attention as well. He could feel her breasts pressing against his back – a most agreeable sensation. Altogether a most remarkable and agreeable woman, he thought. When she finished his back, Beth put the soap down and used both hands on him. She cupped his balls with her left hand and used the right to very good effect on his stiff cock. Before too long he began to wonder if there could be too much of a good thing. If she carried on much longer he was going to lose it in the shower.

Beth sensed the same thing, and she let go of him with a terse, if enigmatic, 'Do me now.'

13

'Your back, or some of the more interesting bits?'
'You can start with the back, and if you're good enough I'll let you try somewhere else.'

Tom soaped her back and let his hands trail suggestively over Beth's round, tight bottom as he worked down her legs. Tom considered himself somewhat of a leg man. He had read somewhere that the mark of a discerning lover was a preference for legs over breasts: those men who were fascinated by women's breasts were put down as immature – mother-fixated, as the shrinks would say. He liked breasts well enough. He had never disdained them. But the subject now was legs. Beth's were long and well shaped: not the spindly type so prevalent among models and famine victims. The delicate veins in the hollows of her knees seemed made to be kissed. He did, surprising both of them. He had never showered with anyone who permitted or encouraged such attentions. Showering was just a means of getting clean, something you did after sex, a way to wash out the memory, the stigma of it. No matter how liberated his other lovers claimed to be, they were still their mothers' daughters. They could never quite shake off the idea that sex was dirty. Wasn't that what their mothers had taught them? And who were they to doubt?

Beth was surprised, but enjoyed the attention to this hitherto neglected area of her anatomy. Her fingers wound into his hair and he was acutely aware of their gentle weight on his head like a benediction. There was a trace of her perfume lingering in the delicate hollows. He had read somewhere that truly discerning women put a dab of perfume in the hollows of their knees, just in case someone happened to be in that area, he guessed. Beth seemed to be a very

14

discerning woman, amongst her other, more obvious attractions. Tom's hands were on her thighs, holding her steady while he nuzzled. Beth's pleasure was made evident by the small tremors that travelled her legs. He could feel them come and go.

She turned and Tom found himself facing an entirely different proposition. As he knelt he was on a level with her vulva. The dark reddish hair was glistening with drops of water and streams were running down the front of her thighs. Beth shifted her stance slightly and parted her legs – an invitation he couldn't mistake, and certainly didn't want to refuse. 'Venus rising from the shower tray,' he remarked as he shifted his hands to squeeze her bottom and draw her closer to his lips.

Beth smiled at the sally. 'I'm not sure this is what Botticelli had in mind.'

Then once again he found his face buried in the fragrant cavern at the apex of her thighs. What he did there made her tremble even more. And heave. And pant. She gripped the back of his head with both hands, holding on to him and pressing him tightly against herself. Tom's tongue was very busy indeed. He interspersed the licks with gentle nips at strategic points. When he took the time to look up quickly, Tom could see that her nipples had erected and her areolae were crinkly with excitement once more.

Tom beavered away and presently Beth shuddered and clasped his head tightly against her crotch. Her breath was loud and ragged and her face was flushed. Her knees threatened to give way, and Tom supported her with his arms around her hips as she came. When Beth stopped gasping she raised Tom to his feet. His cock rubbed against her belly and she reached down to guide him into her. When he was

15

aimed in the right direction Beth wrapped her arms around his shoulders and whispered, 'Lift me up.' Tom lifted her and slid fully home. Beth gave a small gasp of pleasure and twined her legs around his waist, crossing her ankles behind his back as he braced her back against the opposite wall of the shower cubicle. Their bodies were all slick with the soap and the sliding sensation as they made love was a rare pleasure.

Beth brought her face down to his and they kissed with the water running down their bodies. Her mouth was open and her tongue darted into his when their lips met. She planted hot kisses over his lips and eyes and chin. He kissed her with equal fervour, and when they broke he nuzzled her ears and the sides of her neck. Beth's legs around his waist held her straining body against him. Tom lost track of her orgasms. Once again he was concentrating on holding his own back for as long as possible. When he could wait no longer he spent inside her, barely managing to keep to his feet and support her weight as she bucked and heaved in her own climax.

They spent the weekend at Beth's flat, dressing only to go out for the newspapers. They didn't get around to eating much beyond the odd sandwich. Somehow there never seemed to be enough time to devote to cooking a meal, though once or twice they made half-hearted offers. Tom hadn't expected anything like this encounter when he met the stranger at the market. Her eagerness matched his own, which was rare in his experience. He had never made love so often with any other woman he had known in such a short space of time, nor been so absorbed by the bizarre sex games she introduced to the encounter.

In the early hours of Sunday morning Tom woke up needing a drink of water. Beth slept on as he got carefully out of bed. When he was done he made his way over to the bureau where she had laid the handcuffs. He examined them to see how they operated. He went carefully back to the bed and got in beside Beth with the handcuffs. He waited a few minutes more to be sure she was asleep. When she rolled over Tom caught one of her wrists. She grunted sleepily as he locked one of the cuffs on her. He waited until she settled down again. There was no way to accomplish the next step without waking her, but he wanted to give himself as much time as possible. He rolled her over onto her stomach and pulled both her arms behind her, locking the cuff onto Beth's other wrist. As he had expected, this brought her fully awake. Beth tried to bring her hands up and failed. She grunted in surprise as she realised that she was now Tom's prisoner. Tom was ready to clap his hand over her mouth in case she screamed, but she didn't cry out. On the whole she seemed to take the whole thing rather calmly. He was surprised. Most women, he guessed, would make panicky noises and thrash about if they woke up in the dark in handcuffs. Since she didn't, Tom wondered if this was a commonplace event for her.

'What do you plan to do now?' she asked. There was no fear in her voice.

Tom hadn't thought about that. His plans had gone no further than making her helpless. Now he had to think of something else. He realised that the next move had to come from him but had no experience to guide him.

Beth came to his aid when she saw him hesitate. 'I don't suppose you have much experience with bondage, do you? Is this your first time?'

'Yes.'

'I thought so. How are you at rape fantasies? I have several in which a man overpowers me and has his way with me when I can't resist. Like now. Or if you haven't recovered from our last bout, we can lie here and talk. Or sleep. I can wait until you feel up to something more athletic. And by then you may have developed some ideas of your own. I can play the role of the captive beauty for you. Or the slave girl waiting for her master to free her, or take her. Name your fancy.

Tom could think of nothing more imaginative than to manoeuvre Beth until she sat astride him. He reached up to fondle her breasts and squeeze her nipples. He found himself enjoying the idea that she couldn't stop him from doing what he liked with her. Before very long his erection was rubbing suggestively against her bottom and Beth was beginning to look preoccupied with inner matters. She lifted herself off him so that he could guide himself inside her, then sat back down with a sigh of satisfaction. Tom knew by the ease with which he glided in that she was already wet and aroused. They made love for what seemed like hours, at first with Beth sitting upright and later lying on him with her breasts pressed against his chest.

And then they slept. And woke up to repeat the process. Beth never complained about the handcuffs or the pace of his lovemaking. She had placed herself in his hands and she allowed him to do what he wanted with her. This was something new as well. In his encounters with other women Tom had found that they wanted certain things, and resisted other things. Beth went along uncomplainingly, encouraging him to try whatever took his fancy when he showed signs of slowing down. And she didn't engage

18

in the verbal put-downs he had heard from others, no matter how well they fitted together in bed. Almost always there were implied comparisons. Sometimes these were more than implications, and always in the background was the notion that the woman was granting an undeserved favour.

Chapter Two

After making love to Beth during that stay-at-home weekend Tom found it hard to concentrate on business on the Monday morning. And in the following weeks the condition worsened – if that is the right word. There were frequent reveries of a particularly erotic nature. He imagined what Beth was doing at that moment: shopping; eating; visiting; waiting for him. Since she had not told him what she did, he could imagine almost anything he wished. He would form a mental image of her dressed in lacy underwear with her stunning legs sheathed in sheer nylon. Her lips were parted and there was an unfocused stare in her eyes as if she were thinking of making love. The erection these thoughts produced made it embarrassing to stand up too abruptly, but more important he found it hard to wrench his thoughts back to the task in hand. The naked body of his strange new lover seemed to come between him and everything he had to do, so that he began to see everything else as something devised by a perverse reality to keep him from her.

The weekdays stretched out endlessly before him. The time from Monday to Friday was entirely too long to contemplate as a single span of time: an eternity before he could lose himself once more in her body and their wonderful sex games. For she seemed to take a special pleasure in devising new ways for them to enjoy one another. Her willingness to dress erotically and her skilful use of the slow strip made her the fantasy goddess that inhabits the dreams of even the mildest of men. Her alternation between dominatrix and slave, and his own similar alternation, confused and delighted him at the same time. Never before had he been with a woman who tied him helplessly and then used him so thoroughly. Nor one who urged him to bind her, gag her, ravish her. She fulfilled his rape fantasies, and when she took charge of him she took all responsibility from him. When he was tied to Beth's bed he gladly relinquished all control over his body and his actions to her. All responses were provoked by her. He had nothing to do with the process of his arousal or with his satiation. He became an instrument upon which she played, evoking some very strange harmonies and discords he had never suspected lay in him. And when it was his turn to play the master she gave herself, as completely, over to his control. Each time he saw her they did something different.

At first he had to be shown how to pose her, how to bind her. When at length he found his own inspiration, he began to do things to her he had never dreamed possible while she urged him on to make ever greater use of her body. Her helplessness under his hands and the abandoned writhing of her body drove both of them to new heights. It wouldn't be inaccurate to say that he saw her through a haze of lust. In everything he did the image of Beth bound hand and foot and heaving under his hands as he teased her or pleasured her was before him. And he as often found himself imagining how she dealt with him. It seemed to him that he had a permanent erection. Certainly his mental erection was permanent. In the increasingly fewer calm moments he wondered at the power she exerted over him. But he never considered that they should be, or do, anything different. He was losing himself in her. The aroma of her perfume, her body, her sweat, her musk would return to haunt him at any time throughout the age-long time when he had to be away from her so that he couldn't be sure if it was an actual smell or merely the memory of one.

But there was one thing Tom couldn't help noticing. As their games unfolded he found himself more often the one in charge. Beth never complained about that. In fact she seemed to become more and more the submissive partner as he assumed the active role. The change was slow, but it was there.

One Friday, as he was preparing to leave his flat to go to her, there had been a knock at his door. Annoyed, he had gone to answer it, thinking that he would have to deal quickly with whoever it was so that he could return to that darkened bedroom which was such an important part of his world – indeed the centre of his world. When he opened the door Beth was standing in the hall. She was wearing a long coat buttoned up to the neck. Beneath the hem, which reached to her knees, Tom saw that she was wearing his very favourite pair of high heels and a pair of sheer glossy black stockings. He remembered that it had been a cool day, but certainly not cold enough to wear such a heavy coat. Before he could recover from his surprise, she said, 'Well, aren't you going to ask me in? A girl could get the idea that she was unwelcome standing out here. Cat got your tongue?'

In the end he simply stood aside and motioned her to come in. He closed the door and was about to turn to Beth when she told him to lock it. He felt surprised and happy because she had come to him. Up until now it had been the other way around. All the confusion of the past days faded from his mind as he turned to face Beth as naturally as a sunflower follows the course of the primary across the daytime sky. And then he stopped abruptly. Beth had unbuttoned her coat and stood before him: she wore nothing under the coat save her stockings and suspenders. The idea of Beth travelling across town to meet him in this state gave him an immediate erection.

'I planned it as a special treat for my first visit to your place.' Beth slipped out of the coat and let it fall to the floor at her feet. She smiled wickedly at him as she opened her arms. 'See anything you like?' she teased. Tom nodded dumbly and they kissed for what seemed like forever, standing there in the entrance way. His senses swam with the combination of her woman smell and the heat of her body as she pressed herself against him. He held her tightly to himself with one hand while the other roamed over her naked body. She gasped in pleasure when his hand slid down her back and cupped her bottom, lifting her onto tiptoe and pushing those magnificent breasts more firmly against his chest. She put her face close to his ear and whispered, 'Why don't you take your clothes off too? Then we can start equal.'

She began to unbutton his shirt and pull it out of his jeans. He let go of her long enough to let her slip it off. Beth took the opportunity to unbuckle his belt. The zipper of his trousers purred open and he felt her warm eager fingers grasp him and tug him free from the confines of his clothing. Tom felt himself hardening under her skilled fingers. He felt the cool air of

23

the room on him and found that a stimulant. When he spoke of it later to Beth as they lay upon the disordered bed, she observed that almost anything turned him on. This was said with a curious, proprietary smile as she caressed his face and breathed softly into his ear. The warmth of her breath made him shiver in anticipation. She had always been able to arouse him by almost everything she did.

But on this occasion Beth tugged him towards the bedroom by the cock, holding him firmly and squeezing gently as he hardened under her hand. Somewhere between the entrance hall and the bed his jeans disappeared so that when they lay down he was naked.

He felt the cool brush as her stockinged leg touched his hip. Then she was kneeling astride him and guiding him into herself. That must be the shortest foreplay on record, he thought fleetingly as he was surrounded by warm moist flesh. Beth had learned the trick – from an Indian woman, she once said laughingly – of contracting her vaginal muscles. Tom felt himself being squeezed by that warm tunnel in which he was buried to the hilt. He reached up to fondle her breasts as she sat back on her haunches and fondled his balls in her turn. Beth's nipples were hard and crinkly already.

Later she admitted that she had been in a state of almost constant arousal as she rode across town. She described the looks she got from the men who passed her. Most men look assessingly at women they pass in the street or ride with on a bus, but she had felt their gaze much more acutely in her novel state. 'If some men mentally undress you, I must have been very easy to disrobe,' she commented. Tom gazed in admiration at the glory of her bent knees and the swell of her thighs beneath the smooth stockings.

Beth lifted herself up his pole and slid down again with a sigh of pleasure. Tom watched the play of her leg muscles and the changing highlights on her stockings as she wriggled herself more fully down onto him. He had to think of something else – almost anything would do – if he wasn't to lose it in the first instance.

Tom considered himself a gentleman because he tried to make sure his partner had a good time too, but as always with Beth he was having a hard time holding back. She had that effect on him. The very unexpectedness of her arrival and her nudity under her coat had raised his blood almost to boiling point. He had felt himself about to explode from the first time her fingers had found him, and he suspected that Beth knew it, and was enjoying the effect she had on him. He loved to give her pleasure, because she was so uninhibited in showing him all of herself – all sides of her personality. And this time it looked as if Beth was having almost as much trouble holding back as he was. But of course she didn't have to wait. Nor did she. She raised herself and slid back down again and again as he continued to cup her breasts and squeeze her taut nipples. Her breath became ragged and shallow with the onset of orgasm. She arched her spine and threw her head back, eyes closed as she concentrated on what was happening between her legs and in her belly. She clenched herself tightly around him and began to pant – a steadily increasing 'Hahh! Hahh! Haaaaahhh! Heeeaaahh!' She shuddered as she came. Tom could feel the dampness of her skin as sweat broke from her. Her eyes were closed tightly and she slumped forward suddenly so that the weight of her upper body was supported by his arms as he cupped her breasts.

As soon as she had recovered a little she opened her eyes and gazed down into his face. He found her glance hypnotic and couldn't look away. Gradually her breathing slowed and she resumed playing with his balls, reaching behind her to rub them gently with her fingers. Abruptly she caught the tender skin with one of her long fingernails and gave a pinch that made him jerk in surprise. At the same time Beth clenched her vaginal muscles and he felt himself enveloped by the heat of her body.

'Again, Tom? Can you do me again?' she asked. In reply he shifted his hands from her breasts to the folds where her legs joined her body. With his thumbs he alternately spread her labia and pressed the lips together, slowly kneading the tiny button of her clitoris as he did so. He fancied he could feel it swell beneath his fingers. Beth certainly felt the effects. Once more her breath became rapid and shallow and her body grew taut with the onset of her next climax. Teasingly he removed his hands. Beth groaned, 'Don't stop now, please don't stop!' She shuddered and began to thrust herself up and down on his cock. Once again he watched the play of her thigh muscles as she rose and sank. Beth reached for his hands and placed them between her legs, pressing them there to urge him to resume the massage of her clitoris. When he did she gave a muffled shriek and slumped as she came. But this time he continued. He didn't intend to let her relax and recover. When she realised that he was going to drive her over the top once again Beth began to cooperate. She sat up straighter to allow him to reach her and at the same time resumed her own thrusting. 'Aaahhh! Ahhhhh! Ah God, ohhhh Tom, Tom, Tom,' rising to a scream as she came. He couldn't hold back any longer and in seconds he felt himself spurting inside her. When it was over she slid down until she was lying atop him. Their sweat mingled as their breathing slowed and their bodies cooled. Still locked together, they fell into a doze.

It was dark when they woke up, ravenous. Tom went to the kitchen to make supper. Beth headed for the loo and he could hear splashing sounds as she cleaned herself up. He thought he heard the shower running and some time later, as Tom was peeling the potatoes, Beth came into the kitchen. She was drying her hair and there were glistening drops of water on her back, but she was wearing her stockings and suspenders once more. She had taken the time to slip her shoes on as well. Once more Tom was struck by the small touch of eroticism implied by her choice of clothing. She could have used one of his bathrobes but instead had chosen the more provocative outfit in which she had arrived. It was almost as if she had read his mind and had known that this would please and excite him.

'Will you dry my back, please,' she asked. Tom took the towel and she turned away from him to present her wet back. Tom rubbed her down and draped the towel over one of the chairs. When his hands were free, Beth leaned back against him and rested her head on his shoulder. Tom put his arms around her from the back and held her breasts in his hands. Beth brought her own arms up over his, hugging him to her tightly. Her damp hair was cool on his chest.

'You really don't have to cook an elaborate meal. A sandwich would be fine and takes less time anyway.'

'I wanted to do something elaborate. And anyway, I'm getting tired of sandwiches. We always eat something fast. This time I'll take the time to make a proper meal for you, and I can put in the time admiring your bod. You go sit there,' he said, indicating a chair across the table, 'where I can see you. I'll get on with the food.' He released her and gave her a gentle shove.

'Do you really want to just look?' Beth asked with a grin. 'I can think of other things I'd enjoy more.' That was the kind of remark which he'd remember at odd moments during their time apart, when he was supposed to be doing the things that made up the other part of his life, and he'd lose himself in reveries of their last encounter – to the dismay of the other people he had to deal with. His absences and vacancies were becoming more marked. His work was beginning to suffer. He was close to believing that Beth was the most important thing in the world, and their weekend trysts the only reason for getting through the rest of the time. Understandable in a teenager; not so in a man of thirty-four who had to earn his own living.

'If you're absolutely committed to the idea of cooking, I have an idea that may liven up the process for both of us. Do you have any rope in the flat? Grocery string or clothes line, for example?'

Tom thought for a moment, mentally taking an inventory of his closets. 'Have a look in the airing cupboard. There should be something left over from my linen line.' He knew that she intended some sort of bondage, but couldn't guess exactly what she had in mind. It was characteristic of Beth's approach to sex that she was always full of ideas which he would have called bizarre in someone else. Indeed he had found them so when he first met them in Beth, but the bizarrerie had become commonplace, helped by Beth's matter-of-fact approach to whatever she had in mind, and by his increasing reliance on her judgement in matters sexual. He was much readier to suspend his own judgement and bow to Beth's whims than he had ever been with any other woman. She was very close to becoming the arbiter of his taste and the major influence in his life.

Beth went to search the cupboard and Tom continued with his preparations. He heard the sound of doors opening and the sound of her high heels rat-tat-tatting on the floors as she searched the flat. Eventually she came back with a little grin of triumph. In her hand she carried a coil of clothes line. She uncoiled it and measured it by eye. 'About 30 feet,' she said. 'That should do. Tom, I want you to take enough time out from your cooking to tie me to one of these chairs. Then you can use your imagination about where to go from there.' There was an impish grin as she looked at him. 'You'll probably need to cut off some convenient lengths, but I'll leave the details to you.' She handed the rope to him and sat down on the chair nearest the stove.

She crossed her legs with a whisper of nylon and he felt his stomach lurch with the glory of her. And she's here with me, he thought. The ball was in his court. Tom picked up the rope and ran it through his hands, taking the kinks out of it. There was a carving knife on the draining board. He picked it up and cut a length of rope, then put the knife down on the table and went around behind her.

With a dry mouth and a constriction in his throat Tom said, 'Bring your hands around behind your back.' Wordlessly, she did as he asked. Tom crossed her wrists and tied them tightly together. Beth gave a low grunt as the rope bit into her flesh but made no other comment. With another length of rope he lashed her elbows together, drawing her shoulders back and causing her to thrust out her breasts.

'Where did you learn that trick?' she asked, smiling up at him over her shoulder. She wriggled about on the chair and her breasts jiggled with the movement.

'Oh, sudden inspiration,' he replied. 'I'm glad you like it. On you it looks good. Now hold still before I do something rude to your tits.'

'Oh, would you, please. I'd really like that.'

'Yes, I imagine you would, but I have to make something for us to eat. Got to keep up the strength for the weekend.'

He tied a length of rope around her narrow waist and pulled it tight around the chair. Beth was pulled against the chair back, and sat up straight, waist nipped in and breasts jutting out invitingly. He stepped back to admire the effect and then returned to peeling the potatoes and seasoning the steaks he had bought earlier, intending to take them to her place. On the whole, he was pleased that she had come to him. It made a change in their usual routine (if that was the proper word) and seemed to indicate to him another stage in their relationship. Having her in his kitchen while he prepared a meal for them made him feel closer to her. He was perilously close to falling in love with her, but he didn't want to use the L-word because she had never even raised the subject. He set the steaks aside to marinate and turned to admire Beth.

She sat up straighter when she saw him looking in her direction. Her breasts jutted out aggressively as she drew her shoulders even further back. 'What are you going to do to me?' Beth asked, giving a good imitation of a romantic heroine in the hands of the villain. 'Please, please, just let me go,' she continued in the same vein. 'I promise I'll tell no one about this abduction.'

Stepping around behind the chair, Tom knelt on the floor and whispered roughly in her ear, 'Let you go? What makes you think I plan to let you go? I've only just got you here.'

He reached around her and cupped her breasts, squeezing hard so that she gasped in surprise. 'Nice ones, nice titties,' he whispered. His fingers slid down to tweak her nipples, which grew hard beneath his touch. Beth inhaled deeply, gasping in pleasure as his hands continued to tease her flesh. Her breath began to come hard as she became aroused. She twisted in her bonds and the rope bit into her waist. Abruptly he let her go and went back to put the steak under the grill. Beth sat red-faced and breathless in the chair.

'Don't bother with food now! Come back and finish me off!' she urged in a strangled whisper when she recovered her breath. She was tugging at the ropes on her wrists and was bent forward in her eagerness to offer herself to him.

'Be patient. Neither of us going anywhere. You'll feel much better after you've had something to eat. And I don't intend to neglect you totally while I cook for us. Sex with you always gives me an appetite. As William once said, "Where others satiate, she but makes more hungry." You can spend the intervals anticipating the next grope.'

Tom slid the steaks onto the grill and put the potatoes into the microwave to begin baking. Meanwhile he set to work on the salad, chopping the onions finely and making an elaborate show of wiping the tears from his eyes. He sliced the tomatoes, washed the lettuce and put everything into a bowl. After he had added oil and vinegar, he set it aside and returned to Beth bearing a small bowl of olive oil. He dipped his fingers into it and oiled her nipples gently. The effect on Beth was instantaneous. She drew in her breath sharply and thrust forward as far as her bonds allowed. Teasingly he drew back out of range.

'Damn you!' she hissed. 'Get on with it!'

Tom bent to kiss her taut nipples and suck the oil off.

'Ahhh,' Beth sighed contentedly. 'Ohhhh, ohhhh,' she added as he continued alternately licking her breasts and applying more oil.

When he was free to speak he informed Beth that olive oil was supposed to be good for the complexion: 'A zillion Italians can't be wrong. Though I don't know how many people will be able to notice the improvement in yours. Have you ever thought of joining a nudist colony?'

Beth didn't answer.

When he was satisfied that he had her undivided attention, Tom took a quick look at the steaks, turning them over and replacing the grill before he turned back to Beth. She was heaving in the chair and her eyes were closed. This time he applied the oil to other regions. Not to put too fine a point on it, the new target was her labia and clitoris. Beth was duly appreciative – not to say frantic. She spread her legs to allow his hands free access to her centre. Nothing loth, Tom slipped his finger into her crack and massaged her clitoris gently. If she had been frantic earlier on, Beth was now beside herself, writhing and struggling against the ropes that held her to the chair.

When he bent forward to lick and suck at her slippery flesh, she thrust her hips against his face and closed her thighs about his head, holding him against her. If her hands had been free, she would have used them as well. Judging by the sound effects, Tom knew

32

that she was close to climax. He reached up to tease her breasts, and the combination of his mouth on her clitoris and the manipulation of her engorged tits brought on a shattering orgasm. Small whimpers escaped her, and she clasped his head tightly with her straining thighs. The chair creaked as she flung herself against the ropes that bound her.

When she went limp, Tom gently extricated himself from her legs and stood up to regard her fondly. Beth was breathing heavily, occasional shudders passing through her body. Her head lolled and she was bent forward as far as the ropes allowed. He went behind her and gently pulled her upright against the back of the chair. Her head fell back and he bent down to kiss her on the mouth. He didn't linger because she needed all the air she could get. The smell from the grill told him that the steaks were about ready, and he left her to recover her breath and her composure while he set dishes on the table and served the food.

By the time he was done, Beth had recovered some of her breath and most of her composure. She sat erect on the chair and the flush was fading from her throat and face as her breathing slowed, although she still shuddered occasionally. She gave him a tentative smile when she caught his eye. 'If the meal is as good as the sex, I'll make sure you get into the *Good Food Guide*. Untie me now?'

Tom opened a bottle of white wine and poured a glass for each of them. He held one to her lips and Beth took a small sip, and then a larger one as the cool wine slid down her throat. As she was drinking, Tom said to her, 'You have the best seat in the house. No point in giving it up just yet. I'm going to feed you. All you have to do is relax and enjoy the service.' He set the glass on the table and got a pair of candlesticks from the cupboard. He set them on the table and lit the candles, then went to turn out the light.

The candlelight gave the small room a cosy and intimate air. The soft ruddy glow and the velvet shadows on Beth's naked body made him catch his breath in wonder. Tom let his hand trail gently across her cheek, feeling the softness of her with an unexpected tenderness after the earlier passion. The traffic noises from the street that filtered to the back of the house sounded far away. A background, like the noise of surf breaking on a distant beach. The sense of fulfilment he felt when he was with Beth came back to him again as he savoured the sight of her seated at the table. He drew up another chair facing her and began to feed her, taking a bite of his own food between times. From time to time he paused to wipe her mouth with a napkin, or to offer her a swallow of wine. Tom felt intensely proprietary as she literally ate the food from his hand. Also excited. He had enjoyed giving her pleasure and at the same time holding himself back for later. He had been almost painfully erect while Beth was having her orgasm. He had enjoyed the sight of this beautiful woman in the throes of passion as she strained in her bonds.

When they were finished he stacked the dishes in the sink and opened another bottle of wine. Washing up seemed a waste of time when his lady in waiting was – well, waiting. 'Something to sustain us for the rest of the frolic,' he remarked with a smile as he got fresh glasses.

'That sounds promising, but I'll have to go to the loo pretty soon unless you want to clean up after me. Afterwards you can work your evil will upon me.' Beth smiled widely and, he thought, wickedly at this idea.

Tom untied the rope around her waist that held her to the chair. He did not, however, free her hands. Instead he escorted her to the bathroom and helped her to pee, which she did copiously. 'Must have been the combination of wine and sex,' she remarked. Indicating her bound wrists, she asked, 'What now?'

'Something's bound to come up if we allow enough time,' Tom replied. 'In fact I believe I've got just the glimmerings of an idea that will amuse you and while away an hour or two. Come on into the front room and we'll watch TV before the next round. Too much dessert and you lose the taste for it.'

Beth sat down on the edge of the settee in front of the TV. Tom went back into the kitchen and returned bearing the bottle of wine he had opened earlier and the rest of the rope she had found. 'Yes, you've guessed what's next. But contain yourself for a bit yet. There's a programme I'd like to see.' Using the remote control, Tom adjusted the set and then settled back on the couch next to Beth. He poured a glass of wine and offered her a drink. Then he took a swallow himself and pulled her closer to him.

She didn't resist. And he wasn't all that serious about watching TV. Not many people have the chance of an evening's viewing in the company of an attractive woman wearing nothing but stockings, suspenders and heels. And even fewer have the opportunity to tie her up beforehand.

Tom wore his ever present jeans and shirt. 'Aren't you a bit overdressed?' she asked. 'A gentleman should never try to upstage a lady.'

Wordlessly Tom got up and took off his clothes. Then he settled down again on the couch. 'Where were we?' he asked. 'Was I after your tits or your legs? I forget so easily.'

'You mean we aren't going to watch telly? I was getting interested in the programme.' Beth squirmed about in an attempt to find a comfortable position – not easy with both hands bound.

That produced some interesting seismic effects in her wobbly bits, an effect not entirely lost on Tom. He moved to the end of the settee and braced himself against the armrest. Then he lifted Beth and arranged her so that she lay in his lap. This had the additional effect of bringing her into easy reach. He began to stroke the backs of her thighs, enjoying the warm feel of the firm flesh beneath the smooth nylon of her stockings. Beth grunted contentedly and settled herself in. He ran his hands up and over her stocking tops and then back down again, gradually paying more attention to her bottom and the smoothly curving cheeks. From there he worked his way around to her vulva and the crack immediately adjacent thereto. He found her already moist, and when Tom very gently insinuated a finger into her cunt she became even wetter. The button of her clitoris hardened beneath his probing.

About then Beth's attention began to stray from the TV and onto more immediate matters. Her breath began to catch in her throat whenever his fingers touched a particularly sensitive spot. She squirmed a bit more and must have felt the hard evidence of his own arousal against her back. She pressed backwards against his erection. Her hips undulated gently. When he began to tease her nipples into erection, Beth could wait no longer. 'Now, Tom. Take me now. Please. I can't hold back much longer.'

Tom lifted her quickly to a sitting position on the couch and shifted himself so that there was some space on either side of him for her legs. His cock stood at full stretch, and Beth seemed hypnotised by the sight. She couldn't take her eyes off it. Hampered by her bound hands, Beth struggled awkwardly to her feet and moved until she could stand astride his knees. Tom grasped her bottom and guided her down onto his cock. As she felt herself impaled, her knees buckled, but he supported her.

As he slid into her, Tom imagined he was sliding into a heated cave. He gave a short gasp as he felt the slight resistance change to a liquid sliding. Beth knelt astride him with her legs spread wide to help keep her upright. She braced her knees against the back of the settee. Tom slid forward to meet her urgency with his own, sliding fully into her, and she swayed as if dizzy and fell forward against his chest. Her head rested on his left shoulder and her breath was loud in his ear. Tom put his arms around her and pulled her fiercely forward and down onto his erect cock.

Beth gasped once more as her taut nipples made contact with the crisp mat of his chest hair but re-covered quickly and began to thrust herself up and down on the spear between her legs. He moved to meet her thrusting and the world contracted to con-tain just two people.

Her whimpers gradually became full-throated inar-ticulate cries that rose in pitch as she came. She shud-dered as the waves of release swept through her, but he felt as if he could go on forever. Tom continued to slide in and out of her with single-minded purpose, and Beth was swept away toward yet another climax, almost without pause. How lucky, he thought fleet-ingly, that she was one of those women blessed with multiple orgasms.

But there was no more time for thought. Tom's hands were on her bottom, teasing the crack and finding their way unerringly to her anus. He pressed the bud of her contracting arsehole as she rose on each up stroke. It was a new idea to him, one that he had never tried with any other woman. Beth seemed to enjoy the friction and pressure on her tight ring. He pushed a bit harder and felt the tight muscles yielding to the insistent pressure. Suddenly they relaxed as she reached the bottom of her stroke and his finger slid into her back passage. Beth yelped in surprised pain and made as if to rise off him, but his free hand was around her shoulders holding her down.

'No, Tom. It hurts. Take it out,' she gasped.

'Relax,' he replied, 'and wait a minute.' He kept the finger inside her as she squirmed and bucked. And gradually he felt her muscles relax so that his finger slid fully inside. He waited so that she could get used to the feeling, and then began to thrust again with his hips and hand. Beth picked up the rhythm and was soon back in full cry. She seemed to be excited by the novelty of the double penetration, and the earlier discomfort was forgotten. He no longer had to hold her down, and he put his other hand to use in teasing and hardening Beth's nipples. 'Ohhhhh!' she exclaimed. Tom could feel her vaginal muscles in spasm around his cock, until it felt once more as if she were milking him and he knew he couldn't stop himself from coming. Just as well that she was coming too. When he ejaculated inside her she was still in full cry. It seemed an age after he had come before Beth finished. But finish she did, and she lay limply against his chest as they regained their breath.

Tom withdrew from her and helped her to sit down on the couch, then got a towel from the bathroom and wiped them both down. Then he untied her hands, which were numb from having been tied for so long, and she couldn't move them for a while. He rubbed her wrists and hands until the circulation returned, and she groaned with the pain of it. But she never complained, apparently accepting the pain as a natural consequence of her own actions. When he apologised she reminded him that it was she who had asked to be tied. And then they went to bed. This time to sleep.

They made love several times before she had to go, late on Sunday evening. Neither kept count, the hours passing in a haze as they woke, ate, screwed and slept again. And this time it was Beth who took the lead, inventing new delights for them both. She seemed to be a thousand women. When it was time for her to go, Beth got up straight from the bed and put on her stockings and shoes. She buttoned her coat and bent to kiss Tom goodbye. He had watched her dress, feeling the return of dreary reality as she covered up the body he had enjoyed so much.

'Do you want me to see you home?'

He was reluctant to let her go and hoped she'd let him enter the hitherto closed portion of her life; across the boundary of Sunday evening into the rest of her week. Tom felt jealous of the time she spent with others, wanting all of her time for himself, and the thought of his lover travelling through the streets naked under her coat made him uneasy. And excited. Someone else might detect her state, or she might reveal herself to another. Instant jealousy mixed with real concern, but she was firm. She left and he went to take a shower.

Chapter Three

A note from Beth, posted on Wednesday, arrived early on the Thursday morning: *I want you to come over to my place on Friday afternoon as usual, but you needn't bring anything to eat.*

Tom wondered briefly what she had in mind, but forgot the last part of the instructions as he contemplated the first part. Another weekend with Beth was on the cards. That made the rest of the week worthwhile. Thursday went by normally but Friday dragged badly. He couldn't wait for quitting time. When he left the office, Tom drove directly to Beth's flat, not even pausing to change his clothes.

'My, we are eager, aren't we?' Beth said when he presented himself at her door. 'But I have to disappoint you slightly this weekend. You won't be staying here, at least not the whole time. I will be here alone most of the time.' Seeing the puzzled expression on his face, Beth explained, 'I want you to leave me here bound and gagged over the weekend. You will leave me here alone, and I want you to be sure to tie me well so that I can't escape. I'll tell you beforehand that I shall try, and you lose points if I get free unaided. As a reward for doing what I ask, you can come back at odd times, but it's important that I don't know when, or even if, you will come. You'll have to check up on me – to see that I'm all right, or if I need to eat or drink anything, but when you go for the last time in the evening I don't want you to come back until the morning. It's an important part of the game that I am left helpless through the night.'

Tom was taken aback by the request, though it was no more bizarre than many of her other whims. He wanted to spend the weekend with her, and now it looked as if he wouldn't be able to. He wouldn't refuse her request. He never did that. But he did try to dissuade her. 'What if you have to go to the loo? And what about losing circulation in your hands while you're tied up?'

She smiled. 'You don't talk me out of it that easily. If I have to go, it's up to me to hold it in. If I can't, you'll have a mess to clean up. Don't worry,' she said, seeing the sudden look of alarm on his face. 'I'll hold myself. I don't like the idea of lying in my own mess any more than you like cleaning up after me. But that's another part of the game. There's always the danger that I will have an accident to add spice to the act. Just make sure I go before you leave me in the evenings.'

He tried again. 'But there might be a fire. Or a burglary.'

'All part of the risk I'll be taking. Don't you ever want to tempt fate? You can't play it safe all of your life.' When he didn't reply she continued, 'Now that you mention it, I might not mind a burglar so much. It's part of every girl's rape fantasy. You can leave the door unlocked if you like. I won't be able to stop you.'

Once again he felt a stab of alarm, which must have shown on his face.

Beth said, 'Oh, go ahead and lock me in all secure then. But there's nothing I can do to prevent you from doing the burglar act yourself. You mightn't be able to sleep very well imagining me lying here helpless for anyone to find.' She laughed. 'But please don't come back at night. I want to be alone. Should I write all this down, or can you remember it?'

'I'll remember. Anything else?' Tom knew he would do as she asked. He always did. He had tried the objections for form's sake, but now that he knew she was determined to go ahead with her scheme, he began to think of how to aid her. Thinking positively, as she would say. And as he thought out the implications and possibilities before him, he realised that Beth had once again opened another avenue of sexual adventure to him. Several refinements and improvements on the original idea began to occur to him and more would probably come later, making the weekend another time of discovery.

'There are a few more things, but we can work them out as we go along. I don't want to do everything. You should be free to work out some variations of your own within the broad scenario. Just remember that you can't let me loose until Sunday evening. The later the better. I like the idea of not knowing in detail what you are going to do. I just want you to be sure to avoid the things I've mentioned. Once the gag goes in, you'll be in charge of me. I won't be able to tell you what to do next or stop you from doing what you like to me.' At that idea Beth gave a little shiver of delight. She smiled wickedly at Tom. 'I'm sure you can think of something to keep up your interest and prevent the weekend from being a total bust. Shall we begin? I'm really looking forward to this.'

Without waiting for his reply, Beth led the way into the bedroom and waited for him. Indicating a coil of quarter-inch nylon rope lying on the bed, she said, 'I've been busy today. That little lot came from the yacht store down at the harbour. I rather fancied being tied with something nautical.'

Tom followed her into the room. 'I guess this will be the best place for it. You can lie on the bed and be as comfortable as possible. Unless you'd prefer to be left in the front room? Or I could tie you to one of the kitchen chairs,' Tom mused. 'How do you fancy yourself?'

'I'm in your hands, Tom. Do what you think best.' Beth's voice had lost the edge of command and she averted her face.

A quite remarkable change had come over the usually self-possessed woman he had come to know. It was strange to have Beth seem so passive. An air of abstraction had settled over her. She seemed detached from the scene she had so carefully constructed, as if it had nothing more to do with her, or she with it. Did she regret speaking so plainly, Tom wondered. She never had before. It was hard to see how he could have proposed the idea to her, even if he had thought of it. He decided that it was time for him to take charge. 'Here then. The bed.'

Both glanced at him and her hand strayed uncertainly to the top button of her blouse, but Tom shook his head. Through the silky cloth he could see the darker areolae. Her nipples were half erect. 'It will get cold in here during the night. You'd better wear something. I can tuck you in before I go, but if you lose the bedclothes after that you'll be very uncomfortable. I don't really want to read a lurid headline on Sunday morning: beautiful redhead found dead in freezing room.'

As he picked up the rope, his eye was caught by a

carving knife on the bedside table, obviously left there by Beth for this session. She had been thorough in her preparations. Tom cut the rope into convenient lengths. There were several of her headscarves ready to hand, on the table, and a tightly rolled ball made from old stockings stuffed inside one another. This was the gag, he realised.

'Do you want to go to the loo before we start?' Beth shook her head. 'Lie down on the bed then.' Beth did so. 'On your stomach, woman. Move.' Tom allowed his voice to roughen, almost barking at her. She quickly rolled over onto her front. He found himself slipping into the character she had outlined. It was easier for him to play the casual intruder than to retain his everyday self. Less embarrassing. 'Hands behind your back.' He pulled her left arm to emphasise the words. Beth brought her hands behind her and he quickly tied them together. Remembering her instructions, he was careful to keep the knots out of her fingers' reach. He tested the ropes. Not too tight but he didn't think she'd be able to work them loose. He tied another piece of rope around her arms just above the elbows and put a bit of tension on it. If she did get her hands free, she'd still not be able to reach that.

Tom helped her to sit up and guided her until she was sitting on the side of the bed. He tied her ankles and knees next, then raised her skirt to admire the view. Beth was wearing stockings and suspenders, and no pants. More evidence of her thoroughness. If she was trying to look like a sexy package, she was certainly doing well. Tom ran his hand up her leg and toyed with her pubic hair. Her breath caught as he stroked her, and he felt his own crotch tighten in response. He stopped abruptly, leaving Beth aroused, and gagged her. He twisted the rolled-up tights into one of the scarves and pushed it into her mouth, pulling the ends together and tying them behind her head. The silk scarf pulled her cheeks back in a grimace. Despite that Beth still managed to look desirable. Tom retained enough sense to know that he would find her desirable in almost any situation.

With one last glance at Beth, Tom walked out and left her sitting on the edge of the bed. He made a quick inspection around the flat to be sure there were no obvious fire hazards, then checked the windows and made sure the back door was locked. Satisfied, he made his way back to the living room. As he opened the front door to leave he heard the bedsprings creak and he guessed that Beth was settling herself. He was reluctant to leave, and he resisted the impulse to take one more look. He'd come back later this evening, he promised himself.

It was only early evening when he left, and he was at a loose end. He had been planning to spend the time with Beth, and now he had no other plans. Tom knew from experience that he had to find something to do with the time if he didn't want his mind to dwell continually on Beth. He walked into the town centre with the idea of finding a restaurant or a congenial pub for his evening meal as he didn't feel like cooking for himself. Nor did he feel like going back to his own flat, but eating out alone wasn't much fun either. There was nothing else to do. The pub was full of strangers, and there was no reason to stay after he had finished his drink. He picked up his car outside Beth's place, looking up at her door. The windows were dark and blank. Tom imagined her lying alone in the dark, the room lit only by the reflected glow of the street lamps, and the muted sounds of the traffic drifting in through the windows as it had done on the many past weekends they had spent together. Was she struggling to free herself? Had she somehow got loose?

Later, I'll come back later, he thought once again. She won't want me to come around so soon. He started the engine and drove off. The drive home was slow because of the evening traffic. It had been some time since he had been out at this time. Usually he was with Beth and they were indoors making love or getting ready to make love, or recovering so they could make love again. His life since meeting Beth had been spent largely indoors. Tom was not a true outdoorsy or sporting person, but he realised with a start that he had not ridden his bicycle or taken a walk for literally months. He had not missed these things until now, suddenly on his own at a time he had expected to be occupied. His activities had revolved around the twin poles of work and weekends with Beth. And the weekends with Beth were becoming the more important of the two. They could easily become the centre of his life. May already have done so.

Tom parked outside his flat and locked the car. There were couples strolling past on their way out for the evening. He saw no single women, and only a few men. He went inside and spread the paper on the coffee table. He made a cup of coffee and tried to read, but was too restless. The television was, as always on a Friday evening, appalling. They seemed to save all the worst stuff for weekends, he reflected. The time crawled by. Each time he looked up to see if it was time to go back to check up on Beth it seemed that only minutes had passed. How he would get through the night after he had seen her and come home, he had no idea.

Finally it was time to leave. He quickly drove back to Beth's apartment. The streets were quieter now, fewer cars and people about. It was the indeterminate hour between the pub and theatre closing time and the quiet of late night. There would be one more brief flurry of activity as people made their way home, and then the quiet would be unbroken until the morning. When he parked the car Tom noticed a light was on in Beth's apartment. He felt a stab of alarm. Had she got free? Had there been a break-in while she was helplessly bound? He understood then the nature of the game she was playing. It was a war of nerves. Beth deliberately put herself at risk to see what it was like. Tom remembered her earlier remark: 'Don't you ever tempt fate?'

He hurried up the front steps and fumbled with the key. He dropped it and swore beneath his breath. It wouldn't do to burst in if there was an intruder there. More quietly he fitted the key into the lock and eased the door open. The front room was dark. There was no sound from within. As he eased the door shut he heard the creak of the bed springs, a short sound as of a sleeper shifting position. Or a bound female moving around. Quietly he made his way to the bedroom. The door was as he had left it. The light came from the kitchen, and Tom remembered that it was on a timer which operated it after dark unless it was reset. The light filtered into the bedroom and, with the outside lights from the street, allowed him to discern Beth lying on the bed. She was still bound and gagged, and the duvet was hanging halfway onto the floor, probably from her movements.

A floorboard creaked under his weight, and the figure on the bed stirred suddenly at the noise. 'Only me,' he called. The figure relaxed. Tom moved over to the bed and switched on a table lamp. He shared with Beth a dislike of overhead lights. She lay on her left side, her back to him as he stood over the lamp. Tom could see that her hands were still securely tied. He would lose no points for sloppy workmanship then. Her wrists were slightly reddened, probably from her attempt to free herself. He wondered what she would look like as she struggled, and felt a stirring in his crotch at the thought.

Before Beth came into the picture, he had not been particularly interested in bondage. He had not thought about tying anyone up for sex or for any other reason. Now he enjoyed both the artistic and sexual aspect of it. Beth had described it as packaging your partner. She herself made an attractive package as she lay on the disordered bed with her skirt up around her hips and the ropes pressing into the flesh of her legs. Tom was glad she had worn stockings and suspenders, he liked the effect.

Beth slitted her eyes against the light and tried to sit up. She failed and fell back with a little shrug of helpless resignation. Tom lifted her with his hands beneath her shoulders. He felt her back muscles tense as she tried to help him, and he admired the way her legs tightened and then relaxed when her weight shifted. He set Beth once more on the side of the bed with her feet on the floor, then bent down to untie her knees and ankles.

'Let's go to the loo before bedtime. Can you stand?'

Beth nodded, but her legs were stiff from being tied, and she almost fell. Tom caught her and steadied her into the bathroom. He helped her raise her skirt and sit down on the pan. From the splashing which ensued, he guessed that she must have been bursting

48

for a pee. When she finished, he wiped her dry and removed the gag.

'Are you hungry? You can't have had anything since about tea time.'

Beth worked her tongue around her dry mouth and croaked, 'No, nothing to eat. But I want some water, and I'd like to clean my teeth.'

Tom gave her a glass of water, holding it while she drank. Then he brushed her teeth. She drank another glass of water when that was done. 'Not too much water now, or you won't be able to hold out until morning,' he cautioned.

Beth nodded and said, 'You're right. My mouth is dry from the gag. Would you mind wetting it before you put it back?' She made her way back into the bedroom and sat on the edge of the bed.

Tom rinsed out the gag and left it wet with fresh water. It gave him a curious sense of satisfaction to learn that Beth hadn't been able to think of everything beforehand. Making his way back to the bedroom, he asked her, 'Are you okay now, or do you want to call it off?' Half-hoping she would.

'I'm okay,' she replied.

He replaced the gag and picked the rope from the floor where he had let it fall. Once more he tied her ankles and knees together. He laid her down on the bed, checking the ropes on her wrists and elbows. They seemed all right. Tom placed the pillows under her head and drew the duvet up over her body. Bending down, he brushed her eyes with his lips. 'All right. Sleep well. I'll be thinking of you.' It occurred to him that this may have been one of Beth's motives, although she had never been out of his thoughts the whole time.

Once more he made his way to the bedroom door,

closing it behind him. He turned off the light in the kitchen and left the apartment. He locked the front door and walked to his car. It was late now, and the drive home through the quiet streets was relatively quick. He was feeling a bit sleepy now, despite the undercurrent of excitement. When he got home he parked the car and went inside. Despite the lateness of the hour, he knew that he wouldn't sleep for a while. He put 'Eine Kleine Nachtmusik' on the tape deck and sat down to think, inevitably, about Beth. How was she enjoying the game? He remembered his first encounter with her, when she had handcuffed him to the bed and they had made love. He had enjoyed that, as well as the enforced idleness while he waited for her to do something. He imagined she was experiencing something like that now, and he hoped she was enjoying it. By her rules he could do nothing about it until tomorrow morning.

He slept fitfully and woke just after dawn. He sat for a moment wondering why he was in the chair and not in bed. Then he remembered last evening and was abruptly on his feet. He switched the tape machine off and tuned into the early morning news. While he listened he hurriedly splashed water on his face and made a cup of coffee. It occurred to him that he should call Beth, but then remembered that it wouldn't do any good. Instead he changed into a fresh shirt, brushed his hair and headed for his car. He would shave at Beth's place. The streets were not crowded and he made good time, stopping only once for pedestrians. But he couldn't go fast enough. Once he pulled himself up abruptly: no point in getting a speeding ticket. He pulled up at the kerb outside Beth's and hurried to open the door.

As before, the place was silent. He pushed through

into the bedroom. Beth was lying on the bed, still bound and gagged as he had left her the night before. She looked a bit dishevelled. Her hair needed brushing and her skirt and blouse were crumpled from having been slept in. Her eyes over the gag were sleepy looking, but she smiled when she saw him. 'Ummnnh,' she said.

'I guess that's meant to be "good morning", unless it means you have to go the loo rather badly.'

'Oooooo,' Beth said, nodding her head so vigorously her hair swept over her face.

'I thought that might be it,' Tom remarked as he untied her ankles and knees. He had to practically carry her into the bathroom. Her legs refused to support her after being tied all night. Tom arranged her on the toilet and held her erect. The sound of splashing from the pan told of a very full bladder indeed. When she was done, Tom wiped her dry and said, 'I guess you need some water, and maybe a toothbrush. I'm going to take your gag off so you can drink. Then I'll brush your teeth and make some breakfast for both of us.'

When the gag came off, Beth worked her tongue around her dry mouth and croaked, 'Water.'

Tom held a glass to her lips and she drank it down in a gulp. 'Another?' Beth nodded. She drank the second glass a bit more slowly, and refused a third. He put the glass down and picked up her toothbrush. She opened her mouth at a sign from him and he brushed her teeth for her. He rinsed her mouth and put the brush away. 'Breakfast?' She nodded. 'Can you walk?'

'I'll try,' she said, rising unsteadily to her feet.

He supported her through into the kitchen and drew out a chair for her. She sat down awkwardly across the chair. She couldn't sit back in it with her

51

hands bound behind her. Tom began to make coffee and to set out the things for breakfast. 'Are you all right, Beth?' he asked as she sat down.

'Yes. I'm okay, just a bit cramped. No, don't untie my hands,' she said quickly as he moved in her direction. 'I stood it all night and I can stand it for the duration. You can untie me tomorrow evening, not before. Remember the rules.'

'All right,' he agreed. 'Coffee?' He set his cup down on the table and held hers to her lips. A bit trickled down her chin and he wiped it away with his fingers. He set the cup down and turned her face up, holding it as he bent down to her lips. The kiss went on and on, their mouths seeking each other. He felt her tongue in his mouth, and her breath was warm on his cheeks. He felt her shudder against him. His own breath was beginning to come hard, and there was a tightness in his crotch.

Beth pulled her lips away from and gasped, 'Not now. Home Office rules forbid sex with prisoners, especially when they are restrained and can't offer resistance. Let's wait until tomorrow as we agreed.'

'I didn't make any agreement about sex,' he said. 'You can't change the rules in the middle of the game, and I rather like the idea of having you helpless. But we'll wait a bit if you like. There's plenty of time.' He could see that she was aroused. Her nipples were taut under the silk of her blouse, and she was breathing heavily, almost panting. 'What do you want to eat?' he asked, turning back to the stove.

'Just cereal and milk. I'm not all that hungry now. Maybe I'll have something else at lunch.' Her voice was unsteady and the breath rasped in her throat.

'Okay. In that case I'll just have coffee. No point in cooking for myself.' He set a bowl of muesli in front of Beth and poured coffee for both of them. Pulling up a chair, he sat down and held the coffee to her lips. When she had drunk a bit he began to feed her. He noticed that her breath had slowed, but her erect nipples were still outlined under the blouse.

Beth raised her eyes and looked at him. 'Enjoying the game?' she asked. She wriggled a bit on the chair and her breasts jiggled slightly with the motion. She knew what effect she was having on him, and seemed to be enjoying her power.

'Yes. I like it. I never thought not having sex could be fun, but this is the way to do it. Do you have any more bright ideas?'

'A few,' Beth replied enigmatically. 'Stick around for a week or so and we'll see what comes up. In the meantime feel free to try out some of your own fantasies with me. I don't want you to feel left out. I'm open to most things and I like surprises every now and then.' After a pause Beth asked for another sip of coffee. Afterwards she resumed eating from the spoon he held for her. When she was done, she asked him how he planned to spend the day, adding, 'I'm lucky. I don't have to make any plans.' Beth wriggled a bit more on the chair and her skirt rode up so that her stocking tops were visible.

Tom tore his gaze away from her thighs and replied, 'I hadn't made any definite plans. You caught me on the hop. I had been planning to spend the weekend doing what we usually do – screwing our brains out. Shopping, I suppose. I've been neglecting that lately. And maybe a cinema. I really don't know.'

'Why don't you give what's her name, Valerie, the girl at the office, a call? You could use my phone if you like. I can't stop you. And maybe you two can have a nice evening while I'm lying bound and gagged in my lonely bed.' Beth assumed an air of mock resignation as she made this proposal.

Tom remembered how his account of an earlier tryst with Valerie had aroused Beth. She had been interested in the details of their lovemaking, and had asked endless questions. He guessed she would be imagining their sweaty exercises while she lay helpless in the dark bedroom if he were successful in making a date for the night. He realised it was rather late – Saturday morning – to make a call! He didn't want to give Valerie the impression that she was an afterthought or a last resort. In fact he had rather enjoyed the times with her. She was lively and interesting and he might have spent more time with her if he hadn't been so deeply wrapped up with Beth.

'Okay. I'll try it. I might enjoy a bit of company tonight. Much better than spending the time on my own. And we get on well,' he added, to see what effect it would have on Beth.

She frowned momentarily but recovered her earlier interested manner. In order to cover the lapse she said, 'I've had enough for now. Can we go through into the front room?' Tom nodded and helped Beth to her feet. She moved ahead of him through the door, teetering slightly on her high heels when she stepped onto the carpeting and it gave beneath her weight. Beth recovered her balance and moved across the room to sit on the settee. 'The phone's just there on the table,' she reminded him as she settled back awkwardly.

'I know. I've been here before. When I'm ready, no, when I've got you ready, I'll make the call.' Tom went through into the bedroom and emerged with the rest of the rope. He dropped it in a pile at her feet.

Beth smiled up at him and asked, 'Are you going to leave me here for a while? I'm all for a change.'

'That thought had crossed my mind,' Tom replied as he turned away to reenter the kitchen.

She heard him opening cupboard doors and called out, 'Is there something I can help you find? Shall I come through?' Beth was struggling to her feet as she spoke.

'No. I've found what I want.' Tom came back to her side just as she was rising to her feet. He turned her one-handedly so that she had her back to the sofa and gave her a gentle shove. Beth sat down abruptly with a bump. Tom had brought a cucumber from the kitchen. 'You're getting low on vegetables, but fortunately there was this. I don't suppose I have to tell you where it's going, do I? This is part of the initiative programme you recommended to me earlier on.' Roughening his voice, he asked, 'Are you going to spread your legs, or do I have to use force?'

Beth spread her thighs as far as her skirt allowed. Tom knelt and pulled it all the way to her hips. He paused to admire her legs, then felt inside her with his finger. She was wet, and she caught her breath as she felt him probing her. Withdrawing his finger, he picked up the cucumber and thrust it slowly into her cunt. It was the knobbly variety, and she seemed to feel each one of the bumps as it slid inside her. This penetration brought another, more prolonged sigh from Beth. Tom tied her ankles and knees once more. With an extra piece of rope he tied her thighs together as well, pressing her legs tightly around the cucumber and holding it inside her. Once more he toyed with her, rubbing and stroking her vulva until her hips began to rise and fall gently. Tom guessed she could feel the cucumber sliding back and forth inside her as

55

she moved. Her face and neck were suffused by a flush which spread its warmth quickly over her entire body. She looked as if she would have parted her legs if they hadn't been tied together. She leaned back against the arm of the settee so as to present herself more fully to his hands.

As the arousal continued her nipples became erect. They looked acutely sensitive, almost painful, as they rubbed against the soft material of her blouse. Tom used one hand to tease and harden them further. With the other he continued to stroke her thighs and belly. Her nostrils were flaring widely as the breath sawed in her throat, and she was beginning to heave and writhe on the settee. He fumbled at the buttons of her blouse and eventually got them open. He pushed it aside, exposing her taut breasts to the cool air in the room. She gasped at the caress of air on the heated flesh. Beth heaved herself about until she was more or less lying on the settee. Only her legs hung over onto the floor. Tom paused to lift them up and to arrange her in a more accessible manner. 'Oh, Tom, don't stop,' she gasped, mistaking his intentions.

'I should do, but this time I think I'll go on. Are you really enjoying this?'

'Don't ask silly questions. Can't you see I am?' Beth gritted out between bouts of heavy breathing.

'Now who's asking silly questions?' he retorted. He resumed stroking her belly. Occasionally he forced a finger between her bound thighs and toyed with her labia and clitoris. He could tell whenever he found the spot by her increased movement. When she thrust herself against his finger, he could feel the hard rind of the cucumber inside her. Whenever he moved it Beth drew in a deep shuddery breath and strained against his hand.

56

Tom shifted his hand so that the palm lay on her vulva and his finger rested on her clitoris. Beth clenched her thighs tightly together as if to hold him there. He guessed that she was clenching herself around the cucumber as well. He bent over her body and took one of her nipples between his teeth, nipping gently and running his tongue over the engorged flesh. Beth seemed to go mad. She bucked and jerked at his touch, crying out her pleasure as the waves of her climax swept over her. 'Aahhhh, oh God. Tom! Go on! Go on! More, more! Haaaahhhh, haahhhh!' She became incoherent at the end, not to say inarticulate, and a good time was had by at least one of the participants.

As he brought her to orgasm, Tom felt a sense of power over her – something the feminists would doubtless resent and decry, but pleasing none the less. Bound as she was, Beth had done nothing to bring about her pleasure. She was helpless and completely in Tom's power. He had done this to her, and she had not been able to prevent or control him. Rather he had driven her until she had lost control of her body and became inarticulate. Beth had thought up the game and had urged it upon him, overcoming his initial objection. But now she was caught up in it and couldn't escape or influence what happened to her. It came to Tom in a disturbing flash that he could do anything he wanted to with Beth. She was in his power until he decided to end it by untying her.

But what if he decided not to let her go? There was nothing she or anyone could do. He imagined keeping Beth a helpless captive for days and weeks. At first she would not realise her predicament, then would come the dawning of understanding – and fear. She would struggle to free herself and plead with him to let her go. He would have to keep her gagged so that she couldn't cry out or scream for help. It occurred to him that he would need to find a place to keep her so that she would not be found or heard no matter what outcry she made. A secluded house, perhaps with a cellar where she could be confined. Somehow he would have to get her into the car unseen to move her to her place of incarceration. He would probably be better hiring a closed van. And the transfer from house to van would best be done in the early hours of the morning. The memory of his trip through the quiet streets just last night flashed into his mind.

How best to avoid the enquiries that were sure to follow the disappearance of such an attractive woman? He imagined the newspaper stories: *Local Beauty Disappears*. Newspapers always talked of beautiful women. They sold more papers than merely attractive ones! Would they miss her at work? It occurred to him that he knew nothing of Beth's work – if indeed she did anything. Her strict injunction against seeing her during the week had prevented him from making enquiries. He marvelled for a moment at how docile he had been, never trying to exceed the limits she had set. Never questioning the scenarios she provided for their trysts; never thinking beyond the erotic possibilities of their closed relationship. Now this same woman whom he had never disobeyed lay beneath his hands, helplessly bound and out of control as he played upon the instrument of her body. Where could he find a secluded place to confine her? And where . . .

The thoughts tumbled through his mind as his hands and mouth continued their play over Beth's heaving body. He had retreated to another fantasy world for the moment, one whose existence he had never suspected, such was the influence Beth was beginning to exercise over his thoughts. Tom had never thought of making Beth – or anyone – his captive, his possession, his slave. But he did now. New ideas presented themselves to him as Beth gasped and moaned in her bonds. For a fleeting instant he thought he had better gag her in case she screamed out in orgasm, but he didn't stop. Her cries were choked back in any case, the sounds of passion rather than fear or pain. The infrequent newspaper stories of people who complained about the noises their neighbours made when making love occurred to him. Would there be complaints today? He dismissed these thoughts and returned to the task in hand. Beth was in fact now a double handful. He was having trouble keeping her from wrenching away. Only the need to keep herself under his hands kept her from making any more violent movements.

Once more Beth cried out, a guttural moan of pleasure as his forefinger massaged her clitoris and his palm rubbed her vulva. Her cries rose in pitch and volume as yet another climax shook her. She slipped from the couch and landed with a slight bump on the floor, half on the carpet and half on Tom. He was perilously close to a climax of his own. Tom used one hand to ease her to a more comfortable position, half on the floor and half on his lap. He cradled Beth's head and shoulders and leaned back against the settee to watch her contortions in an interested manner: look what I've done. Beth rolled over onto her side and drew her legs up. She bent herself almost double at the waist, trying to fold herself around her centre and hold onto the ecstasy for as long as possible.

Eventually, though, the feelings subsided and her taut body relaxed against him. 'Mmmmm, that was nice,' she said dreamily. 'Do you have any more good ideas?' She arched her back like a cat and rubbed her breasts against his idle hand.

'Not at the moment, but something else will occur sooner or later. Anything you'd like to suggest?'

'Well, now you mention it, I was feeling bad about leaving you out of the action all weekend, and especially just then when I was having such a good time while you worked so hard over me. If you'd like to get undressed, or just unzip your trousers if you're in a hurry, I think I can make some of it up to you, Tom. Unless you've got other plans,' she added with a wicked grin.

'No, nothing that won't keep. Shall I untie you?' Tom asked with just a hint of eagerness.

'No. The original rules still hold. You have to keep me tied up until tomorrow evening. I'll think up some suitable reward for your patience then. This will be just a slight foretaste to keep you in suspense until tomorrow.'

Tom eased her to the floor and stood up. He realised he was getting excited merely looking at Beth as she lay at his feet. Her bare breasts poked out through the open front of her blouse, jutting out even more with her hands tied behind her back. Her skirt had rucked itself up to her waist and he admired the curve of her thighs and calves with the ropes biting into the flesh. He wanted to fling off his clothes and have her there and then. She always had that effect on him. But something made him go slowly, draw out the act of undressing. He felt Beth's glance on him as he unbuckled his belt and let his trousers drop. Stepping out of them, he slowly removed his shirt and underpants.

He was erect (had in fact been painfully erect since

they began), and Beth made admiring noises when she saw him. 'Is that on account of little old me?' she asked coquettishly.

Her words reinforced his urge to prolong the foreplay. Normally he would have been on her in an instant, but he was entering into the game she had proposed: postponing the pleasure and making her wait as she was making him wait. When he was naked Tom sat down on the floor with his back against the settee once more, but at some distance from Beth. She must have had something in mind, and he wanted to let her reveal it to him without any urging.

She looked quizzically at him. When he still did nothing, Beth appeared to reach a decision. She shrugged her shoulders and began to inch across the floor to him. At the first movement she must have felt the cucumber slide inside her and she gasped at the sensation. The friction and the sense of being stuffed full were probably arousing her again even after the extended stimulation she had already undergone.

Tom watched her slow progress, admiring the play of muscle beneath her skin as she inched across the floor. There was something intensely arousing in watching this bound woman crawl towards him. His cock stretched itself until it felt as if it would break the taut skin. His breath came harshly as he tried to control it.

She too was breathing heavily by the time she reached him. Her thighs were clenched tightly around the cucumber and he imagined she felt it massaging her clitoris as it moved inside her. She raised herself and manoeuvred herself until her head lay in his lap. From there she could reach his cock with her lips and tongue. Beth leaned toward him and kissed the underside of the shaft. The sharp intake of his breath

61

told her she had found a sensitive spot. She kissed him there again, using her tongue as well this time.

Moving down slightly, Beth used her tongue to lick his balls. That brought a groan from Tom. Encouraged, she continued to use her lips and tongue to arouse him. Tom responded, gripping her hair tightly in his hand and pressing her face against his scrotum. He could smell the odour of his musk and he guessed the same smell was strong in her nostrils as she gasped for breath. She tried to draw back and catch her breath but he held her firmly against him.

Finally, sensing her difficulty, Tom relaxed his grip slightly and she was able to breathe again.

Tom lifted her shoulders until she could reach her goal. Beth took his erect cock inside her mouth and Tom felt himself surrounded by the wet warmth. She teased with her tongue, licking him gently. With his free hand he pinched and rubbed her breasts and nipples. Beth continued to arouse him with her lips and tongue. She must have felt him swelling until he seemed to fill her mouth, but she made no effort to avoid what was sure to follow. When he came, she was forced to swallow quickly to prevent herself from choking on his semen. He held her tightly against him for a long moment as he shuddered and emptied himself into her mouth. Then he relaxed and loosened the grip on her hair.

Beth rolled slightly away from him and he watched her face. He guessed he would remember this day for a long time. He hoped she would too. She tried to sit up without success. As she wriggled and heaved, the cucumber must have been sliding about inside her. Tom wondered how long he could leave her like this. If he went away now, she would be in a state of continual sexual arousal. Not an unpleasant prospect, but he guessed it would be very tiring if it lasted all day. He lifted her off him and stood up. Then he bent to lift her back onto the settee.

When she was comfortable Beth reminded him of his promise to call Valerie.

'If you insist,' Tom said. 'Will it make you hot to hear me talk to her while you're here? Though you might well burst into flames if you get any hotter.' Even as he spoke Tom found himself once more marvelling at how natural it seemed to do whatever Beth asked. If he had his way, he would spend the time with her, but she had ruled that out most firmly. He went over to the telephone and reluctantly dialled Valerie's number. He heard the phone ringing. It rang for a long time, and Tom knew she was out. He was relieved. But he had to keep up the act, so he engaged in an imaginary conversation with the absent Valerie, hoping he sounded as if he weren't talking into a dead phone.

Finally he put the phone down and turned back to Beth. She was sitting up on the settee and showing every sign of interest in the evening's arrangement. Her lips were parted and wet. Her nipples were half-erect. 'Do you get turned on just by listening to me talk to someone else?' he asked.

'Some people do,' she answered. 'I like to imagine you and Valerie together. I want you to tell me what you do when you see her.'

Tom heard this but didn't understand it. Not for the first time, he thought that Beth was a very complicated woman. He was very lucky to have found her, but he wished she wouldn't disturb him quite so much as she did with her novel schemes. In fairness, he reflected that he always enjoyed her bizarre behaviour, after he had got used to the idea. She led him into unfamiliar territory again and again, opening him to ideas and acts he had not considered before. That was the basis of his fascination with her.

'Where will you and Valerie go tonight while I lie here helpless?' Beth asked with mock dismay. 'I expect you'll forget all about me.'

'Well, if you want me to I can bring her with me when I come to look in on you.' Tom walked back and sat on the floor next to the settee where Beth lay. Idly he fondled her breasts as they talked. She heaved herself around until she was lying conveniently to hand and looked steadily at him. He didn't meet her gaze, pretending to be preoccupied with other areas of her anatomy. She managed to look both helpless and appealing at the same time. He knew why he felt so attracted to her.

He lifted Beth from the couch to the floor and arranged her so that she was kneeling with her back to him and her upper body resting on the seat. Her bottom was presented invitingly to him. Then he went through into the kitchen and searched until he found the olive oil. With this he lubricated her anus and the divide of her bottom. Then he slowly stroked the area, noting Beth's reactions. She seemed to be happy enough. From time to time she sighed contentedly, especially when he paused to prod the pink rose of her arsehole. When she shuddered and drew in a particularly deep breath he knew she was coming along nicely.

At the same time he was noting his own reaction, which became more and more pronounced as he fondled Beth. When he was erect he used some of the olive oil to lubricate his shaft before rising to his knees behind Beth. He eased forward until he could press the head of his cock against her arsehole.

Gradually he increased the pressure, working silently. It was a tight fit with her legs bound together, but Tom finally managed to slide his prick into her anus. Beth jerked in surprise and tried to get away, but he held onto her until she quieted down and began to respond. He could feel the cucumber inside her cunt through the thin wall separating her two entrances. He used his other hand to caress her nipples and breasts. Doubly penetrated, Beth was heaving under him and crying out. But she wasn't asking him to stop. The situation was new to both of them, and Tom found himself trying to hold back until Beth reached orgasm. She didn't take long. Her orgasm was acccompanied by loud moans and low strangled cries. Tom came as she did, and Beth's body seemed to leap beneath him.

He slipped from her body and leaned back against the front of the couch. He waited while his breathing slowed and the sweat dried on his body. Beth lay face down, half lying on the settee and half kneeling on the floor. Her skirt was up over her hips and she was breathing in gasps. From time to time she shuddered. Tom thought of the aftershocks that followed an earthquake, and was tempted to ask her if the earth had moved for her. But he said nothing. By now he knew enough about her reactions to judge how she had enjoyed it. After a few more minutes she was breathing normally and he lifted her down until her head rested in his lap.

'I'm not complaining, mind you,' Beth remarked as she stared at his prick just in front of her face, 'but isn't this where I came in earlier? I hope you're not expecting a re-run. You've worn me out, and I can't say that about many men.'

Tom accepted the compliment with a smile. 'Me

too,' he said. 'We could use a break, but if I stay here we aren't going to get one. You look too good to let alone. Ready to call it a day? Can I let you loose?'

Beth smiled and shook her head, the red hair sliding across her face. 'Not until tomorrow evening. We agreed on that.'

Tom brushed her hair aside and looked into her face. He could read the familiar determination there. He knew there was no point in trying to change her mind, so he stood up and lifted Beth to her feet. He steadied her when her legs refused to bear her weight, setting her down on the couch. She lay back against the cushions as he untied her legs. The rope had left angry red marks in the flesh at ankles and knees. Apparently the circulation had been restricted, because Beth whimpered once or twice as she flexed her legs.

'Pins and needles,' she said when she saw Tom looking at her. 'I'll be all right soon.' When he continued to look concerned, she told him, 'Don't worry. It's a small price to pay for that experience. An occupational hazard among us B&D freaks. But it looks as if I've laddered my stockings. You'll have to help me change them. I need to look my best at all times. Your average passing rapist just won't look twice at a girl with ladders in her stockings.' The lightness of her remarks made Tom feel easier. She really *was* enjoying all this.

Finally Beth made as if to stand. Tom helped her to her feet. He guessed she wanted to go to the loo. They went through into the toilet with Beth leading. There she asked Tom to unplug her so she could pee. She relaxed and he pulled the knobbly thing out of her. Beth sighed with regret, but it had to come out sometime. She said, 'I don't think I'll be able to pass a greengrocer's shop without thinking of cucumbers.'

66

She sat on the loo and let go at once. She shivered with the relief of it. Tom wondered if there was anything she didn't enjoy. It was another facet of her attraction for him.

Tom wiped her dry and steered her back into the bedroom. Beth sat on the side of the bed. 'I keep my tights and stockings in the top bureau drawer. There should be another pair like these somewhere near the top. Would you get them and help me change out of these?'

He opened the drawer and began to search through the contents. The faint aroma of Beth that clung to her underwear rose to his nostrils as he moved the neatly paired stockings to find the ones she wanted. Tom was amused by her neatness. Not every woman, he guessed, took such pains with her lingerie. It was another of the small touches that made Beth special. When he found what she wanted he took them across to where Beth sat docilely on the bed. Raising her skirt, now quite wrinkled and damp from their lovemaking, he unclipped the laddered stockings and stripped them from her legs. As he smoothed the new stockings up her legs and secured them to her suspender belt, Tom thought that there was something especially erotic in performing this intimate service for a woman. Beth helped him as much as she could, lifting her feet or raising her leg for him to get at the suspenders that came from the rear of her belt.

When he was done, Tom paused for a moment to admire the effect. Then he stood up to replace her gag. Beth opened her mouth obediently and he thrust the damp ball of tights and stockings inside, making her cheeks bulge. With the scarf he secured the gag in place. He retrieved the rope from the front room and once more tied her legs at the ankles and knees. When she was bound he turned and left without another word. Let her sit or lie down as she wished. He thought the abrupt and silent exit might add to the air of mystery and menace she seemed to relish. A few weeks ago he would never have thought of that touch. Tom drove home to shower and invent the story of the date with Valerie for Beth's titillation.

There was plenty of time for the task. In fact there wasn't much else for Tom to do at home. Since meeting Beth he had dropped out of most of his social habits, preferring to spend the weekend with her. So now he was high and dry. He made a few notes, watched TV and went to sleep in the armchair, but not before he had set the alarm to wake him in time to get to Beth's place.

In the early mornlng darkness the streets were quiet as he drove to her flat. It was dark, but there were lights beginning to show in several of the surrounding buildings. Terminal insomniacs, Tom thought. Or the inveterate early risers. He let himself into the silent flat and headed straight for the bedroom. Beth lay bound and gagged as he had left her, but he caught the sharp odour of urine as he bent over her. She was a damp, untidy mess, as he had suspected she would be. He had been trying to give the impression that he had spent the evening with Valerie, and had left it a bit too long. Beth hadn't been able to hold out.

First things first, he thought as he took off her gag. If she was going to be angry, he'd deal with that later. 'We'll have to get you cleaned up. I'll have to let you loose for a bit. It's almost morning and you need a shower. A proper one, I meant; not the golden shower you've already had.'

When she could speak, Beth made it clear that she wasn't angry about the mess. 'I knew this might

68

happen. It's one of the risks you take when you get into long-term bondage. We groupies call it humiliation, and I'm now finding out how it feels. A large part of the fun is the attempt to hold off when you are almost sure you won't be able to. And then when you wet yourself you can imagine you've been forgotten and that no one will come.'

This was something Tom had heard of without believing. But Beth seemed all right. Damp and smelly but not reproachful. He untied her and helped her into the bathroom, where he had her stand in the shower with her clothes on, rinsing away the worst of it. Then he helped her undress and take a proper shower. Tom got undressed himself for that bit, and joined her in the shower. He scrubbed her clean and shampooed her hair, admiring once more the rich red sheen and the weight of it. Beth began to dry her hair but Tom took over. He enjoyed the task, and Beth sat quietly as he worked at it. Then Beth asked Tom to get a clean skirt and blouse for her.

'And stockings and suspenders, too,' she called after him. 'I know how you like them.' When Tom brought the clothing she dressed herself. Tom admired her body even as she covered it. He had deliberately chosen a silk blouse that allowed her nipples to show through.

When she was dressed again, he used the damp rope to tie her wrists and elbows again. Beth didn't protest. They went into the kitchen where Tom made breakfast for them. He fed Beth between bites of his own toast and marmalade. He paused to rearrange her skirt so that she was showing more leg. Beth only smiled.

Breakfast over, he took Beth through into the living room and switched on the TV for her. She settled on the couch and when she was comfortable he tethered her to the coffee table by her ankle. Then he raised her skirt until he could see the tops of her stockings and the smooth flesh above them. Tom went into the bedroom to gather up the soiled bedding and clothing to be washed. Each time he passed through the front room she gave him an encouraging smile. The damp hair trailing over her face and shoulders gave her a dishevelled look which made her more appealing.

Tom paused on one of his trips to open the top buttons of her blouse and bare her breasts. He teased her nipples until they were erect and her breath was becoming rapid. Then he stopped to allow her to simmer. She looked like the classic captive maiden of romantic fiction awaiting with trepidation the pleasure of her captor: very exciting, thought Tom. He sometimes wished she'd struggle or protest, to give added piquancy to the game. But she didn't. Tom carried on with the chores.

Finally the washing was all in the machine and the breakfast things put away. Tom went to sit beside Beth and they watched the awful Sunday morning shows. When the boredom was too much to bear he turned to fondle her breasts and slid a hand between her legs, liking the feel of the smooth nylon on her thighs. Beth always parted her legs obligingly when he did this. But soon it was time to go. He wanted to stay but her rules were still in effect. He tied her legs again and replaced her gag. Beth gave him an encouraging smile as he left.

Tom was at a familiar loose end when he got back to his place. The condition aggravated by the dreary atmosphere of Sunday afternoon. In desperation he drove to the zoo – not because he particularly wanted to see the animals. But at least there were people there. If nothing else he could play the game of watching and assessing them until it was time to go back and let Beth loose. He idly watched the families (and the single parents) strolling with their children. And as he watched these more or less complete family groups he realised just how far he was from their pre-occupations. He had never thought of having children, and had never seriously contemplated marriage and family life. That alone was enough to isolate him from the normal run of social contacts. And it made him a loose cannon. Isolated from the usual concerns of the family group, he prowled on the fringes, looking for loose females. And they were thin on the ground.

He was lucky to have met Beth as he had. She didn't demand to be taken out to shows or restaurants. She seemed to be content to stay indoors and play erotic games. By the usual standards theirs would be considered an exotic, greenhouse lifestyle, focused as it was on sex and bondage. Some (maybe most) people would regard their preoccupation as unhealthy, even perverted. But that didn't make him any less eager to get back to his lady in waiting. These were definitely not Sunday-at-the-zoo thoughts. He was probably exactly the kind of man mothers warned their children against. He imagined Beth would carry a similar health warning. He was a sex maniac and she was a scarlet woman. Too bad there weren't more of them around.

Tom found Beth as he had left her. He removed her gag and untied her. Beth wanted to know about his evening with Valerie. She asked him for the most intimate details of the supposed encounter, and Tom found his powers of invention very strained indeed.

71

He wondered (while hoping that she wouldn't notice any discrepancies in his tale) why she was so interested in his behaviour with other women. At the end of the tale he found out why. Beth asked him if he wanted her to find someone else to share their sex games.

Tom was taken completely by surprise. It wasn't an easy question to answer. A 'no' was the expected answer, and would brand him as conventional – something he didn't like. A 'yes' could bring on a fit of jealous rage. Instead of answering he asked, 'Where do you think you'll find another one like you?' In addition to being an implied compliment, the question was intended to allow him time to think about a totally new subject.

Beth accepted the compliment and told him that she would ask around. She looked preoccupied.

Ask around where? Ask who? Tom wanted to know. There was something vaguely alarming in Beth's question. And in her persistence. It wasn't jealousy, else Beth would be obviously furious. No, not Beth. Any other woman, yes, but she was different. Wasn't she? This made her question all the more alarming. She was not one to be easily diverted from her course. Tom didn't know if (assuming Beth managed to find a kindred spirit) he would be able to handle a triangular relationship. And what if the someone she found was male? It might be his turn to fight against jealousy and all the other problems he might bring to the relationship. Tom preferred to believe that the someone Beth had mentioned would, if found, be female.

For some moments Beth said nothing. She appeared to be thinking. At length she looked up and began to speak. She was uncharacteristically hesitant.

'I had planned to handle this differently, but there isn't any way to make it easier for either of us. I thought having you spend time with someone else would make it easier for you.' Beth paused to give Tom a wan smile. She resumed quickly before he had time to interrupt with questions. 'I have a job offer in Canada and I'm going to take it. I have to take it.'

Tom opened his mouth to protest. He was dismayed by the prospect of not seeing Beth again. He wanted to say all the conventional things that he imagined women wanted to hear, the things that would assure Beth that he wanted her to stay. But even as the words came to him he knew that he couldn't say them. Beth was not an ordinary woman. An appeal to the more conventional emotions would not work. And he was not ordinary either, but he knew he didn't want Beth to go, for reasons they must both already know. But even if she knew these reasons, she had still announced her intention to leave.

'No, don't say anything, Tom. Let me finish. Please. I promise you it's not as bad as you think. I'm going to Montreal for a while: five or six weeks, maybe two months. I don't know how long, but it's not permanent. I'll be coming back here. I just want to make sure you'll be all right in the meantime. I know someone who will take care of you while I'm away. She'll be able to give you a lot of helpful instruction in B&D. It will be like going to a college of further education. You can get your A levels!' Beth said in an attempt at humour.

Tom saw that she was serious. 'When are you going?' It was his way of saying he accepted her decision. It didn't imply he liked it, which he didn't, and that was putting it mildly. Dismay might not be too strong a word. Beth's weekday persona, the things she did during the time she would not let him share, had finally caught up with them. He remembered how he had met Beth at the street market. It was possible that she would meet someone else in the same easy way in Montreal. But he couldn't say that either.

'Tomorrow,' Beth said quietly. 'But remember, it's not permanent.' She looked unhappy but he knew she had made up her mind. 'I don't think it will do any good to talk about it. You ought to go now. But be ready to meet a friend of mine soon. And remember, I'll be back sooner than you think. And I'll miss you while I'm away.'

In a daze Tom got up and went out the door. He didn't know how he got home. Nor how he got through the rest of the evening. The next week at work passed somehow. If someone had asked Tom what he did in that time, he wouldn't have been able to say. He barely noticed the blank looks he got from his colleagues. The weekend didn't promise any relief. There would be no more games with Beth to give shape to the time. Tom worked and ate and slept and tried not to think. He knew how rudderless ships felt – if ships could be said to have feelings.

Chapter Four

On the Friday after Beth's departure Tom had the afternoon off work and was at home wondering what he was going to do with the time when there as a knock at his door. He was not expecting anyone, so he was surprised when he opened the door to find himself confronted by a sturdily-built woman who seemed to be both supremely self-confident and slightly impatient. He had been listening to a recording of 'The Water Music' and had taken the time to switch it off before answering the door. Hence his visitor's impatience.

'Tom Clark?' she said without preamble.

Tom nodded.

'I'm Harriet Jones,' she said, advancing as though he had stood aside and invited her to come in. She looked as if she expected him to be expecting her. He hurriedly stood aside and she walked into his front room. She surveyed the place with an air of summing up its occupant, and finding him wanting in some obscure way.

'Harriet Jones,' she repeated, as if she expected the name to ring a bell.

Tom looked blank. He had not been thinking too clearly since Beth left.

Harriet Jones looked annoyed. 'I suppose Beth neglected to tell you about me. She often forgets things,' she said, with the air of one who never forgets anything. She went on, 'I'm going to take over from her. She must have said something about that.'

The penny finally dropped. This must be the someone Beth had mentioned in their last conversation. But she had said nothing about her friend 'taking over'. That must have been Harriet Jones's own phrasing. Tom looked at his visitor and saw a short, sturdy woman who wore a brown tweedy two-piece suit and dark brown tights (or stockings). She was not in the same class as Beth for glamour. But she was pretty in her own way. Her legs were heavier than Beth's, one of the first things Tom had noticed about her, but well-shaped. She wore high heels which made them more attractive – though that may only have been Tom's prejudices showing. Her hair was brown, like her eyes. But the most striking thing about her was her air of command and self-possession. She was not someone you would lightly cross.

Tom recovered and offered her a coffee, or a drink, if she preferred. Harriet accepted a coffee and sat down on the settee without being invited. Tom went through to the kitchen to put the kettle on. He called back through to Harriet to ask if she wanted sugar and milk.

'Both,' she replied laconically.

When he came back with the coffee he noticed that her short skirt had ridden up her thighs. He paused to admire the view and to compare her with Beth. Harriet went up considerably in his admiration, as the owner of that pair of shapely legs, but Beth was undeniably the more attractive. Best not to make too many comparisons. Beth was gone. Harriet was here.

Harriet noticed his glance but said nothing. She did, however, allow herself a brief smile as though accepting a compliment. 'Set the coffee down on the table and take off your trousers. Your pants too, if you're wearing any. Beth wasn't too clear on that point.'

Tom found himself unbuckling his belt before he thought about the bizarre nature of her command. With a shrug he continued until he stood before her naked from the waist down. Himself, unsure of the occasion, was inclined to sulk.

Harriet looked appraisingly at him. 'Come here,' she commanded. When he stood before her, Harriet casually reached for his cock and began to fondle it. Obligingly, it became erect under her hands. 'That's better,' she said. 'Hold that while I fix you up.'

Harriet fished in her handbag and came out with a tie wrap. She threaded the end of the plastic strap through the locking head and slipped the loop over his balls. She slid it up until it touched the underside of his cock, then she drew it tight.

Tom winced a little as the strap pinched him slightly. Harriet paid no attention. She dug a pair of side cutters out of her handbag and snipped the excess length from the strap.

'Be careful with the family jewels. I haven't got another set,' he warned Harriet. She gave him a scornful look and continued to adjust the strap.

When she was satisfied, she gave him a dismissive nod. 'That's to remind you that you're with me now. Put your trousers back on and drink your coffee. Then we can go.'

Tom did as he was told. He didn't ask her what she meant by his being with her, nor did he ask where they were going. Later he wondered why he was so docile. At the time she seemed to be an irresistible force.

'I need an assistant, and you've been volunteered for the job. By Beth, in case you haven't guessed that already. She told me you might be at a loose end about now, and would be interested in some congenial work. With me. Of course you'll require some more training and experience, but I will attend to that. She told me you had taken her sugestions readily enough.'

Tom felt a stab of regret at the mention of Beth, but he didn't say anything. He hoped his feelings didn't show. It didn't seem like a good idea to appear weak to this resolute woman who had marched into his house as if she owned it, and him. He recalled how Beth had urged him to experiment sexually with her. He wondered if Harriet would fill the space left by his departed lover and tutor. He wondered how Beth was getting along in her assignment. He hadn't heard anything from her, and he guessed he wouldn't for some time. And he didn't want to be the one to beg her to return.

Harriet didn't appear to be interested in his moods or his expression. When he had come to know her better, he learned that she never bothered to study her subjects closely. She was a member of that self-assured group of women who assumed that others would do whatever she asked as a matter of course. She assumed from the start that he would be her 'assistant'. She explained later what she wanted him to do in that capacity, but she never tried to persuade him to do anything. She took his acquiescence for granted.

'Get your trousers on. It's time to be going along to my place,' she repeated.

Tom buckled his belt and followed her out the door, conscious of the tie wrap constricting his scrotum and wondering (though not asking) what she intended to do next. They drove through light traffic to Harriet's place in Chelsea. It was a three-storey terraced house with a basement. There was no front entrance to the basement, and Tom concluded that there was no separate flat there. Most of the other houses on the street had basement flats. They went up the front steps with Harriet in the lead. As she opened the front door he noticed the unusually heavy door and the strong locks. Women had to be careful if they lived alone, as Harriet apparently did, but even so the locks seemed more than adequate.

Noticing his glance, Harriet said, 'These locks are intended to keep people in as well as out. You'll have the run of the house for some of the time you're here, but you won't be able to get out short of breaking down the door. And you won't have the tools for that. It's difficult to break out of even ordinary houses without tools, and this is no ordinary house. All the windows are locked, and those bars aren't just ornamental. I hope you'll settle in quite quickly, but if you keep on trying to get out I may have to employ stronger measures. On the other hand, I eventually reward good behaviour.'

When they were inside the front hall Harriet closed and locked the door. She turned and said, 'Come along and I'll show you some more of the place.' She went past the stairway that led up from the entrance hall. Apparently he wasn't going to be shown the first floor. Harriet turned into a lounge off the hall with a window overlooking the street in which she had parked the car. The room contained a comfortable looking three-piece suite. There was the usual television and video recorder. Tom also noticed a video camcorder on the coffee table in front of the settee.

The walls were papered in complementary shades of pale blue. It was a sunny room, at least in the afternoons. The plants and ornaments all seemed ordinary, but the house didn't feel ordinary. That may have been due to the manner of the woman who lived there.

An archway led into a second room which was both an extension of the lounge and a dining area. At the far end there was a table and chairs. The kitchen to which Harriet led him opened off the dining area and occupied the back of the house. It overlooked a courtyard with a garage which could be entered from the passage that ran behind the house. She showed Tom where things were kept: pantry, fridge, pots and pans, china and cutlery. It all seemed neat enough, and he said so. But he wondered why she was going into such detail. He learned the answer when she ordered him to cook a meal for them.

'This will be one of your responsibilities while you're here. You have to keep things clean and tidy and prepare the meals for me. You are going to be my housekeeper. There are other things I prefer to do. But before you begin I want you to take off your clothes.'

Tom was taken aback by her calm belief that he would do anything she asked. He also found himself taking his clothes off. When he was wearing nothing but the tie wrap she had placed on his scrotum, Harriet collected his jeans, shirt and underpants and took them away – to keep them safe, she said. He didn't ask, safe from what? She continued, 'I'll keep them locked up until you're ready to leave. While you're here I'd like you to begin feeling naked and defenceless. This is your first lesson.'

'Do I get to look at you as well?' he ventured.

'Only when I want you to,' Harriet replied. 'And I will decide what you can see. We will both dress as I think fit.' Changing tack, she continued, 'Would you like to look at me?'

'Well, yes. I find you attractive, and . . .' he trailed off, not certain how to finish the remark.

Harriet prompted, 'And what?'

'Well, attractive . . . I intended it as a compliment.'

'Then thank you. Now get on with the job while I get into something more comfortable. I think I'll enjoy having some help around the house. And some company,' she added as she went out bearing his clothes.

Tom opened cupboards and began to assemble things for a meal. There was enough in the fridge and pantry to see them through several days. He wondered how many days he should plan on. He decided on steak and baked potatoes with a tossed salad and, after a glance in the fridge, white wine. There were carrots and broccoli to prepare. As he was putting the potatoes into the oven Harriet returned. She was wearing the 'something more comfortable' she had spoken of, though Tom would have argued about the more comfortable aspect of it. He heartily approved of the effect, however, and recalled the remark another woman had made about how looking stunning and feeling comfortable were the same thing. Or had she said that when your appearance struck the observer dumb with admiration, matters of comfort receded into the middle distance? No matter.

Harriet looked stunning to him. She wore an outfit based on the one-piece swimming costume, but made of smooth black leather instead of the softer fabrics more familiar to the connoisseurs of ladies' underwear and the swimsuit-watchers' league. Tom thought it an improvement on the original idea. Harriet's outfit gave the impression of having been sprayed on. It was cut high on her thighs, revealing her really nice legs to the hips on the outside, while the crotch area was framed and accentuated by the V of skintight leather that dived between her thighs. It re-emerged behind, where it ran between her buttocks in the manner of a thong, dividing those generous hemispheres from one another as decisively as the Red Sea had been parted. Though her parting was by far the more attractive, Tom thought. At the top it plunged low as well, cupping her full breasts tightly and thrusting them up and out, an enhancement they scarcely needed. *Served up on a platter* was the impression he got. But he approved of that effect as well.

In fact his approval was unmistakable. He got hard simply looking at her, and was reminded of that fact by the tightness around his balls where the tiewrap was making itself felt.

Harriet wore sheer black tights and high-heeled shoes to match. Her waist was nipped in by a wide leather belt, accentuating two other measurements that didn't need emphasis. This was the dominatrix outfit the sex magazines and books went on about. Even though the domination looked like being exercised over him, he still liked the effect.

He had always liked women to wear things that outlined their figures. This preference doubtless came from an early fascination with adverts for ladies corsets. All of his schoolmates had lingered over them – the only pictures of semi-naked women they had been able to get in their younger days.

Harriet also carried a riding crop. 'To teach you your manners and duties,' she said, with a nod toward his erection. 'I'm glad you like the outfit, but don't touch. Tonight will be looking only.' She produced a pair of leg-irons from nowhere, seemingly, and indicated he was to put them on. Of course she had been carrying them all the time, but he hadn't noticed them. That was a measure of how deeply he was engrossed in her appearance.

Obediently, Tom sat and locked the irons on his ankles. Harriet nodded her approval and stooped to check them for tightness. She tightened them one more notch and then double-locked them with the key she carried on a ribbon around her neck. She tucked the key back into the top of her outfit. 'Carry on,' she said, turning to leave the room.

He was left alone in the kitchen to finish the meal. Shortly thereafter he heard the TV from the front room, and he guessed she was relaxing. When dinner was ready he brought the plates through to her. Harriet was seated in an armchair with her legs splayed out before her. He got hard once more when he looked at her. Tom brought the wine from the kitchen and poured a glass for each of them. Harriet nodded for him to sit down and they began to eat, Tom pausing to stare and Harriet seemingly oblivious of him.

After she had eaten a bit Harriet spoke to him. 'There will be many evenings at home like this, so I thought you should begin to get used to the idea from the first. I want you to get used to the fact that I set the rules around here, especially about sex, but also about the daily routine. I like you to look and admire, but you mustn't touch me without my permission, and then only as I direct you. Later on, when you finally do get to sleep with me, you'll enjoy it much more for having waited. And I will enjoy having made you wait. So I hope it will be fun all round. In any case the discipline will do you good. I don't like slackness in my lovers. I'm sure you understand.' Harriet added as an afterthought, 'You will address me as "mistress" unless we're in the presence of strangers who might not understand how the word is meant. My name will not be used without my permission. And I'll remember any lapses.'

Tom nodded silently. He watched Harriet as they ate, admiring the tautness of her body beneath the tight leather garment, and listening for the sibilant hiss of nylon against nylon as she crossed or uncrossed her legs. Tom thought of himself as primarily a leg man. He enjoyed ogling the legs of all the women he knew – and of many he didn't. As he put it, there was no harm in looking. He enjoyed the way the light now shifted and played on her smooth tights. There was a tightness in his groin every time she shifted her legs. So they ate their dinner, Tom growing more aroused by the minute. Harriet contrived to ignore the evidence of his excitement. When they were done, she directed him to clear away the dishes and wash up. He did so in silence. When he was done he came back from the kitchen with a freshly brewed pot of coffee. She accepted a cup and held it while he poured for her. Then he stood near by while she tasted it. When she nodded her satisfaction, Tom sat down once more.

Harriet noticed that he was not drinking and asked him if he cared to join her.

Tom replied that he was waiting for her permission. This seemed to please Harriet. 'You're learning quickly. But go ahead and have some if you like. I couldn't possibly drink all of this by myself. I wouldn't be able to sleep for having to run to the loo. Coffee always has that effect on me.'

It was Tom's turn to be pleased by the admission of this small detail to him. He found himself eager to learn more of her moods and habits. Harriet struck him as a woman who didn't chatter lightly about herself. Slow to give confidences and reluctant to let out intimate details. There was a lot to learn about this stranger who had entered his life and taken charge of him. He wanted to know more, but Harriet was silent. She turned her attention to the TV, paying him no more mind than the furniture. Nettled, he drank his coffee, hoping none of this showed on his face.

When he finished his coffee, Harriet stood up and crossed the room to him. So she must have been watching me, he thought. That was gratifying. She opened a drawer in the sideboard and produced a pair of handcuffs.

'Remember these?' she asked. They must have been the ones Beth had used on him at their first meeting. Otherwise there would be no reason to recognise a specific pair of handcuffs. One set looked exactly like any other set of the same type. Tom wondered if Beth had borrowed them from Harriet, and how much influence Harriet might have had on him through Beth. She had never mentioned Harriet, but she had seemed to have more than just a cursory knowledge of (and interest in) B&D.

Harriet motioned him to place his hands behind his back, and when he had done so she snapped the cuffs on his wrists. Instead of returning to her chair across the room, she sat down beside Tom and let her nylon-sheathed thigh brush against his bare leg. The touch was electrifying. He felt as if his whole skin were specially sensitised and waiting for just such a contact. She settled herself more comfortably against him. Tom looked at her in pleased surprise, remembering her earlier admonition about looking but not touching. As if reading his thoughts, Harriet said, 'Relax and let me do the work. You're not breaking any rules. You won't be touching me. I'll be the one doing the touching – wherever I like, and you can't stop me. Not that I think you'd want to stop me, unless you're more prudish than Beth described.'

He didn't reply, wondering again just how much Beth had told this strange and exciting woman who now sat beside him. He could feel the warmth of her body against his side, through the tight leather she wore. The smell of leather and warm flesh filled his nostrils, a heady combination. He wondered briefly if he were dreaming. This was just the sort of erotic dream he had been having lately, more so after Beth had gone. More and more he imagined himself as the prisoner of a masterful woman who would toy with him, showing him new heights of sexual experience. Beth had opened him to sexual experiments, bizarre acts he had not thought of, and then she had gone, leaving him wanting more.

Now was apparently the time for more. Harriet snuggled against him, her arm around his shoulders, holding him to her. Not that Tom intended to escape. The taut roundness of her breast pressed against his shoulder as she moulded herself to him. She leaned over and began to lick and nibble his earlobe, blowing softly into his ear at intervals. Her breath was warm on his cheek, and he could smell the aroma of the coffee she had just drunk. He felt Harriet's lips brush the angle of his jawbone and continue down the side of his neck into the sensitive spot below his ear. She licked him gently, the saliva making cooling patches on his skin that only seemed to make him hotter. With her free hand she stroked his scrotum, teasing the crinkly flesh until it grew tight. She toyed with the tie wrap around his balls, which felt as if they could swell no more without cutting through the flesh. The plastic gripped him like a steel band as Harriet's hands continued to arouse him slowly.

As she stroked and rubbed his balls, Harriet whispered into his ear, 'When rape appears inevitable, relax and enjoy it. Wouldn't you like to feel how warm and wet I am between my legs? Or are you a tit man? Would you like to get your hands on mine? Shall I take off everything for you?'

These were rhetorical questions so long as she kept him handcuffed, and so he made no reply. But her words had the effect she had calculated. His breath sawed in his throat as she whispered these enticements in his ear.

She continued, 'I'm going to test your resistance, Tom, so keep your chin up and don't let the side down.' Harriet appeared to have a fondness for mixed metaphor. 'I'm going to give you a case of what our American cousins call blue balls.' Seeing his uncomprehending look, she went on, 'You really ought to read more widely, Tom. Blue balls is the term they use to describe how a man feels when a woman teases him but won't allow him to touch her. In extreme cases (and this will be an extreme case, I assure you), she plays with him until he's ready to burst. And then she leaves him to stew while she enjoys his frustration. I admit it's a nasty practice, developed before the feminists came along and substituted their own version of it. The game is usually played in a car. That's partly because the Americans are more mobile than we are, and partly because the woman who tries it indoors where there is a bed handy is at a big disadvantage when she decides to disengage. She can always make a run from the car and get inside before he can react. Usually she will promise him more later as she makes her escape. She may or may not be sincere in her offer. They usually don't tie their partners. It's only perverts like me who do that. They rely on a quick escape, and on his sense of honour and male pride: "You wouldn't take advantage of little old helpless me, would you?" Since we're indoors, and because I don't know if you have a sense of honour yet, you will have to be restrained, but I promise to make this as enjoyable as possible. Incidentally, that's something *they* don't often do.'

As she spoke, Harriet continued to stroke his scrotum. His erection was huge. Quite noticeable, in fact, and Harriet noticed! 'Are you getting excited, Tom? Would you like me to talk dirty? Shall I tell you what I'm going to do?'

Tom didn't say anything. He was busy experiencing things, and talk seemed superfluous.

Her fingers moved to his cock. She ran a fingernail up and down the sensitive underside, and he jerked reflexively. 'That's a good way to test reflexes, don't you think? Much better than hitting your patella with a rubber hammer, though I guess they're testing for a different reflex when they do that. But let's see how your other reflexes are.' Harriet circled his erect cock with her fingers and squeezed him gently. His breath came in a gasp. 'Like that, do you? Let's continue.'

Tom was agreeable. He had reached the uncritical stage by now. Anything she wanted to do was all right by him.

Harriet resumed nibbling his earlobe. He found that pleasant now rather than arousing. What was going on further south – now *that* was arousing. So he was disappointed when she abruptly ceased her attentions to his cock and balls. She seemed to sense that he was near to bursting point, and she had no intention of letting him get that far. She shifted back to kissing: the corners of his mouth; his chin, and his neck, where she planted a lovebite. A brand, she called it. 'Proves you're owned. By me.' She kissed him hard on the mouth, thrusting her tongue inside. Tom responded readily.

Then she drew back. 'That's enough for now,' she said. She got up and crossed back to the chair she had occupied earlier. As she sat down she remarked, 'You can carry on admiring the view now if you like.' Harriet crossed her legs and Tom heard again the whisper of nylon as she resumed her temptress-in-repose posture. Tom felt tempted, but he knew better than to get up and cross the space between them. Even if Harriet had not forbidden it (and the handcuffs prevented it), he still didn't want to appear to beg or fawn over her. He thought how very nice it would be to rise and bury his face in her crotch, breathing in the mingled aroma of Harriet and leather. They can't put you in jail for thinking.

But he did nothing, ruefully contemplating the erection she had given him. Blue balls indeed. He wondered what else she had in mind. So far the afternoon and evening had gone like the erotic dreams of a teenager. He didn't want to wake up. It would be so much nicer to string things out for as long as he could hold out, though Harriet was the one who controlled that. He could do nothing to guide or prevent her. Even his cock was out of reach and control. He couldn't even touch himself. Harriet had made him helpless with his cooperation. Tom had never contemplated the pleasure of being powerless until Beth had led him down the paths of her own sexual adventures. Now he realised he was ready for more. Perhaps Beth had sensed that and had turned him over to Harriet – much as one used to be sent off to finishing school. He remembered that she had made a remark very much like that.

Harriet herself seemed to be inordinately interested in the television programme, or it may have been a pose of studied disinterest. Another test of his endurance. It wasn't easy to sit across the room from an attractive woman dressed as provocatively as she was and not think of sweaty sex. To Tom it was like being told not to think of elephants. Immediately the words were said he could think of nothing else. He was sure he caught Harriet stealing sidelong glances at him from time to time, studying him covertly beneath her pose of indifference. But he was never quick enough to catch her actually looking at him. If his own inability to tear his thoughts away from her was any indication, she must at least have been glancing at him as well.

His cock stayed at attention for a long time, even though it wasn't receiving any attention. And when his erection subsided a bit it was only necessary to stare at Harriet, or even catch the creak of leather or the whisper of nylon as she changed her position, to restore it. He had wondered, in an idle and relaxed way, if he were a leg and stocking fetishist. He always ended the enquiry by agreeing that he might be slightly obsessed, but that didn't matter. It was at least an agreeable obsession, one he could manage to gratify frequently enough to keep him from having to steal ladies underwear from clotheslines.

And sometimes, like now, he got to stare at a woman in tights for hours. Or what seemed like hours. Harriet gave no sign of ending the tableau

anytime soon. He remembered the long session with
Beth, when she had asked him to tie her up and had
dressed specially for the occasion. Along with the
nostalgic regrets he found himself remembering the
excitement of calling on Beth, not knowing what new
scheme she had in mind. Those memories did nothing
to lessen his excitement now with Harriet. Nor did
they do anything to lessen his erection.

At length Harriet stirred, breaking his reverie. She
stood and walked out into the kitchen as Tom admired the movement of her hips and legs. She wasn't
out of the room for long, and when she came back
she moved behind the settee, reaching down to fondle
his half-erect cock.

'Have you been keeping this for me?' she asked.
'How thoughtful,' she continued, answering her own
question. 'I'm not sure just what I should do with it.
I could put you out of your misery, but I don't think
I will. Instead I'll just turn the screw a bit more and
see how you react. Remember not to let the side
down.' As she spoke she moved into Tom's line of
sight. He saw that she had brought a riding crop back
from her foray into the kitchen. Harriet swished the
crop once or twice for effect, then brought it down
abruptly across his stomach. Tom whuffed and lurched forward, but he didn't cry out. This seemed to
please Harriet. 'I'm glad to see you're not a cry baby.
Did you like that?' Before he could even think of an
answer she struck him again, this time across the tops
of the thighs. The tassel at the end of the crop dealt
his cock a glancing blow. Along with the pain and
surprise he felt a thrill of pleasure. In all their explo-
rations Beth had never used a crop on him.

Harriet raised the crop to strike again. 'Where
would you like me to hit you now?' Tom didn't

answer. 'Can't decide? Or are you just leaving things up to me? I think that's wise. I know what to do – what you'll like.' Harriet carried on her one-sided conversation, not bothered by his lack of response, or by the bizarre proposal she was making. Tom thought that Beth was never so cool and sure of herself. She had seemed faintly embarrassed at times. Maybe if she had stayed a bit longer things would have eased still more. Tom snapped back to the present when he heard the swish of the crop in Harriet's hands.

Instead of striking him again Harriet leaned forward and kissed his nipples. Tom was surprised and aroused. He had a clear view down her cleavage at the swelling of her breasts. He fancied he could even see her nipples, and he imagined how they would feel in his hands. He wanted to reach out and touch them, but of course he couldn't. He stirred restlessly on the couch, wishing she would do something about his bursting cock. Once again Harriet seemed to read his mind. She knelt before him and reached for his erection. Tom let out his pent-up breath, noting how her tights swelled tautly at her bent knees. He admired the ripe contours of her thighs and calves. Yes, I'm definitely a leg and stocking man, he thought as she leaned forward and took him into her mouth.

And then he stopped thinking about even that as her tongue left a scalding trail up and down his cock. She nipped delicately at the head of his shaft with her small, even teeth. He managed to gasp out, 'What sharp teeth you have, grandma,' before he lost all interest in conversation. If this was a time of trial and testing, as Harriet had averred, he wondered what the reward for successful completion of the course might be. Harriet cupped and stroked his scrotum with her left hand. She scratched him sharply, abruptly at the base of his cock with her fingernail. Tom grunted, more in pleased surprise than in pain.

'Is that another sensitive spot?' Harriet asked unnecessarily. 'You seem to be all nerves tonight. Anything to do with the company?'

'Must be the company,' Tom managed to grunt. Harriet continued the manipulation of his cock and balls and once more Tom felt his scrotum grow tight beneath the constricting band. He gave a low groan, which Harriet took as a sign of pleasure.

She took his cock into her mouth once more and bobbed her head so that he slid in and out. Her lips closed tightly around the shaft and her tongue teased him as she moved. Harriet could feel the tension building in him as she continued the arousal. She continued until he felt as if he could hold out no longer, then, judging the moment nicely, she drew back and looked at him.

He tried to thrust himself closer to her, wanting Harriet to continue. She closed her lips primly in reproof, but the effect was spoiled the next moment when she grinned mischievously and licked a few drops from the corners of her mouth. 'You're doing well, Tom,' she remarked. 'I didn't think you'd be able to hold out this long.'

'I'm not the one holding out. You are,' Tom grunted. 'Aren't my balls blue enough for you yet?'

'Not quite. We'll go for navy blue tonight. I think we can go on for hours yet. But I'm not holding back. Wouldn't you just love to feel how wet I've become under all this leather?' Seeing the expression on his face, she continued, 'Yes, I can imagine you wanting to get at me. But not just yet.' Harriet sat beside Tom on the settee and began to run her hands up and down her legs, stroking herself as she knew he wanted to do. 'These tights are really sheer and glossy, aren't they? They feel so smooth. Do you like them? Yes, I can see you do. Watch while I stroke my legs and imagine what it would feel like if you could do it.'

As she spoke Harriet's hands moved slowly up and down her thighs, from knees to crotch and back down again, as if she were gathering herself into her centre. His eyes followed her hands. Harriet kept her own fixed mainly on her legs. Now and then she looked up at him to see if he was still watching. His erection told her he was paying attention. The stroking hands seemed to be having the desired effect. His gaze was fixed on her legs and his breathing was clearly audible.

'I'm glad to see I have your undivided attention. You should always pay attention when someone is trying to teach you something. You'll know a lot about self-restraint before we're done. You'll be quite virtuous, as such things are mistakenly called.' With a lascivious grin Harriet continued stroking her thighs. Tom could hear the whisper of her hands as they slid over the smooth nylon. His hands twisted behind his back and there was a faint grinding from the chain, but the handcuffs were unyielding.

Soon it became apparent that Harriet was concentrating her efforts on the tops of her thighs, where the black leather ran tautly between her legs. She began to stroke herself gently from front to back, making her fingernail rasp on the leather from time to time for emphasis. After a few minutes of this she wormed a finger beneath the leather at her crotch and worked it around. When she pulled it out, she held it up to Tom's nose. He could smell the musk of her arousal.

'Harriet,' he began, but stopped when he saw her expression.

'I told you not to call me that without permission, didn't I, Tom?' She raised the crop and struck him a stinging blow on the underside of his erect cock. He yelped in surprise and jumped away as far as he could. His face went red, and there was a faint red stripe where she had struck him.

Harriet watched him as he writhed and strained at the handcuffs. Doubtless he wanted to hold himself. She waited until he subsided. 'Don't worry. There won't be any permanent damage. But you'll have to learn to do what I tell you. Now, address me properly if you have anything to say.'

'Mistress,' he began again, 'take these handcuffs off.' Instantly she raised the crop, and he added a hasty 'please'.

She lowered the crop and his eyes followed its descent. 'That's better, but you'll have to be more careful in future. Now where were we? Yes. There,' she said, bending to plant a kiss on his cock. 'Just this once I'll kiss it better, then we can take a break and you can stare at me some more while thinking sexy thoughts.'

Harriet turned her attention then once more to the TV, not unaware of the effect on Tom. He was becoming something of an expert in blue balls by the time Harriet decided to go to bed. He had been hoping that she would relax the look-don't-touch rule for their sleeping arrangements. He found he had been assuming that they would sleep together. But she didn't relent. There was one more session of kissing and fondling which almost made him explode but, as before, Harriet knew just when to stop. Tom was sweating and trembling when she finished with him. Harriet gave one more playful squeeze to his cock before she stood up.

'Bedtime,' she said, using the remote control to switch off the TV. 'Let's be having you. She motioned for him to follow her. Tom got awkwardly to his feet, his cock sticking out stiffly and throbbing. Harriet struck it a light flick with her crop and it bobbed comically. Tom grunted, more in surprise than in pain. He was even more surprised by what came next: he did!

He felt the familiar wave of excitement pass through him, and then he realised he was going to lose control. He shuddered and his knees bent as he started to come. With his hands behind his back he swayed, almost lost his balance, and would have fallen if the settee had not been there to lean against. Some of the semen landed on the floor, but the rest ended up splashing Harriet's thighs, staining the smooth black of her tights. He was too preoccupied to notice it at the time. It was one of the most intense orgasms he could remember. Later, when he had time to think about it, he assumed that the intensity must have been due to the prolonged cycle of arousal and denial to which he had been subjected throughout the long afternoon and evening. At the time he was too busy to do much else but utter a prolonged groan. His hips jerked as he moved in time with the orgasm.

Caught by surprise, Harriet didn't move quickly enough. She glanced down at the sticky mess on her legs and back at Tom, who was still hunched over as he finished. She looked annoyed, as much at herself for misjudging his tolerance as at Tom for his lack of control. She recovered, and said, 'Dirty boy. You'll have to clean this up tomorrow, you know. So I hope you enjoyed that little lot. Stick with me and we'll see if we can't improve on it as we go along.'

She took Tom's elbow and led him to the

downstairs toilet, where she dampened a cloth to clean herself. She sponged the semen off her tights, the water leaving darker blotches on the nylon. Tom stared at her legs in fascination. When she had cleaned herself up, she sponged his still-erect cock. 'You can put that away now, but you'll have to practise more self-control in future. I was about to say you shouldn't go off half-cocked, but you weren't at half-cock, were you? However, there's a price to pay, even for accidents. I was going to let you sleep in a bed tonight. Not mine,' she added when she saw his look 'but a bed none the less. Now you'll not be so comfortable. Still,' she said, talking as much to herself as to him, 'you'll be all the better for a little *Unruhe*. It helps to drive the lesson home.'

'*Freude durch Schwierigkeit, Fraulein?*' he asked sardonically.

'None of that, now. It is a far cry from the excesses of our German friends during the war to the thoroughly scientific training regime I administer. You'll soon grow to like it. After all, the rewards are better,' she posed for him, 'not just an extra crust of bread. Man doesn't live by bread alone. Sex is also part of the diet. The dessert, you might say. Life is uncertain, so better order dessert first! However, in your case you'll have to earn your dessert. A bit of the old *Arbeit* will make you more free.'

Tom couldn't imagine how, but he said nothing.

Harriet drained the hand basin and hung the face cloth neatly on the towel rail. She was beginning to look like an everything-in-its-place person. 'Want to pee before beddy-byes?' Before he could answer she took him in hand and led him by the cock over to the toilet. Harriet lined him up and declared, 'Fire when ready!' When he was done she led him, still by the cock, down the hall toward the stairs. She stopped beside the door to the cupboard under the stairs and dropped his lead. Or rather let go of it. It wasn't yet ready to drop.

The door and its frame looked much heavier than was usual for interior doors and cupboards, and the door opened inward against substantial stops. There was a light switch near the door frame. Harriet switched on the light and opened the door. Inside, Tom saw a thin mattress on the floor. These were apparently his sleeping quarters. There was no latch or handle on the inside of the door, nor was there a keyhole. There was also a stout bolt on the outside of the door and Tom concluded that it wasn't meant to be opened from inside. There was no light switch inside either. The cupboard was actually more like a cell. He didn't think he'd have much luck breaking out.

'This is my little holding tank for visitors,' Harriet remarked as she pushed him inside. 'Sit down.'

The ceiling barely cleared his head when he stood inside. He sat awkwardly. Harriet knelt beside him and he smelled her perfume as she reached past him, brushing lightly. Tom felt his desire for her grow again. He wanted to have her then and there.

As before, Harriet seemed unaware of his need. She grasped a ring protruding from a hole in the floor near the foot of the mattress. It proved to be attached to a short chain, which she pulled up. Harriet unlocked one of the irons on his ankles, slipped it through the ring at the end of the chain, and relocked it on him. This left Tom chained by the ankles to the floor of the cell. She withdrew in a whisper of nylon and a gentle creaking of leather. She went back to the downstairs toilet and returned with a bucket. 'In case you need to go again in the night,' she declared. She withdrew again and closed the door. Tom heard the key turn in the lock. There was a metallic scraping as she slid the bolt home, Harriet's muffled 'sleep well' came through to him as the light was switched off.

It was almost totally dark. Only a small chink of light came through beneath the door. He listened to Harriet's receding footsteps. Presently there was the sound of a toilet flushing, and then splashing noises. Presumably she was washing before bed. She had apparently forgotten about him and Tom felt another kind of excitement rising in him as he lay chained in the dark closet. Harriet was going to leave him there while she slept. If he could, he had better sleep too. The stairs creaked overhead as she went up to her bedroom. He imagined the play of her legs and bottom as she climbed. That exercise didn't make him any calmer.

Tom tried to make himself as comfortable as possible for the night but soon found that it wasn't going to be all that comfortable. The handcuffs prevented him from lying on his back or side. He could lie face down but that felt unnatural because he couldn't use his arms to pillow his head. He found that he could lie half on his side and half on his front, but after a short time his hands went numb behind his back and woke him. He was about to resign himself to a sleepless night when he hit upon the idea of propping himself into a seated position in the corner. The wall behind him supported his back and he used the adjoining wall to lean his head against. He slept fitfully, waking up from time to time to shift his position fractionally. He dreamed he was in prison – which in a way he was, but with a most agreeable jailer.

In his waking moments Tom thought of Harriet

lying in her bed out of his reach. He imagined her sleeping in the leather corselet and tights. That made him get hard. It was disturbing not being able to reach his cock. If he couldn't have Harriet, he could at least relieve himself, or he could have if his hands had been free. Perhaps Harriet had anticipated just this situation when she had left him chained; she seemed to think of most things.

At some time in the night Tom woke and had to pee. He tried to remember where the bucket was in the dark closet, and after a good deal of squirming he managed to locate it and made his slow way over to it. He got awkwardly to his knees and knelt beside the bucket. He aimed by centring it between his knees, hoping his calculations were correct. His aim was good. Though still frustrated, he felt some relief afterwards. There was a faint odour of piss in the confined space, but he couldn't escape that. Tom worked his way back to the corner and settled down once more. The rest of the night passed in fitful sleep and lurid dreams.

Even before he heard the first faint sounds from upstairs, Tom knew it was daylight by the light filtering through the crack under the door. Then there came the sound of Harriet's footsteps and the sound of a toilet flushing. Tom wondered if she was coming for him and what she had in mind for this day. He felt the now-familiar mixture of anticipation and dread that coloured all his contacts with Harriet. The sounds from upstairs ceased. It looked as if she was going to lie in. He would have to wait for as long as it took Harriet to decide what she wanted to do. The sense of being in someone else's power came home once again to him as he settled in the closet to await her whim. But even as he waited he could sense his excitement growing once more. His cock, out of reach, was most definitely *not* out of mind. It grew stiffer by the moment, until it positively ached, but there was no relief for him, only more waiting.

Eventually there were more sounds from the upper floor. Footsteps coming down the stairs, the treads of the stairs creaking over his head. Dominatrix descending a staircase. They stopped outside the door. There was the rattle of a key in the lock and the sound of a drawn bolt. The light was switched on, dazzling Tom after the hours spent in darkness. The door opened and his mistress stood over him, looking sleepy but still somehow daunting. Her brown hair was tousled and she stifled a yawn as she bent over him. She was wearing an ordinary dressing gown, belted at the waist but with enough of the top open to allow a generous amount to show. There was no trace of the working gear she had worn the previous day, and Tom felt a small stab of disappointment. He had been expecting to be greeted by Harriet in her form-fitting leather costume. Only as he looked at her now did he realise how much he associated her outfit with her role. He recalled his dream about Harriet sleeping in her tight leather corselet and wearing her high heels. That fantasy had excited him greatly.

As she came into the small closet to free him, Tom smelled her fragrance and felt a rush of desire for her. He said, 'Good morning', the only thing that came to mind. Even as he did it he realised how banal it sounded in these bizarre circumstances. Just what was the proper greeting for the woman holding you prisoner after a night in chains? The etiquette books were silent on this point.

Harriet did not respond to this sally, but when she noticed his erection she gave a small smile of

101

approval. 'Been thinking creatively, then, haven't you?' As she unlocked the leg irons and freed him from the tether she wrinkled her nose at the smell from the bucket. Tom had grown used to it but it must have seemed quite strong to someone who hadn't been living with the odour all night. Harriet took the leg-irons off and then reached behind him to unlock the handcuffs.

Tom got to his feet slowly and stretched his arms and legs. They felt stiff after the night in chains.

'Come out of there. I need coffee desperately,' Harriet ordered.

Tom came out into the hallway and stretched some more. It was a dull morning. Silvery rather than golden sunlight. Not dismal. Not rainy. Just not the sort of morning one usually called glorious. He felt happy, though, as he stood before Harriet at the start of this new day.

'Coffee now,' Harriet repeated, half-mockingly but with an undertone of seriousness, 'before I do something you'll regret.'

With a shiver of anticipation Tom remembered the riding crop. He knew she would use it on him if he didn't please her. Last night had shown him that. He moved toward the kitchen to make the coffee. Harriet went through into the sitting room. As he filled the coffee maker with water Tom wondered if he was going to spend every night at Harriet's house in the cupboard. When he remembered the erotic dreams of the night before he thought that another night there wouldn't be so bad. Certainly better than sleeping alone. And even, he realised with some surprise, better than a night with Beth. When he compared her with Harriet, she seemed more ordinary. He realised with a start that he was beginning to enjoy this far-from-ordinary situation much more than he had enjoyed the nights with Beth. It wasn't that she was unattractive. But the memory of their relationship was beginning to pale when set beside the Harriet alternative.

As he waited for the water to boil, another thought struck Tom: he had better go empty the bucket in the closet. Harriet had said nothing but he sensed that she expected him to slop out. Better that than risk her displeasure. After he had emptied the bucket down the toilet he rinsed it out and splashed some disinfectant into it. Then he replaced it in the closet in case she decided he needed another night there. She didn't look forgetful, but he wanted to be sure he had some place to go if he needed it. Another night in the cupboard might not be so bad, but he caught himself thinking that a night or two in Harriet's bed would be much better – if he dared aspire to it. She had hinted that this might be his ultimate reward, but she had set no time limit on how long he might have to wait for it. Doubtless, in her scheme of things, she thought the wait would be good for him. Character building, she might say.

When Tom got back to the kitchen the water was boiling, so he made coffee and looked about for something to prepare for breakfast. He didn't know how Harriet felt about cereals and such things, but he sensed that she liked a prepared breakfast. Prepared by someone else, him, in this case! He was doing his best to please her, something he had never done so thoroughly for the other women in his life. Tom wondered idly if he was becoming the 'new man' that the feminists were always on about. No, he concluded, he was pretty much the old man but was being introduced to a new mode of sexual reality. Harriet had

103

never said anything about changing the status of women by teaching him the pleasures of subservience and submission. She had never said anything about the political or social aspect of domination. Rather she seemed to be doing it because she enjoyed the experience. And so did he, although that was not her main concern.

When the coffee was ready, Tom made up a tray for Harriet and took it through to her. He remembered last night's session and her remark about cleaning up in the morning. He took a damp sponge and a saucepan of water with him when he went into the sitting room. Tom poured the coffee, then knelt to clean the small crusty patches left on the carpet from his unexpected loss of control. This action gained him another small smile of approval from Harriet. Tom smiled in return, pleased that he was doing what pleased her as well. As he worked he wondered if she would *really* use the crop on anyone rather than employing it mainly in a symbolic fashion, to underline her wishes. He concluded that she could well apply it in earnest. She seemed the type of determined person who would.

Harriet stirred on the settee, rattling her cup and spoon. Tom heard and asked, 'More coffee, Mistress?' The ritual words of submission still seemed strange to him. Unfamiliar. They stuck in his throat. Tom got to his feet and waited for her next move.

She noticed his hesitation and smiled encouragingly at him. 'Don't feel too awkward, it's early days yet. You'll learn how to behave as you go along. Think of the movies you've seen with servants in them, then try to behave as they did. I'll help with advice from time to time.'

Tom wondered again how often her advice might consist of an application of the riding crop.

Harriet continued, 'I don't expect you to learn everything at once – though it might be nice if you could. In time you'll learn to anticipate my wishes as a good servant should.' She went off on a tangent: 'It's so hard to get good servants nowadays. They want respect, and days off, and exorbitant salaries and fringe benefits. It all comes of this madness for democracy and equal rights. Trade unions are largely to blame for it, giving workers the idea that they can set the rules instead of following orders. It wasn't that way a hundred years ago,' she mused, sounding as if she had wide personal experience with Victorian master–servant relations.

Tom wondered if her idea of proper relations with workers extended to lowering urchins into chimneys to sweep them. He reflected that even she might have some trouble finding an urchin nowadays. Children seemingly went directly from squalling infants demanding constant attention to shouting yobs requiring constant guarding.

Harriet once more cut across his thoughts. 'More coffee, please,' she said, holding out her empty cup.

Tom poured for her and added cream and sugar, earning another nod of approval. She didn't offer him any. Doubtless her idea of proper mistress–servant relations. Servants eat in their own place, not with the mistress of the house. Feed them enough so that they can perform their duties adequately but show no sign of familiarity. Tom assumed that the lecture was over and returned to cleaning the white crusty patches from the carpet near her feet. As he worked he stole glances at her legs. Harriet had crossed them in a seemingly careless fashion allowing him to peer up to her crotch. She wasn't wearing pants. Tom didn't think she had forgotten them or that she was unaware of the display she was creating. Even in his short experience with her Tom had come to believe that Harriet rarely did things unwittingly. She appeared much too organised. Almost everything she did had a purpose, like a good teacher teaching by demonstration when she wasn't lecturing. Tom appreciated her legs while he worked.

'I wonder if it would help to have a uniform for you.' Harriet spoke as if there had been no pause after her last remarks. 'I was thinking of letting you do a little TV. A French maid's uniform for you might do the trick. You can hire them from the fancy-dress people. Would you like to dress as my maid next time?' Harriet's tone made the question into a statement.

Tom was startled. That idea had never occurred to him. He knew there were clubs for transvestites in the same way there were gay clubs and even sado-masochistic clubs and groups, but he had never imagined himself wearing women's clothing. It looked as if he had better get used to the idea of doing things he had never thought of as long as he remained with Harriet.

'I might even have you go in and hire the outfit. Would you like that? Then you could shop for underwear and tights for yourself as dessert. Have you ever bought women's lingerie? You must have done. All men like to make their girlfriends presents of what they think the girl of their fantasies should wear. They, the men I mean, rarely stop to think if it is indeed what the woman wants to wear. It's always black stockings and suspenders and a black bra. No other colour will do. Don't men have any imagination? No, I suppose not. Can't be helped. It must be your early upbringing and toilet training. Men can be so square and predictable. I like red occasionally.

Even a nice light green is a pleasant change, though for important occasions I think there's nothing like a polished steel and brass chastity belt to really turn their heads. On me, I mean,' Harriet added. 'Not that I'm all that hooked on chastity itself. But I *do* like the trappings now and then. And the implied contrast. Something that makes men wild to tear it off you is my idea of a successful outfit. And something they can't tear off you makes them wilder still. Would you like me to drive you wild with unfulfilled desire, Tom?'

'I thought you did rather a nice job of that last night,' he replied when she paused. He saw that Harriet was pleased with the compliment. He was also pleased with the calmness he managed to put into his remark even while his mind was busy with the implications of what she had been saying. Harriet had a knack of making remarks calculated to startle or keep him in suspense. Willy-nilly he had been going over the idea of wearing women's clothing. The idea of having smooth nylon covering his own legs and body was disturbingly vivid and, he admitted to himself, pleasant and arousing.

Tom didn't believe he would be particularly good at dressing and looking like a maid. The closet transvestites and those who did it only occasionally rarely managed to look as female as the public TVs who practised their craft almost daily and who had received professional help with hair, make-up and fashion. And Tom had no desire to be seen in public as they did. Still, the idea, now that Harriet had planted it, began to grow and seem more attractive. It seemed of a piece with the submissive role she was teaching him. He would submit to her choice of clothing and the role of a woman. He knew that, like most transvestites, he was firmly heterosexual but the idea of looking female still appealed to him. If Harriet had been trying to teach him that the male should be submissive and the female dominant, she would not have suggested he wear the clothes of the dominant sex. He imagined that she was telling him that *this* man was submissive and that *this* woman was giving the orders. A local phenomenon rather than a general statement of policy.

'That's something to think about while you wait for next Friday,' Harriet said, interrupting his train of thought again. 'I'll let you know what I decide in the next week or so. It'll be fun for you to wait for my word. Half the fun's in the suspense, don't you think?'

Her question didn't seem to call for a response, so Tom made none. Silently he finished cleaning and took her coffee cup into the kitchen, where he began to prepare a breakfast of scrambled eggs, bacon and toast for his Mistress. The word sounded more natural to him now. As he worked he thought about Harriet's proposal with more equanimity and a certain eagerness. It would be another new adventure for him.

He served Harriet and ate his own breakfast at the kitchen table. There was the rest of the Saturday stretching before him, and he wondered what Harriet had in mind for that day. Last night would be a hard act to follow, but she would have to do something. Usually there wasn't much to do at the weekend except go to the pub or join the divorced parents visiting the zoo with their children. Neither idea seemed appealing. Harriet didn't look like the zoo type anyway. But the decision was hers. Tom was glad he didn't have to think up something to entertain her. That was the nice part about his situation. He didn't have to make executive plans or decisions.

Which was just as well, as after breakfast Harriet announced that he wouldn't be needed any more that weekend and he could go home. She got his clothes from wherever she had put them and handed them back. From her manner Tom gathered she had other things to do. He felt a momentary stab of jealousy when he imagined Harriet with someone else, even though he wasn't sure she was going to see anyone else. Nor did he know what business she might have with whomever she did see. But he at least knew better than to ask. For one thing, she didn't seem to want to discuss her business, and he didn't want to lose face by asking questions.

As she handed his clothes to him, Harriet said, 'Get out of here and earn your living,' with mock severity. 'Go home, get some sleep. Come back next Friday after work. Don't bring anything. And don't call me. Just show up on time.'

This sounded like the deliberate fencing off of the weekends with him from the rest of her life that Beth had enforced. He felt resentful and excluded, just as he had with Beth. Dismissed, he got dressed and took a cab home. He found the weekend very long indeed. He contrasted the empty days with the erotic play of the last twenty-odd hours at Harriet's place. The only encouraging sign was Harriet's demand that he come back next weekend. At least he was not being banished forever. On Sunday night he dreamed once more of Harriet as she had looked in her black leather outfit. She was offering herself to him and he could feel the tight smooth fabric as he undressed her. She was panting with the need for him. 'Fuck me, Tom, please! Now! I can't stand it. Do me!'

Chapter Five

The alarm clock woke him, and it was Monday. It was like every other Monday when he woke up to the workaday world after a weekend with Beth. She would occupy his dreams, and then he had to endure the routine of his job until he could see her again. It looked like being the same with Harriet. The main difference between them was that Harriet gave definite orders whereas Beth had led or suggested. Tom had the feeling that with Harriet he had given the control of his life over to someone else. He knew he had to see her again. There was no question of not turning up next time. Besides, there was the promise of becoming her assistant. Tom wondered if this included becoming her live-in lover. That was certainly implied. Or was it? Hard to tell with Harriet. Well. Wait and hope.

As he showered and dressed Tom thought about assisting Harriet in her business. Almost certainly that would involve plenty of B&D. Would he have access to and control over other women in his role as her assistant? Would he be expected to bind them? Lash or torture them? Abduct unwilling women? He found the possibilities incredibly exciting. Fantasies like these had certainly never presented themselves so strongly to him before. He would have been seriously disturbed by these ideas before Beth and Harriet had shown him the way. Or he felt he should be disturbed, but was turned on instead. And what about men? He found that idea off-putting, tinged as it was with the unease he usually felt about homosexual dealings. That idea broke the spell and dropped him back into the Monday morning routine.

The next week at work went as slowly as the earlier ones had gone when he was with Beth. He received the note from Harriet to attend her that Friday, which happened to be a holiday, so it would be a long weekend. He was commanded to bring nothing but himself.

On the appointed day he knocked at her door. She let him in and told him to take his clothes off. As before, she took them away to be locked up and he didn't ask where she put them. It was not the sort of question she would like. By now he was getting used to her lack of ceremony. She had just got up and was wearing her dressing gown, which was promising, Tom thought. But she had still not decided to sleep with him. As he went into the kitchen to do her bidding, she went upstairs again. She didn't say anything about the plans for the day.

By now Tom knew were things were kept, and so it didn't take long for him to make a pot of coffee. As he was arranging the coffee things on a tray, he heard Harriet coming back down. When she came into the kitchen, he saw that she was wearing the same outfit she had worn on his previous visit. What she called her uniform.

'Like what you see?' she asked, twirling round for effect. 'Yes, I can see that you do,' she continued without waiting for his reply. 'It sticks out all over you.'

Tom looked down at his stiff cock when she called attention to it. He saw her point.

111

Harriet went through into the front room, beckoning for him to follow with the tray. She sat on the settee and Tom placed the tray on the coffee table in front of her. She poured a cup for herself. Tom felt as if he should have done that for her and he hurried to make amends by offering cream and sugar.

'Ah, good. You did that just right,' she said as she tasted the coffee.

Harriet settled herself more comfortably, crossing her legs. Tom thrilled once more to the hiss of nylon on nylon. He never got tired of the sound, he reflected. He remained standing. It seemed the natural thing to do: if Harriet wanted him to sit down, she would tell him. He watched as she sipped her coffee with every sign of enjoyment. When she had finished half of it, she seemed to notice him standing there for the first time.

Harriet turned to him and said, 'Could you just go to the closet under the stairs and fetch the chains you'll find there. The ones you wore last time.'

Tom felt his stomach lurch with excitement as he remembered the last time he had worn the chains. Silently he moved to do her bidding. He thought about that phrase. Not so very long ago he wouldn't have chosen that expression. Bidding wasn't a word he used often, but now it seemed quite natural to him in these circumstances. The handcuffs and leg-irons hung on a hook just inside the door. He took them down and returned to the front room. Harriet set the cup down as he entered. He saw it was empty and asked, 'Would you like another?' He almost added 'Mistress' but hesitated at the last moment. That word wasn't natural to him yet.

Harriet noticed the omission and looked quickly at him. 'Manners. Did you forget so soon? You really

112

should be more careful, or Mama spank next time. I just don't feel like doing it now, so we'll put this one on the account and settle it later. But please don't go on that way.'

He felt his stomach lurch again in anticipation. The 'please' had the emphasis of the 'if you please' that followed military orders when the officer was trying to appear calm and polite.

'Pour me another cup and then go sit down over there,' she said, indicating the armchair across from her. 'Put the leg-irons on your ankles for me.' She didn't add, 'There's a good boy,' but she might as well have done.

Silently Tom picked up the coffee pot and filled her cup, not trusting himself to say anything. He guessed his voice would have shaken with suppressed excitement, and he didn't want to give that away. This was the moment he had been waiting for the whole week. He set the pot down and crossed to the chair. He sat down and locked the irons on his ankles as Harriet had ordered. Then he looked questioningly at her. 'The handcuffs too?' 'Mistress,' he added hastily, seeing her look of exasperation.

'Not just yet.' Harriet removed a light graceful chain from her neck and tossed it to him. There was a key on it with a short spike on its head. 'Double-lock the irons, please,' she said in her matter-of-fact way.

Tom examined the leg-irons and noticed a small button about the size of the spike on the key's head. He used the spike to press it and found it went in with a definite click. He repeated the process on his other ankle. Then he looked questioningly at Harriet, who nodded in approval as she held out her hand for the key and chain. He guessed that she wouldn't like him to toss it back to her as casually as she had given it to him. That would be just too cavalier and democratic a gesture. The moment seemed to require more ceremony. He stood, crossed over to the settee and handed the key on its chain back to her.

Harriet nodded once more and indicated he should clear away the coffee tray. She recrossed her legs, and Tom once more caught the hiss as she slid one over the other. Once again his heart lurched as he imagined how it would feel to run his hands over the smooth glossy material of her tights, and over what lay at the apex of her thighs. He shook his head to clear the thought away. Not yet. But soon, he hoped. Maybe this very weekend. Harriet had given him no sign that she was ready to allow greater intimacy, but he found himself hoping against the odds that she soon would.

As he washed up Tom thought he was turning into the proper domestic. Apparently this was what Harriet had in mind for him. A reversal of roles, something entirely different from what he normally thought and did. He realised he was being taught to please someone else, to think of himself later, if at all. Harriet gave no sign that she was aware of his desires and that too was part of the lesson.

Tom thought back to Harriet's earlier remark about a uniform. Was this going to be the weekend with the maid's costume? Had she already got it for him? So soon? Somehow he hoped not. He wasn't sure he was ready for that yet – not that Harriet seemed to worry much about his state of readiness. A part of him wanted to save something for later. Don't gulp it all down at once, was how he put it to himself. He had an entire two days to make discoveries about himself. And, he hoped, many more days beyond that. He was looking forward to that with anticipation and hope. He would just have to be patient and see what Harriet had in mind. She gave the impression of someone with long-term plans.

Harriet's voice cut across his reverie. 'When you're done in there, please go upstairs and tidy my room. I have to make some phone calls, and I'd appreciate it if you didn't come down until I'm finished. The cleaning things are under the sink and in the pantry.'

Tom hung up the tea towel and searched around in the kitchen until he had found the furniture polish, the dusting cloths and the Hoover. With these he climbed the stairs, being careful not to trip over the chain between his ankles. Harriet had not shown him around the top floor on his first visit, but he had no trouble finding her bedroom. It was the only room with the bed unmade, and there was a pair of high-heeled leather lace-up boots beside the dresser. The curtains were drawn back and the late morning sunlight slanted in through the window.

The faint lingering odour of her perfume came to his nostrils as he fluffed the pillows and began to make the bed. Tom imagined her lying in the bed and waiting for him to caress and pleasure her. Just what would she like him to do to her? He found he had no clear idea. Harriet was different from anyone else he had ever known – truly unique. Did she want him to treat her roughly? Somehow he thought not. If anything, she would be the one to deal roughly with him, and he knew he'd let her do whatever she wished. The only question was how he should respond. He imagined he'd pick it up soon enough. And if he didn't Harriet would be there to drive the lesson home. That thought excited him too. Tom wondered if there was anything about this experience that wouldn't.

He put the boots in the closet, glancing through Harriet's wardrobe as he did so. There seemed to be an awful lot of leather and rubber gear. That looked promising. No sign of the promised maid's costume, though. A momentary disappointment was quickly overlain by an image of Harriet wearing a constricting rubber leotard and matching tights. The rubber-clad dominatrix advanced ominously as he lay helplessly bound. She had a whip in her hand. Her mouth, beneath the mask that hid her features, was twisted into a grimace – a parody of a smile – as she looked down on her victim. On her long legs she wore tight boots with stiletto heels. The image faded and he remembered that Harriet's legs were rather short and full. Not the long-legged ones featured in the stocking adverts. He still found them entrancing, as he did the rest of her compact, well-made body.

He dusted the top of the furniture, moving her make-up items and perfume to pass the cloth under them. He tidied the top of her dressing table and closed a drawer left carelessly open before he plugged in the vacuum cleaner. As he passed near the door he heard Harriet's voice on the telephone. The words came up in snatches. 'He's here now . . . busy upstairs . . . tomorrow? All right.' Obviously she was talking about him. But to whom? And to what end? Tom briefly considered listening in, but thought better of it. It would be undignified, to say the least, to be caught eavesdropping when Harriet had told him she wanted privacy. Best get on with his work. He would find out whatever Harriet wanted him to know when she was ready to tell him.

When he switched it on, the noise from the vacuum cleaner drowned out her voice. He vacuumed the carpet and ran the machine under the bed as far as it would go, then he went out onto the landing and did the carpet there. Harriet was still on the phone when he switched off, but she was apparently talking to someone else – or at any rate she wasn't talking about him. Tom opened the door to the second bedroom, intending to show willing by doing more than she had ordered him to do, and also wanting to keep busy until Harriet was done.

This room was fitted out as a cell. There was no handle on the inside of the door, nor was there a keyhole on that side, though there was a sturdy mortise lock with a keyhole on the outside. Like most doors, and like all cell doors, it opened into the room it served. The door stopping was unusually heavy, which would make the door difficult if not impossible to force outward. And there was nothing on the inside of the door with which to pull it inward. Even if the door were not locked, no one on the inside would be able to open it against the latch. With the door as a clue, he quickly became aware of some of the other features of the room. What appeared at first to be an ornamental column for hanging flower baskets turned out to be firmly anchored to the floor and ceiling. It could be used to truss someone up for a whipping. The bed was heavy and was bolted to the floor.

Tom crossed to the window. It looked down onto a small back garden. It was neatly kept, but seemed out of place when seen from a room such as this one. As a rule cells don't overlook lawns and flower gardens. The nearest house, about three hundred feet away, across some waste ground, presented a blank windowless wall to his view. He touched the glass lightly, experimentally, with his fingers. There was no give to it. When he rapped it gently with his knuckles, it gave off a heavy sound.

Harriet's voice from the doorway interrupted his exploration of the room. 'That's armoured glass,' she said.

Tom jumped back from the window in surprise. He hadn't been paying any attention to the other noises while he was surveying the room, so he hadn't noticed that Harriet was no longer talking on the phone. Indeed she had climbed the stairs without breaking his concentration. He turned to face her, feeling suddenly even more naked and helpless before this woman. In her black tights and leather corselet she seemed very determined and severe.

'I didn't want anyone I put in here to be able to escape by smashing the glass,' she continued. 'Of course it wouldn't hold up against a prolonged and determined attack from a hammer or an axe, but I make sure there is nothing like that in the room whenever I have a guest staying with me.' Harriet smiled as she spoke. Apparently the idea of this as a guest room was amusing to her. She went on, 'My guests usually aren't wearing much more than you have on now, so any successful escape could be very embarrassing to them, but I try to make their stay here as comfortable as possible, so that they don't really want to run away. That is a comfortable bed, and I leave a slop bucket for them in case they have to go to the toilet in the night. I hate to be wakened once I get to sleep. I can be quite unpleasant with anyone who makes a row and gets me out of a warm bed. No doubt you see my point.'

Harriet beckoned him away from the window. 'This room is for my more privileged guests. I have other, shall we say, less salubrious quarters for others. But I see you were about to clean in here when I interrupted you. Carry on, then come downstairs when you've finished. I want to show you the rest of the facilities today.' She turned and went down the stairs.

When he had vacuumed the carpet, Tom switched off the Hoover, carried the cleaning things downstairs and put them away. Then he went into the living room where Harriet waited.

She occupied the armchair again, making it look like a throne. She let him stand in the door for some minutes before she took notice of him. Tom was sure the delay was deliberate – another lesson in who was in charge. When she finally acknowledged him, she said, 'If you think of this as a house of ill repute, you won't be too far from what the general public would think if they knew about it. I try not to let them find out. Not that I feel ashamed of what I do. Quite the reverse. I do a good job for my clients – even if I say so myself. I prefer to think of it as a special place for people with their own special needs. I offer B&D to the discerning few rather than B&B to the masses. Not that they'd want what I offer, more's the pity. This country would be much better off with a touch more discipline. But there you are: they don't run things to suit me.' Harriet smiled ironically and continued, 'I run this place to suit myself. The people who come here do whatever I tell them to do. Once they decide to submit themselves to me, I get to make all the choices after that. It's a heavy responsibility.' Again the ironic smile. 'You'd be surprised how many people want someone else to take responsibility out of their hands. Actually deprive them of choice.'

Tom wasn't sure where all this was leading. It sounded like a confession or an apologia, and seemed out of place coming from someone he didn't expect to explain things needlessly. His perplexity must have showed, because Harriet abruptly changed tack.

'Yes, I imagine all this is a bit abstract. I tend to go on and on when I'm not careful. Too much philosophy and not enough practicality. Perhaps I should make things more concrete.' She stood abruptly. 'Come with me.'

Harriet strode purposefully out into the hall. Following, Tom admired the play of muscles in her thighs, calves and bottom. He was excited by her and her outfit, even though she gave no sign that she was aware of the effect she had on him. Or just possibly she knew that the effect could be heightened if she ignored his reaction. His reaction stood out straight in front of him. She had only to glance over her shoulder to see it. But she didn't.

She threw a light remark his way as they passed the closet where he had spent his first night with her, 'Relax. No need for formality or stiffness here.' Hearing the chuckle in her voice, Tom wondered if she had eyes in the back of her head. Most likely she just knew what effect she was having on him.

Harriet led the way to the door at the back end of the hall. Tom had noticed it but hadn't paid much attention to it. There was a key in the lock. When she turned it she pushed against the door and he could see how heavy it was by the tensing of her shoulder muscles. It resembled the door to the guest room upstairs. Like that door, it rested against heavy stopping, but there was a handle and keyhole on either side. Tom guessed this door was intended to be opened from either side so long as one had the key. Still, it looked like another cell door.

Harriet switched on a light over the landing and descended the steep stairs without pausing. 'Mind your step,' she cautioned him as he followed. Tom stepped very carefully. It wouldn't do to trip over his leg-irons. At the bottom of the flight Harriet switched on the lights in the basement and stood aside for him to see. He was impressed. The basement had been transformed into a combination jail and torture chamber. Or so it would be described by anyone who didn't know of the close relation between pain and sexual pleasure.

Harriet said, 'These are the other quarters I mentioned. The regular guests spend their time down here. It's comfortable enough with the central heating. It has to be since all my guests go nude. If nothing else, nudity deters escapes. Nakedness, on the other hand, tends to make one feel helpless, defensive, submissive – that sort of thing. I like everyone to be both naked and nude. I want my guests to do what I tell them to do. Their being naked while I'm not helps to define the pecking order. The ones with clothes give the orders; the naked ones take them. And there are other advantages to the system. The, er, interesting bits are readily accessible, and there is a certain aesthetic satisfaction – though not with all the people who come here.' She glanced at Tom and continued, 'You're all right in that department. Actually you have a quite acceptable bod. Though I've seen better, so you needn't feel too much satisfaction.'

Tom wasn't used to being appraised so frankly and he was suffering from the disadvantage Harriet had mentioned a moment before. What *had* she done with his clothes? Feeling the need to assert himself before this self-confident woman, he asked, 'Do you damn everyone who comes here with faint praise?' Harriet looked sharply at him and he added, 'Mistress?' rather hastily.

'You're getting the idea, but much too slowly. I'm keeping score, you know. Just because you know that bit from Alexander Pope doesn't mean you're very intelligent. One of my lecturers at university remarked that even parrots can memorise things they hear often enough. But to answer your question, you'll do. Now stop fishing for compliments and go have a look round. Find out what's here and where it is. You'll have to know all about this place if you're to be my assistant. Questions will be asked later.'

As she turned to go back upstairs, the tight leather corselet creaked slightly. Tom's ears were attuned to the sounds of Harriet. He felt a warm tightness in the belly as he imagined how such a garment would feel to the wearer. It was a short jump to imagining himself wearing it. Thoughts of the maid's costume came once again to mind. The tight leather gear under it? Wouldn't that be too hot? Would Harriet care? He pulled himself back to reality with an effort. Harriet had gone and he was on his own with orders to explore her secret place. It felt like learning the intimate secrets of a lover. Going through her bureau while she was away. Feeling eager and slightly guilty as the familiar and not-so-familiar things came to light.

Tom looked first at the two cells that flanked the stairway. They were practically identical, with doors that looked intimidating. The spyhole in each gave them a certain institutional air. Had Harriet actually got hold of real prison doors? It looked that way. The idea fitted the impression he was forming about her thoroughness. So far he had seen no half-measures in her house. He made a mental note to ask her who helped her fit the basement out. It would have had to be someone with discretion.

Unlike the cell upstairs, these had toilets. Harriet's remarks about luxury versus ordinary accommodation weren't strictly accurate. The lingering odour of strong disinfectant lent a further air of authenticity to the small rooms. There were hooks in the ceilings and ringbolts in the walls and their purpose left little to the imagination. Once again he felt a tightening of his stomach muscles as he imagined these fixtures in use.

Tom turned away to explore the remainder of the basement. There were low cabinets built against the wall which looked interesting, if only because they concealed their contents. He opened the doors and found an impressive and varied collection of bondage gear. His Harriet, he smiled as he imagined her reaction to that appellation, was a serious collector of what the B&D groupies quaintly called 'restraints'. Handcuffs of several varieties; more leg-irons of the sort he wore, plus some other types. There were gags and helmets of leather and rubber; bits and bridles; and what seemed like miles of rope of different sizes and lengths. In one cupboard he discovered a pile of light supple chain whose links were chrome-plated and half-twisted to form what is called machine chain. He recognised it from an illustration in an ironmonger's catalogue. He suspected Harriet had seen the same catalogue, or one closely resembling it. The chain was the type used to make dog leads, but here it was in much longer lengths than the pet shops sold. From what he had seen so far, Harriet could accommodate several guests at a time and still be able to service the passing trade. If and when he became Harriet's assistant, he would probably be using all this equipment.

Among the more mundane (if that was the word) bondage gear, Tom came across some of a different sort: this was electrical in nature, and was, he guessed, used to service the more unusual of Harriet's guests. He'd have to ask her about it. Tom was a fair electrician, in the way that people who use computers have to be, and he usually did his own wiring at home, so he could guess in a general way what these devices were for. It was their specific uses he couldn't fathom. One more lesson in the difference between theory and practice.

There was a less ambiguous collection of whips and straps that would be used for chastising those clients whose métier was masochism and the sexual uses of pain. The riding crop which Harriet affected, treating it as a badge of office, would sting rather than wound, but there were other sorts here that could inflict severe injury if they were wielded too enthusiastically. Tom found himself hoping that Harriet could exercise self-restraint when he was on the receiving end.

The collection, which he thought of as a couturier imagines his stock, was completed by a wardrobe filled with leather and rubber garments of various sorts, none of them suitable for street wear. They were designed to confine or restrain the wearer in varying degrees. In the same wardrobe he found a collection of straps with buckles and locks that were clearly intended to tie someone down – more restraints. Tom was impressed by the collection. If she knew how to use all this, Harriet was clearly no amateur.

As he was contemplating the uses of all this gear, her voice drifted down from above: '*Eh, là-bas!* Are you getting on all right down there?' Before he could answer Tom heard her footsteps on the stairs. Shortly she stood beside him. Once again he had to admire the way she stuck out in all the right places. Her timing was good too. He had almost completed his tour and was ready to ask a few questions.

Harriet beat him to the punch. She announced, 'I'm getting hungry. It's well past lunch time. Come upstairs and fix me something you think I'd like. Surprise me. You can even fix enough for yourself. I'm feeling indulgent today, so take advantage of the moment while you can. Later we can chat. Or something.'

Tom felt his pulse begin to pound at the promise implied in her last remark. He found he wasn't all that hungry as he remembered the teasing which had ended in his orgasm. He wondered if she had more of the same in mind, or if she intended to move on from that and join the fun herself.

Harriet opened one of the cupboards and took out a chrome and steel bit with a buckling strap. 'You can have this for afters if you do well,' she remarked as she led the way upstairs.

Tom wondered if she ever walked behind anyone, but he really didn't mind as long as he could admire the rear view of a provocatively-clad dominatrix ascending a staircase.

Once he let his attention stray too far from the matter of treading carefully, and tripped on his chains and nearly fell. He recovered but with an audible bump. Harriet looked over her shoulder to be certain he was still coming. She smiled at his discomfiture, but seemed pleased by the compliment his mishap implied. 'You should really be more careful,' she told him, with more than a trace of irony.

Tom smiled to hide his chagrin. Harriet had a way of making him feel like a schoolboy caught peeking through a hole into the girls' toilet. He reflected that all women could do this if they wanted to. It was a power built into the structure of society. As long as most people treated sex and nudity, or semi-nudity as in Harriet's case, which he thought more provocative than all over bare skin, as dirty and refused to deal

125

openly with the subject, women could make men feel guilty for lusting after their bodies. Men didn't have that power. He wondered how he'd feel if some attractive female let it be known that she had the hots for him. He knew he wouldn't dream of holding out. Probably the reverse, and if the woman in question was Harriet, most definitely the reverse. In the midst of these musings came the realisation that Harriet was deliberately playing the tease. She knew it and he knew it. It was a game whose rules they had agreed upon, at least tacitly, on his first visit to this house. It didn't matter that she made up the rules. She could flaunt herself and he was allowed to look as much as he liked as long as he didn't touch. If he wanted to end it, he had only to say so. He could hardly walk out dressed only in leg-irons, but she would let him go if he demanded it. Wouldn't she? The thought that she might not gave him an added fillip of excitement. In romantic novels the sensation is described as feeling one's heart turn over. His own heart slowly righted itself. A not-disagreeable sensation. He felt he was about to choke with suppressed desire for her. He wondered how much longer he could go on like this, and how much longer she intended to go on. That was just what they were in the process of finding out. Doubtless she would be able to outwait him. Women almost always could.

Harriet reached the top of the stairs and stood aside for him to pass. She closed and locked the door leading to her private dungeons, leaving the key in the lock. Tom went through into the kitchen to begin their meal. He heard Harriet go into the living room. The sound of the TV came back to him as he washed the vegetables for the salad. He imagined her sitting in front of the set, one smoothly-clad leg crossed over the other, as she had done so often since he had come under her influence. Did she pose like that for every one of her clients, or had Beth told her about his stocking fetish? Or did Harriet just sense his mood? He hoped so. It made the game of temptress and tempted more piquant.

Tom decided on sandwiches and salad. Although he didn't say it to himself, he wanted to sit across from Harriet and stare. He didn't want to spend all the time in the kitchen. Tom found a bottle of wine in the fridge and included it in his preparations. When his preparations were done he carried everything in to her on platters. Harriet nodded her acceptance as he set the food before her. When he came back with the wine and the glasses, Harriet was sitting on the edge of the chair with her thighs parted.

'I want you to kneel there,' she said, indicating a spot between her legs. 'You can feed me while I tease you unbearably. Don't lose control as you did last time, or spill anything on my outfit. I don't like changing once I get comfortable.' There was just the hint of a threat in her tone.

'Yes Mistress,' Tom replied with just the right degree of servility. He knelt between her thighs, conscious of their warmth so close alongside him.

Harriet closed her legs until the smooth dark nylon of her tights was pressed against his hips. She bent forward to take a bite of the sandwich Tom held for her. He fed her one bite at a time. She reached down between her legs and grasped his cock, which was already stiffening in response to the smooth pressure of her legs. When he jerked at the intimate contact, she murmured, 'Careful now,' in his ear. 'Don't spill anything. If you do your job well, there may just be something in it for you.' She continued to manipulate

127

his straining cock, running her fingers lightly up and down its length and then making a fist to grasp it more firmly. With her other hand she caressed the tip and scraped her fingernails gently up and down the underside of his shaft. As she played her maddening game with him, she gazed steadily into his face.

Whenever he looked up from feeding her, that level gaze met his. He wanted to look down to where her hands were busy on him, but Harriet shook her head minutely, forbidding him. Whenever his eyes strayed to her tits, thrust up and out by the leather bodice of her corselet, he missed his aim with the sandwich. At those times she would clamp down on his cock, making him gasp in surprise and pain. He became more diligent in feeding her, but those tits so close to his face and those legs clamped around his waist were most distracting. Not to mention the more acute distraction furnished by what she was doing between his legs. It was an interesting variation of the teasing game they had played last time, but this time he found his control being tested more severely.

Tom had had a whole week to anticipate this moment, and now it was here. He wanted her. Now. But he also wanted to show her that he could do what she wished. A lifelong believer in doing what he set out to do, at least sexually, Tom found himself wanting to demonstrate his forbearance to the woman who held him by his manhood and challenged him not to come, even as she did her best to force him. He felt ready to burst at any moment.

Harriet signed that she had had enough to eat by closing her mouth and shaking her head when Tom offered her another bite. She tugged him upright by the cock. He stood between her thighs looking down her cleavage (were those her nipples inside that tight sheath?). Looking up at him, she asked, 'Aren't you hungry? You haven't had anything to eat yet. Eat now and I'll try to keep you amused.' She underlined the order by squeezing him hard. 'Eat now.'

As he bent to take a sandwich for himself, Tom suddenly realised he was no longer hungry, but he ate anyway, mindful of her order. As he ate, sometimes choking on the food, Harriet continued to manipulate his cock. He could feel his muscles clenching as he fought down the orgasm on whose edge he was teetering. He didn't trust himself to look down at her.

Harriet carried on a monologue as she continued to caress his straining cock. 'Do you know the three most frequently told lies?' she asked. When he didn't reply she told him. 'The first is, the cheque's in the post; the second is, of *course* I love you; and the third is, I won't come in your mouth. We're about to see if you're a liar.' She took his cock inside her mouth and ran her tongue round it. She closed her lips around him and moved her head backward and forward so that he slid in and out of her mouth. He could feel the warmth of her breath all around him.

In order to distract himself from what she was doing to him, Tom asked, 'How come you're not talking any more? Cock got your tongue?'

Harriet bit him to remind him who he was dealing with. Tom let out a yelp and jerked his cock out of her mouth. There was a reddening line of teeth marks across the top of the shaft. He couldn't see, but he knew there was a matching line around the bottom.

'Would you rather I talked, or should we continue with the game?' Harriet asked. 'I could bite you again if you prefer,' she added with an air of consideration. Again he didn't answer. She bent forward and took him inside her mouth. Silence ensued, except for the occasional gasp from Tom as she found an unusually sensitive spot.

As she continued to stimulate him Tom began to feel like one all-over sensitive spot. He wasn't going to be able to hold out much longer.

As if reading his mind, although it was more likely she could tell from the feel of his cock inside her mouth, Harriet let him fall free. She looked critically at his cock, only inches from her face. There was a drop of fluid on the end of it. 'Just in time,' she remarked. 'You were about to become a liar.'

Tom could feel her saliva cooling on his cock, which was itself far from cool. So was he. 'I was never a fanatic about telling the truth,' he managed to say when he had recovered somewhat. He resisted the almost overpowering urge to thrust himself back into her mouth. Among other things, there were the teeth to consider.

'Never mind,' Harriet told him. 'You've passed another test.'

Tom replied, 'I don't mind passing tests, but what is the prize for passing them all? And how many do I have to pass?'

Harriet looked annoyed, as if he had asked a really stupid question. Tom gathered that she didn't like him to ask too many questions. Nevertheless, she answered.

'I'll decide when you have passed all the tests. The prize will be your confirmation as my assistant. There are all sorts of fringe benefits to being left in charge of helpless and nubile females. Do I need to draw a diagram?'

Tom said, 'I had one particular nubile female in mind. She's not a million miles from here, either.'

'Why, ah do declayeh,' Harriet said in a fair imita-

130

tion of a Scarlett O'Hara, 'do y' all mean ta say that y' all's lustin' aftah mah own fayeh body? What's a poor girl to do? Here ah thought ah was entertainin' a gentleman in my pahlah and now he's makin' indecent proposals to me. Ah've nevah been so shocked in mah whole entiyeh life.' Reverting to her own accent, Harriet continued, 'Still, I imagine we can reach an arrangement whereby you satisfy your base lust with me.' She looked pleased at the compliment he had paid her. 'If you wish, you can consider me the ultimate prize. I wouldn't mind that so very much. After all, Beth thought you were worth cultivating.'

Tom must have looked disappointed, for she went on, 'Now don't look so downcast. I've made an arrangement for this weekend I'm sure you'll like. But,' seeing he was about to ask, 'don't ask me anything. I don't want to spoil the surprise.'

She changed the subject abruptly. 'If you're not hungry, I'd like you to clear up in here and do the washing-up. I generally give the leftovers to the birds. Put them on the kitchen windowsill if you don't mind. Come back here when you're done.'

As he washed the dishes and tidied the kitchen, Tom wondered what the surprise could be. Given what he knew about Harriet, he guessed it would be something extraordinary. Nothing mundane would fit the atmosphere of the house. He opened the window and put the remains of the sandwiches out for the birds. It seemed incongruous that someone as seemingly ruthless as Harriet should worry about them. He never thought about them when disposing of his own rubbish. He hung up the tea cloth and drained the sink. Then he went through to rejoin Harriet.

She looked up with a smile as he entered. 'Come over here, Tom.' The handcuffs lay on the arm of her chair. Her black high-heeled shoes lay beside them. Tom noticed how clearly her red-painted toenails showed up through her tights. He had heard that when female folksingers removed their shoes on stage, they were telling the audience that they wanted a more intimate relationship with them. He wondered if the same were true of temptresses. And did the red toenails mean that they were more eager? When he stood before her, she motioned for him to turn around with his back to her. He heard the clink of chain as she picked up the handcuffs and anticipated her next order by bringing his hands around behind his back. Harriet gave a small 'Umm' of approval. His groin grew tight as he heard her open the handcuffs with a series of loud clicks.

She locked the cuffs on his wrists, leaving his hands back to back behind him. She remarked, 'Let this be a lesson to you: always put the hands back to back behind your subject when you plan to leave someone for some time in restraint. It's more comfortable for her that way. But you need to develop some judgement of your own, so remember the other things I'm doing as well.' She tightened the cuffs until they fit snugly, and then double-locked them. 'That will prevent your subject from inadvertently tightening the cuffs if she rolls over onto them. Now sit between my legs and you can rest your back against the chair.'

Tom sat awkwardly. The process involved getting down onto his knees one at a time and then falling the rest of the distance to the floor. Once seated he scooted back into the prescribed position by lifting himself on knuckles and heels. When he was seated, Harriet closed her legs around his shoulders. Tom felt an electric shock pass through him as her smooth, nylon-sheathed thighs touched his bare skin. But there was more. Harriet lifted her feet one by one and placed them in his lap. With her toes and the arches of her feet she idly began to tease his cock and balls. The experience was something completely new to him. But he liked the feel of her feet and the smooth nylon on his stiffening cock.

'And they both settled in for a long evening in front of the TV,' she murmured. 'Comfy?'

That wasn't exactly the word he would have used, but he couldn't think of a better one at the moment. Tom merely nodded.

The early evening news was just beginning on ITV. Together they watched the daily catalogue of civil war and starvation that made up the staple diet of the television news programmes. Tom wondered idly what reaction they would get if the newsreaders could look into this particular living room from the vantage point of the TV set. The sight of a nude man wearing handcuffs and having his balls caressed by the feet of a woman in a tight leather corselet and black tights would probably put them right off their autocues. He wondered how many of them would be going home to a similar experience. Not many, he guessed.

Harriet continued to fondle him – manipulate would not be the right word, he thought. Besides being too abstract and clinical, it didn't apply to sexual congress conducted by foot! Feet, he corrected himself. He knew from her previous remarks that she intended to leave him just the wrong side of completion. Harriet was engaged in a tricky exercise in judgement: just when should she stop and leave him hanging? He didn't think her feet were as sensitive as her hands, so how could she tell what state he was in? Briefly he considered relaxing his self-control, already being seriously strained, and shooting his load all over

133

those maddening feet. But he remembered her remark about not wanting to change her clothes once she was comfortable. He decided to hold on a bit longer. The earlier loss of control still bothered him a bit, mainly because Harriet had wanted him to hang on. Not this time, he vowed silently with gritted teeth. Show her what you're made of.

As the main news ended and the local programmes began, Harriet switched tactics. She stood up and motioned for him to do the same. With some difficulty he managed to get to his feet. Standing up without the use of his hands was not easy. Harriet moved over to the settee, pulling the top of her corselet down to free her breasts. Tom admired them, as he was obviously meant to do. They were full and round and only slightly pendulous. He wondered if she did special exercises to keep them taut. Later, after he became more familiar with her ways, he joked, though never to her, that she had ordered them to remain firm and they didn't dare disobey!

Harriet motioned for him to sit. He did so, wondering what she had in mind now. He didn't have to wait too long. She straddled him, her leg outside his own. She reached between them and pulled his erect cock up until it was pointing at his navel, then pressed her lower body (what his grandmother would have called, vaguely and reluctantly, her nether regions) against him, so that his cock was trapped between their bodies and lay against the smooth leather that covered her cunt and belly. Things were looking up, he told himself. When he himself looked up, she smiled into his eyes. A mischievous smile, he thought, as if she were having some private joke, probably at his expense. When he looked down again, he was confronted by her magnificent tits, just inches from his face.

Still smiling, Harriet put her hands behind his head and toyed with the hair at the nape of Tom's neck. He shifted slightly to accommodate her weight more comfortably, feeling his cock rubbing on the smooth garment she wore. That sensation required still more self-control. Tom knew he was on the verge of losing it again. He had to think of putting out the rubbish, think of queuing for fish and chips on a rainy night; lie back and think of England; think of anything but what was staring him in the face at close range.

Harriet gently pulled his head forward, decreasing the range even further. Her intentions were definitely not motherly. Tom did what any gentleman would do when confronted by a pair of tits like those. Since he couldn't use his hands, he opened his mouth and kissed the nearest nipple, running his tongue over the crinkly areola and giving it the gentlest of nips with his teeth. Harriet emitted a sigh of satisfaction. The hands pressing his head to her signalled that he was to continue. Tom pulled back slightly to get another view of her, then nuzzled her breasts and began mapping out the territory with a long series of kisses and nips that caused Harriet to sigh some more and close her eyes. She shifted her weight slightly now and again to bring different parts of herself into range of his mouth. This caused some more agreeable shiftings further south which posed another threat to his resolve not to come.

The fingers rubbing his neck didn't help either. Tom was forced to acknowledge to himself how erotic those fingers could be, and how many women simply didn't know what pleasure they could give. A cynical part of him added that they probably didn't

135

care much in any case. But that way lay danger too: Harriet was not any woman, and she knew quite well what she was doing. She put her knowledge to use against his crumbling defences. Tom had images of sand castles before a rising tide.

Harriet lay her head alongside his, holding him tightly now. Her breath was warm in his ear, and he could hear her sighs and soft moans of satisfaction clearly. He could tell from their rhythm and frequency that she was close to an orgasm of her own. Her scent was strong in his nostrils. Tom wished that his hands were free so that he could use them to help her over the top. Since they weren't, he did the next best thing: he drew back slightly so that he could get her left nipple between his teeth, worrying at it gently.

That was too much for Harriet's self-control, if indeed she was using any. In his ear he heard the rasping of her breath as she drew in great gulps of air. 'Ah, aah, ah, aha, ah, ahhhh, ahh, oooooooooohhh!' She was now writhing against him, rubbing herself and heaving as she came. Tom continued to kiss her breasts as she reached yet another peak. He lost count of her orgasms, but later he told himself he had done a good job for her.

At the time he was busy with other things. Harriet's spasms had been too much for him, and he felt himself explode against the leather of her corselet, the sperm shooting out and dripping off the smooth material onto her tights and his own bare thighs. His body jerked in release against hers.

Harriet held onto him tightly while their breathing slowed and the sweat cooled on their bodies. Tom was glad she had enjoyed the encounter. He was also pleased that she was not prone to drawing herself away quickly after they had come. Many women acted as if, the foul deed done, they couldn't get away fast enough, and many professed to be offended by the mess, especially if the man spent himself all over them. Harriet didn't seem to mind that, but as his own passions cooled, he remembered uneasily her remark about making a mess on her clothes. He would plead the stress of the moment if she said anything.

Eventually she disengaged herself and sat back. 'Well. That was fun,' she said.

Tom thought her choice of words left something to be desired. Fun was not strong enough, though he didn't offer any correction. Maybe it was her way of reasserting her own mastery by playing down what had obviously been a very enjoyable experience. For both of them.

Harriet looked down at the front of her corselet. There was a large dollop of sticky semen in the region of her abdomen, and dark stains on her tights where it had soaked in. Tom, being the underdog, had received his own shower, most of it in his crotch. Mockingly, she said, 'Well, I see you couldn't contain yourself after all. But at least this time you held out longer against stronger provocation. I suppose that's progress. You're learning. Now it's time for you to clean up after yourself. Still, it was nice.'

Tom appreciated the afterthought. He waited for the next move. Not that he had a choice. But he didn't have to wait long. Harriet pulled up the top of her corselet, covering her breasts once more. A pity, he thought. Already she looked more severe, less accessible. Once more she resumed her sergeant-major's demeanour.

Retrieving the key from the armchair where she had sat earlier, Harriet removed the handcuffs and laid them aside. 'Go get a cloth and help me clean up here,' she directed. She was tugging at the shoulder straps of her corselet, settling her tits more comfortably in the cups as Tom went to do her bidding.

In the kitchen he got a tea towel and a saucepan of warm water. With these he went back into the living room. Harriet was still standing by the settee. Tom went to her and began wiping down the front of her corselet. When he had done that he began sponging off her thighs, leaving dark wet patches on the nylon. He rather liked the feel of her legs as he worked away. Next he cleaned up the cushion of the settee and last of all himself. He was conscious of Harriet's gaze on him as he rubbed his crotch and cleaned his cock. In response he began to develop another erection.

'Not now, please,' Harriet said. 'Once is enough. Besides, I'm getting a headache. And it's almost bedtime.' She gave a mocking smile. 'Isn't that what they always say?' She turned off the TV with the remote control and led the way to the door at the back of the hall.

Tom saw that she intended to leave him in one of the cells he had seen earlier. 'When do I get to use the bedroom upstairs?' he asked, more to be saying something than in any attempt to change her mind. He already knew that there were easier things to change.

'That's for special guests,' she retorted. 'You're not one of them. Yet,' she added, softening the rebuke. 'Keep on working at it and you may be promoted. Play your cards right and you could be spending your nights in the room next to it.'

Once more Harriet preceded him down the stairs. When they reached the bottom, she asked him which cell he preferred. The two were almost identical, but he guessed that Harriet didn't offer many choices. He might as well take what ones there were. He chose by

138

walking into the one on the left of the stairs, where he sat down on the cot inside. He waited while Harriet made a short inspection of the room. He didn't know what she might be looking for, and he concluded it was done more for effect: let the other person know that you have to see everything for yourself. Take nothing for granted. Let others know you're checking up on them.

When she was done, she wished him a curt good night. She closed the door and he heard the sound of the key turning in the lock. The staccato sound of her high heels receded, and the door at the top of the stairs closed. The light went out. In the basement it was as dark as a cave. As she had said, it was bedtime. There was nothing else to do. Feeling slightly oppressed by the utter darkness, Tom lay down on the cot. He slept fitfully, dreaming of what they had done that evening and last weekend. And wondering what surprise Harriet had in store for him.

Not too surprisingly, he woke up with a hard on. This was partly the result of his dreams, and partly because he needed to pee. He groped his way to the toilet, guiding himself mainly by feel and his memory of the layout of the room from his earlier tour. He didn't need any light after he found the toilet and had sat on it (not trusting himself to aim accurately in the dark; it wouldn't do to have Harriet find him with piss all over the floor). So naturally Harriet turned the lights on at that moment. Murphy's Law worked as well here as it did anywhere else. The brilliance dazzled his eyes after the hours of total darkness.

He heard Harriet's footsteps on the stairs. He could tell from the sound that she was wearing high heels. They made a different sound from other types of shoe. It occurred to Tom that he preferred heels to flats, both acoustically and aesthetically. He wanted to get off the pot before she came in and saw him in an undignified position, but the sitting posture had told his body that it was time to shit too. She unlocked the door just as he reached for the toilet paper, and he met Harriet's interested glance.

'Haven't you seen someone on the pot before?' he asked, wanting to get in the first shot and so salvage some of the dignity he felt he was losing. 'And what about knocking before you come in?'

'Hundreds of times, to answer your first question. It's an occupational hazard in my business, something lots of people pay for as well. As to the other, I set the rules here. Try to remember that.' She changed tack abruptly. 'Did you sleep well?'

Tom nodded cautiously, not expecting such solicitude after her previous remarks. This morning she was dressed for going out. As he had guessed, she was wearing high heels. A beige blouse and knee-length skirt completed the outfit. She wore matching beige tights (or was it stockings today?). On the whole he preferred her in dark or black tights, and in the outfit she had worn the previous night. But he had to concede that it wasn't exactly something one wore to Marks and Spencer's.

'Good. It's breakfast time out in the wide world. The sun's in the sky, the lark's on the wing, the wolf's at the door, the . . . You get the idea. I'm famished. Hurry up with your business and come get me something to eat. I've a full day ahead of me. Places to be, people to see. But I see I'm running on.' She paused abruptly. With an air of taking a grip on herself, something Tom would have liked to do, Harriet turned and left him to it. 'Come straight up,' she threw over her shoulder as her footsteps receded up the stairs. 'And wash your hands, too,' came more faintly down to him.

When he had finished, Tom went up to start breakfast. It was a clear sunny day, just the sort of day for going shopping if you liked that sort of thing. Harriet clearly intended to do something of the sort. She gave no sign that she intended to take him along, which was just as well. He hated shopplng at the best of times. As he boiled the eggs and made toast and coffee, Tom watched the birds outside the window. The food he had put out last night was gone. Doubtless they had put it to good use making more birds. Tom put marmalade on the tray with the cutlery and napkin and carried it through to Harriet.

She gave him a perfunctory thank you, as if addressing and dismissing a servant. He went back into the kitchen for the coffee. When he had served Harriet, he went back and ate his own breakfast standing at the worktop. As he ate he looked out at the weather. It was just the sort of day that demanded he be up and about. Up he certainly was (in several senses of the word), but he hadn't any idea of what he should do. It was just as well that Harriet had taken over the planning. If I were an existentialist, Tom mused, I would be pondering on the interrelationship of freedom and compulsion. But as I'm not I just have to take whatever comes, which is exactly what everyone else, whether existentialist or not, has to do. He concluded he was no worse off than anyone else. At the least, he was in an interesting relationship which was developing in unknown ways. And at the best, there was the promise of becoming Harriet's assistant in what she called her B&D bawdy house. So far he had only a vague idea of what she wanted him to do, but it was early days yet. The idea of becoming

141

an assistant in what he smilingly thought of as a house of ill repute (relishing the Victorian flavour of the euphemism) appealed to him. He might even be able to quit his job and devote himself full time to it. Become self-employed. After all, the government was always on about becoming self-reliant, by which they meant signing off the dole and taking a job that paid peanuts. They held up the idea of being one's own boss.

'Tom.' Harriet's voice broke into his thoughts. She stood in the kitchen doorway. He hadn't heard her approach. 'You look as if you were miles away. Penny for 'em.'

Tom looked at her. 'Sorry. I was thinking about what being your assistant might involve. I like the idea but still don't know exactly what you want me to assist with. Did you want something else?'

'Never mind. That will come in time. And no, I didn't want anything else. You can clear up in there. I'll be going out shortly and you need to be prepared for being left alone here most of the day.'

Tom looked quizzical. Harriet continued, 'Don't worry about it. Think of this as part of your training: you'll be doing unto others a lot of what I'm doing unto you. The golden rule of good B&D people – watch and learn – another good rule for most things. I'm full of good advice this morning but I do know what I'm doing. I've been at this for some time. You're in the hands of an expert, even if I do say it myself.'

Tom smiled. 'If you say so, Mistress. Excuse me now.' He went into the living room to collect the breakfast things. Harriet stood aside to let him pass and then went down the stairs into the basement. By the time he had washed up and put things away she was back with a carrier bag full of things from her collection. It was beginning to look like time for the next lesson. Tom found he was curious.

Harriet went into the dining area and motioned for him to follow her. There was a table and four chairs. When she set the carrier bag on the table, Tom saw that it contained a fair quantity of rope and some things made of leather whose purpose was not immediately apparent. He imagined he'd find out soon enough, and didn't ask any questions. She drew the curtains and the room darkened. 'That will keep the curious passers-by from seeing more than they're meant to,' she remarked. 'No point in calling undue attention to the operation. Mrs Grundy and her minions are everywhere, and seemingly starved for gossip. I don't like to oblige them. It only takes a word in the wrong ear and we'll have the coppers swarming. In spite of what Sam Goldwyn said, there *is* such a thing as bad publicity – at least in this trade. Oh, I know that we'd have more new customers and more enquiries from the idly curious than we need if the word got around, but that wouldn't help if the coppers were also in the woodwork. You can't deal with customers if you're in court defending yourself.

'I'd have to find a new venue, which is a nuisance and an embarrassment and it's sure to be noted by the police. Once you let them get their teeth into you, become "known to the police" as they phrase it, they never give you any peace. If you can't be prudent, then discretion is the next best thing.'

As she was speaking, or lecturing would be more precise Tom thought, Harriet was laying out her equipment on the dining table. He had been encouraged by her use of 'we' and by the confidential nature of her remarks. He could appreciate the need for discretion as she brought out her selections. He felt his pulse accelerate and his breath become short as she made her preparations as if she were performing some elaborate ceremony. Which she was. They were playing roles: she the mistress and he the slave.

She approached him with one of the tie wraps she had brought with her to their first meeting. 'You know what this is for, don't you?'

'How could I forget?'

Harriet smiled as if to encourage a particularly bright student as she slipped the tie wrap through a brass ring. She passed the strap around his scrotum just above the balls and pulled it snug. After testing it for slippage, Harriet snipped off the excess strap with her side-cutting pliers. Tom winced involuntarily at the decisive snip of the tool so close to home. Harriet noticed, as she seemed to notice everything. 'Not to worry,' she said as she cupped his balls. 'The family jewels are safe in my hands.' The pun came out deadpan.

Harriet knotted a length of rope to the brass ring and let it dangle to the floor. 'Be careful not to step on it,' she cautioned. Next she selected a slim but aggressive-looking dildo with a hole through its blunt end. She lubricated this instrument with hand cream, remarking, 'Our American cousins call this a butt-plug, which is apt but terribly vulgar. What you'd expect from Americans. Bend over, please.' She threaded the rope's end through the hole. 'Keeps it from getting lost inside,' she explained, and slid the plug home into Tom's anus.

Not since the days of childhood enemas had he felt so full back there. He knew that some gay men and some women of either persuasion had anal sex, but he had never been at the receiving end. To his surprise, he found himself getting hard.

144

With a flourish Harriet pulled a chair out into the centre of the floor and indicated he should sit down. When he did so, she pulled the rope through between his legs and tied it fast to one of the vertical slats in the chair back. He felt his balls pulled insistently by the rope. He sat very still. It could prove uncomfortable if he moved too much. Tom was also aware of the plug inside him as it was pressed against the chair seat. An unfamiliar but not an unpleasant feeling. Not all new experiences need be avoided on principle. He wondered if this was how a woman felt when she was penetrated.

With another length of rope Harriet tied his hands together behind him and around the chair's back. Then she bound his elbows to the sides of the chair. 'Now for the fun part,' she said as she knelt beside him and took his cock in her hands. 'Just like last night,' she continued, 'you have to hold on and not come.' She made a fist and masturbated him until he was hard.

Her next move was unexpected – which could be said of most of the things she did. This constituted a good part of the attraction she held for him. Harriet slipped an ordinary condom onto his shaft and taped it securely in place around the base with surgical tape. 'I have lots of this stuff, so I can be lavish with it,' she said as she wrapped him. She finished taping him and produced a pair of scissors with which she snipped off the end of the condom. 'Hold still,' she ordered him brusquely as he squirmed. 'I hardly ever draw blood.'

Harriet inserted a length of surgical tubing into the end of the condom and taped it in place. She was making a crude but effective catheter. 'There,' she said brightly, 'that's you done. Now you won't have an embarrassing accident if nature calls while I'm away.' She dropped the free end of the tubing into a bucket and taped it there so it wouldn't fall out onto the floor.

Finally she tied his legs together at the knees and ankles, bringing a short length of rope from his wrists down under the chair to join them. She was being very thorough, which augured that she intended to be away for some time.

'This is all very nice,' Tom said, 'but what happens if there's a fire or a break-in while you're away? I can't move. And how long will you be out?' Despite his misgivings, Tom was beginning to feel excited by the prospect of being left tied up in the empty house. He remembered the weekend Beth had directed him to leave her bound and gagged in her flat. Had she felt the same excitement? Probably she had. Otherwise why do it?

Harriet responded. 'Nothing is ever perfectly safe. You have to assume some risks – take a chance – with new experiences or become stale. Are you really worried or just trying to give yourself some more excitement? I can't say that a fire would be pleasant, but the house is as safe as I can make it. You must remember that I do this or something similar all the time with other clients. And as to a break-in,' she smiled briefly, 'that would depend entirely on who was to break in, wouldn't it?'

On that enigmatic note she picked up the bit she had promised him for afters the night before and slipped it between his teeth. She pulled the straps tight, forcing it deeply into his mouth and pulling the cheeks back into a grimace. 'You look frightful,' she said as she buckled the leather strap behind his head. 'But you won't have to look at yourself. Or at any-

146

thing,' she said as she blindfolded him with a leather mask with foam rubber pads that fitted into his eye sockets and cut off all light. 'The shrinks call this routine sensory deprivation,' she said as she buckled the blindfold in place. 'And they charge the earth for it. I call it light entertainment; and I don't aim to bankrupt the punter. Relax and try to enjoy it. I'll see you later. Part of the fun lies in not knowing how much later.'

Tom heard her footsteps as she moved about the house. He guessed she was gathering her things for the shopping trip. Then her footsteps moved purposefully away from him. He heard the door open and then close, admitting a gust of air. There was the sound of the key in the lock. Harriet was being thorough as always. Then silence. He was alone in the house and completely immobilised. He shifted slightly on the seat and felt the stir of the plug inside him. The tug of the tie wrap on his balls warned him not to move too much. This must be what Beth had felt in those hours alone in her flat: the faint apprehension, a prickling compounded of worry, fear and excitement. And a sense of utter helplessness. No control over your own body. Unable to stir hand or foot. A feeling of total dependence. No choices to make. A paradoxical freedom to which he surrendered.

With the sense of freedom came a sense of detachment. Unable to move, he began to feel detached from his body, except when he tugged at the ropes or shifted on the chair. Since he couldn't see, he was cut off from the usual things that help us to measure time and its passage. The shifting shadows as the sun changed position; the very quality of the light that told you what time of day it was, even if you had just woken from an unplanned nap. Without these visual clues, which we all take for granted to give order to the hours, he felt cut off, adrift in the stream of time. It was curiously restful to be freed from the tyranny of the clock. He wondered briefly why Tchaikovsky had called it 'The Dance of the Hours'. They didn't dance. They merely passed. Now he was unable to measure even their passage.

He couldn't speak, even if there had been someone there to listen to him. Another of the ties to the ordinary world severed.

His ears brought him the noises of traffic and of pedestrians from the street, but even these sounds were muted. Tom fancied he could tell the difference between men and women from their footsteps, and he bent his efforts to distinguishing their sounds. But none of them stopped or paused by the door. He was alone in a way that few people who live in large cities ever are.

No one knew he was behind that door except Harriet, and only she knew when she was coming back, if indeed she had set herself a time. Some women, he knew, were content to spend the entire day at the shops. The presence of her DIY catheter reminded him that she had allowed herself considerable time to manoeuvre. Her return was not controlled by his bodily needs. She was clearly intending to take her time.

From nowhere another thought came to disturb him. Harriet might have an accident and be taken to hospital. No one would come back for him. It would be days before he was missed. Did Harriet have a note in her handbag saying her assistant was helplessly bound in her house: finder please go release him? He doubted it. But there was nothing he could do.

This train of thought was broken by a noise at the

148

door. Tom sat up in alarm, giving a sharp jerk to the tie wrap around his balls. The sound of the letter box closing told him it must be the postman. He hadn't heard the mail drop onto the mat. He reminded himself to expect the milkman. Perhaps a friend or neighbour of Harriet's as well. When no one answered the door, they would conclude that she was out and away. They couldn't know he was there. He doubted if the strangled noises which were all he could make would carry as far as the door. No help would come.

Tom found he could only strain his hearing and stay alert for so long. Then his attention would wander. He found himself nodding off from time to time despite having slept most of the night. He lost track of the time. Once he recalled waking and having to pee badly. He had to force himself to go, being unused to the position and the catheter. Eventually he managed. He dozed again. The next thing to wake him was the sound of the front door opening. He felt a gust of cool air sweep through the room. He jerked from sleep to consciousness in alarm. He grunted. There was no reply, but footsteps approached him. A woman, by the sound of them. But Harriet? No way to tell. He smelled a faint perfume but couldn't say if it was hers. He hadn't paid much attention to her scent that morning. Now he wished he had.

Tom felt a faint movement of air against his face and body, as if someone were moving quite near to him. Perhaps even breathing on him. He strained to hear anything that would give him a clue to the identity and, more important, the intentions of whoever it was with him. No use; he was not a trained listener. He couldn't mask out the street sounds and concentrate on nearby noise. Tom was discovering

149

the difficulties that came from being deprived of one of his primary senses, nevertheless, he could feel himself tingling with tension and alarm. And anticipation. Was this the surprise Harriet had arranged?

He grunted again. Still there was no reply. Then a hand touched his shoulder and he jumped in surprise, pulling sharply at the tie wrap. He gasped in pain. The hand continued its silent exploration of his body, moving down to his chest and gently stroking his stomach. By now he was sure that his visitor was a woman. The hands were not the hands of a man, and the perfume was definitely feminine. Tom relaxed slightly, for no reason he could put a name to. It only occurred to him later that the sex of the person with him didn't matter. If he was powerless to resist or escape, a person of either sex could do whatever they wanted to him. Still, he felt better after concluding that his visitor was a woman. He assumed, on no real evidence and in the face of several recent incidents which showed otherwise, that a woman would necessarily be gentle with him.

She was standing behind him, because the hand that had first touched him was joined by another from the other side, and he was pulled back against her body. His fingers brushed a silky fabric that had to be a dress or skirt and he explored further and touched her knee. A short skirt, then. And she was wearing tights or stockings, that pleased him. He felt the soft brush of her hair on his shoulder as she leaned over to explore his groin with those delicate fingers. She got full marks for getting straight to the point. A cloud of perfume now enveloped him as she rubbed and stroked his cock.

It responded predictably, even through the condom. He was glad of that. At least they both knew now that he could get it up. It would have been embarrassing and disappointing if he couldn't. Tom took pride in his company manners, they were especially important with strange females, and yet there was something familiar about her. It was most definitely not Harriet. While the manner was all wrong to be her, he had the feeling that he should know who it was. She was evidently the surprise Harriet had referred to, and a nice surprise she was. A part of him wished he could see her, but a different part of him was excited at the idea of being manipulated by this faceless woman.

She was removing the tape and condom from his cock, which was by now standing up on its own. There were sharp tugs as she peeled the tape away steadily and firmly. Next she stripped away the rubber sheath and he was bare beneath her fingers. She touched him lightly on the head of the cock and ran her fingers up and down its length. Suddenly she flicked a finger hard into the side of the shaft. He drew in a sharp breath but remembered not to jerk away. That was doubtless why Harriet had arranged him as she had. She struck him repeatedly from various angles, his cock bobbing at each blow. It began to feel warm and tingly. Tom guessed it was also red. It certainly felt red but it stayed hard.

The blows stopped as abruptly as they had begun. Her hands resumed fondling him. The alternation of mild pain and erotic massage was something new as well. He liked it. The world got fuller every day with things he had never tried. The memory of last night with Harriet came back to him. As then, he tried now not to come too soon, without knowing how soon was too soon. He had no way of guessing this stranger's predilections. So he resolved to hold on as long as possible, if for no other reason than to prolong his own pleasure. He knew it wasn't going to be easy. The combination of sensations sweeping over him were as difficult to resist as Harriet's prolonged teasing had been.

Fortunately for his self-control, the strange woman stopped caressing him. Tom heard the floor boards creak slightly as she stepped away, then there came the rustling sound of cloth nearby. He guessed she was removing her clothing. He found that encouraging, even though he had no way of guessing what she was going to do next. The fact that she was getting undressed suggested that she had something in mind that required them both to be naked. In the present situation there was only one thing he could think of that required nudity.

Which only showed him how wrong a person could be. Nothing happened for some time – more time than was required for her to get undressed and climb aboard, that being the only possible position, unless she untied him, that he could think of. A line of pain was suddenly drawn across his abdomen. It felt like a hot wire had been applied, but then resolved itself into a stinging rather than a burning. Tom realised she had struck him with a lash of some sort. She struck again, lower down, dangerously close to the family jewels. 'Aaarrgghhh,' he said, expostulated rather. The gag prevented further dialogue. She continued to strike him, criss-crossing the blows up and down his stomach and the tops of his thighs. It was all he could do to hold still, but he knew he had to. There were more inarticulate grunts and cries which could only be his own. She must be using a leather thong or a length of rope. The painful blows registered as thin lines of fire on his nerve endings, and there was a low but distinct hiss before they landed. He was breathing heavily and squirmed on the seat. Then everything stopped again.

The sound of her rapid breathing told him she was out of breath from her efforts. Perhaps she had only stopped to recover. The inability to respond or influence what she would do intrigued him, as Harriet had guessed it might. Tom wondered fleetingly how many other people enjoyed this sense of release. It wasn't something people would discuss openly, but he knew he couldn't be the only one to feel this way. There was Beth, for one. She had seemed to enjoy the same sense of freedom while bound.

Then there was no more time for thought. He felt her warm breath on his stiff cock, and then he was engulfed. There was a tongue coiling around his prick, and gentle nips as she used her teeth to arouse him still further. This bondage game certainly got one used to oral sex. Not that it took much getting used to unless one were really uptight, which described many of the people he knew, Tom thought. There were certain notable exceptions, one of them not a million miles away, and another one out shopping, but present company was too present to be ignored. Tom found himself clenching his stomach muscles to hold back. Was this what rape was like – one person helpless while the other did whatever they wished? But this was entirely too enjoyable to be called rape. No resistance was necessary. There was only the minor problem of delaying orgasm.

Even as he thought this, the problem became major. The strange mouth withdrew with a final lingering caress. A fragrant weight as she lowered herself onto him. He felt himself once more taken in hand and guided into a much tighter orifice. A warmer one, too. The strange woman began to raise and lower herself on his shaft, shifting deliciously from side to side for variation. The plug inside him shifted as she did. The sense of being stuffed full while he filled her at the same time was almost unbearable. Tom realised he was *being* fucked. It was an entirely new experience which he could do nothing to aid or counter. Once more he relished the novelty of being entirely in the control of another.

The woman put her arms around him and pulled her breasts against his chest. Tom felt her hair brush his face as she leaned over to nibble at his earlobe. He could feel her tits moving against him, the nipples hard with her arousal. She must have aroused herself by arousing him. It wasn't likely that the mere sight of his body was enough to make her breathe heavily, however nice it might be to think so. In this respect Tom was modest, though he had no use for modesty in its other senses. Luckily, neither did this strange woman.

She was pulling herself strongly against him, and he could tell from her rapid breathing and the low whimpers in his ear that she was about to come. Tom felt as if his prick was engulfed in liquid fire as she slid up and down on it, grinding her hips against him. Knowing that she was close to the edge pushed him closer too. They came almost simultaneously, her cries mingling with his own strangled grunts. The sense of release was wonderful after holding back for so long. He hoped it was as good for her, but couldn't tell from where he sat.

But she wasn't done. Even as he started to come down she began again to move against him. Her low cries continued in his ear and he realised she was going to come again. He tried to keep up. If he had been free he would have used his hands and mouth on her tits. Or would have continued to plunge in and out. As it was he could do neither of these things. But the strange woman riding him didn't seem to mind. Tom concentrated on staying inside her and she pulled herself more tightly against him. He could feel her body quivering as her excitement built up to bursting point. Her cries and gasps of pleasure were loud in his ear. 'Aahhh! Ahhh! Ahhahhh! Aieee!' This last was a shriek as she came again, shuddering against him. From what he could tell she had several more orgasms before she slumped and became a dead weight in his lap. He was reminded disturbingly of the way Beth had enjoyed multiple orgasms like this.

Tom was glad she had enjoyed the ride. And glad and surprised at the strength of his own reaction. He felt a sneaking sense of relief at not having to do anything after that performance. It would have been a hard act to follow, and the usual words would have made it seem banal. He had often found these moments after a good satisfying fuck rather awkward. After the passion there was always a sense of anticlimax. Some women expected more, but he could never figure out what it was, nor summon up the desire to supply it. Declarations of undying love seemed to work for some, but they sounded hollow and insincere to him. It was as if the sexual encounter were not enough, or not proof of some sort of affection. He could just come to like this bondage if it freed him from having to think of what to do next.

So he perforce sat quietly while she came back to an earth which he hoped had moved for her.

At length she stirred and got to her feet. When she moved out of touching range, Tom couldn't guess where she was or what she would do next. Her receding footsteps told him she was moving about, probably going to the loo, as so many women did after sex. At least this woman didn't rush off immediately, she waited a decent interval and didn't give the impression that she was glad to get away. Tom hoped she was only going to the loo. He didn't want her to leave just yet. However, there was no easy way to convey this desire to her unless he worked up another erection and she happened to notice it. At that moment he thought that particular feat was beyond him, unless he had help. He concentrated on waiting and thinking erotic thoughts which he beamed at his visitor.

She didn't seem to be receiving them, however. He heard her moving about the ground floor. She didn't come back to the dining area as far as he could tell, so he concluded that she was stalking about the place in the nude. Now *there* was a happy thought. The mental image of an attractive woman roaming about the house with her interesting bits bobbing about was arousing, and he concentrated on that. Perhaps she was still wearing her stockings and suspenders. He added that to his mental picture and felt a pleasant sense of warmth and reviving interest in his own bits. The noises off continued, now louder and now softer as she went about her rounds.

There was only a limited number of things she could be doing, so she would have to make her intentions clear before too long. She could now be making some coffee, though he couldn't smell anything like that. Maybe she was getting a drink. Or washing after their lovemaking. Putting on more perfume, or repairing her make-up. Even though he didn't like to take too much credit for himself, Tom imagined her make-up would have suffered to some extent during their recent encounter.

Or she could be snooping about the place. Suppose

she went down to the basement and came back with some things from Harriet's collection to try on him? Was she into bondage as Harriet was? After all, Harriet must know her quite well to allow her access to the house (and to him) in her absence. The probability that his visitor was also into the bizarre was having a salutary, if not a conventionally good, effect on his more interesting bits. Yes, there were definite signs that the south was rising again.

Tom wondered if Harriet had given her instructions to leave him as she had found him, or if his visitor was allowed to try out certain of her own ideas. Of course, she could do her own thing and still leave him tied to the chair. He wouldn't tell Harriet exactly what she had done. But what if Harriet demanded to know what had happened? Most women would at least be curious about what they had done. He decided not to volunteer information and so retain some sense of his dignity. He knew what Harriet would say about his sense of pride or dignity, so he resolved to guard it himself as best he could.

The footsteps came closer, and Tom tensed in anticipation. They stopped quite close to him. He fancied he could feel the air stir as she moved. Her scent came to him once more: perfume overlaid with the sharp odour of her musk. She used a warm wet cloth to clean him off: whatever hadn't gone into her had run down onto him. He appreciated her thoughtfulness in several ways, some more obvious than others. It was the most obvious way that she noticed. At any rate she spent a great deal more time cleaning and encouraging his stiffening cock than she did on the rest of him. She was making little wordless noises of approval that did wonders for his ego, and for the other thing as well!

The cloth was replaced by a hand which gently stroked the underside of his cock. Tom wondered briefly if she knew this was one of his specially sensitive areas. Had Harriet told her? But it didn't really matter. It was all very agreeable, and he surrendered himself once more to her manipulation. He could tell where all this was leading but didn't mind. With an inward smile he thought, this new-style sex was certainly addictive. Instantly addictive, was how he expressed it to himself.

This time there were fewer preliminaries. She took him into her mouth and he felt her tongue and teeth working once again on his cock. Although he was trying hard to prevent it, he knew he was going to prove a liar if she didn't stop soon and do something else. He hoped she would appreciate his inability to warn or influence her when he came in her busy mouth.

As if she could read his mind, or maybe she read the signs from his cock, she did stop. But only to sit once more on his lap. As she shifted her weight he could feel the plug shifting inside him as well. This was almost as bad as before – if you thought such things were bad. This time he could feel her thighs resting atop his, and he knew she was wearing stockings from the silky sliding of her legs on his. Her tits were once more pressed against his chest, the nipples taut with her excitement. His cock was pressed between their bodies. Last night's performance with Harriet was in danger of repeating itself. He held on while she cradled his head and licked his earlobes. Her tongue in his ear felt all warm and slippery. It's a pity more women didn't know how this excites a man, he thought.

Just how much did this strange woman know

about him? She seemed to be uncannily well-versed in what drove him wild. Tom wanted to know who she was. He imagined meeting her again in different circumstances, when it was he who was in control of the situation. As it now was, he could pass her in the street and never recognise her. But of course she would have trouble recognising him as well. The gag and blindfold concealed most of his face. He didn't like the idea that they would never meet again.

But now the matter of a solo climax was under serious consideration as his shaft was massaged between their sweaty bodies. Tom would have preferred it if she came too. It seemed ungentlemanly to come alone. However, she once again stopped at the critical moment and stood up. In a flash Tom's thoughts turned to disappointment: she was going to leave him hanging as Harriet had done. Amazing how much conscience a stiff prick doesn't have!

Tom lost track of her as she left the room. It looked as if she and Harriet belonged to the same club. This was just what Harriet would have done at this point.

The sound of the radio being switched on in the kitchen gave Tom some idea of what she was about. He couldn't tell which programme she had chosen, but the sounds of the outside world were reassuring. He had lost track of things after Harriet had gone out. Until this visitor had come, he had been dwelling wholly in his own consciousness. And when they were making love he hadn't been aware of anything beyond that. Now it was good to be reminded that the rest of the world was still there, pleasant as it had been to drop out for a time. He waited for the next move. There had to be a next something, even if it was only her leaving. Somehow he had the feeling

159

that she was not finished with him. But she continued to listen to the radio in the kitchen and paid no attention to him. Noises off suggested that she was getting something to eat. He felt sympathetic hunger pangs but tried to ignore them.

After what seemed an eternity she came back into the dining area. She wet his cock with warm water and soaped it liberally. Then she began to masturbate him. Except for the occasional breaths of cooler air, it felt exactly like being in a warm slippery cunt – almost always a good place to be. Predictably, he began to get hard almost immediately. She continued the slow massage and he found himself approaching the point of no return once again. Tom reflected that he was going to outdo himself this weekend. Harriet was due back some time later, and he imagined she would have further plans for him and the rest of the weekend. Would she join forces with this woman? He had never had two women to deal with at once. It occurred to him that he didn't have to deal with anyone. They would deal with him. He would have to deal with Monday on his own after this session, that might be a hard job, but that was later. Now was more important.

The unknown woman stopped and used a cloth to wipe him dry. When that was done she sat on his lap once again and with no hesitation or preliminaries she took him inside her. As he went fully home Tom thought how wonderfully a naked woman around the cock concentrates the mind. He could tell that she was already aroused. The moist warmth of her was unmistakable. Could that have been from the sight of him, or from her earlier teasing? He had no way of knowing, and soon he ceased to worry about it.

She began to raise and lower herself on the spike

160

of his erection. From the low contented sounds she was making he knew that she was enjoying the ride. She ground her cunt against him on the downstroke, almost losing him entirely on the upstroke until she slid warmly down to envelop him once more. She gave a little wiggle of her hips from time to time, emitting a low groan of satisfaction as she did so. Tom felt her vaginal muscles tense as she came. Tom held on as she gasped and heaved in the throes of her orgasm. She didn't pause. It seemed to Tom that she was coming almost continually, her movements becoming more and more frenzied. With some women it was hard to tell if they were enjoying it. Not so with this one. When he could hold out no longer Tom joined her, shooting inside her as she writhed against him.

Afterwards she seemed to rest a long time, as if the encounter had been especially tiring. He was tired too, but with the relaxed fatigue which follows a good satisfying screw. When she at last got to her feet, Tom felt the cool air against his body as the sweat dried. He didn't think he could do any more that day, and he hoped he wouldn't be expected to.

But with Harriet one never knew what might next be demanded, nor what she would do if someone couldn't perform. Tom wondered if Harriet admitted to a distinction between 'can't' and 'won't'. And what she might do with someone she suspected of being recalcitrant. Dully, Tom realised he was considering how hard it would be now for him to perform for Harriet. Until the arrival of this stranger he had been lusting after her with all the ardour of the lover denied his lady's favours. If a stiff prick has no conscience, he reflected, then a recently stiff one is equally short of enthusiasm.

Tom woke with a start. He hadn't been aware of dozing. But he must have slept through the departure of his unknown visitor. Hardly the gentlemanly thing to do. He felt the condom on his cock, so he knew she must have gone. It was thoughtful of her to fix things so he could pee if the need arose. As it did now. When he had done so he could only wait for Harriet's return, or for the next development. He dozed again.

Some indeterminate time later the sound of the front door opening let in the sounds of the street outside, and also, presumably, Harriet. The gust of wind that accompanied her seemed to sweep the cobwebs from his brain. Harriet had that effect. Curious he had never noticed it before. 'It's only me,' she called cheerfully, emulating Mary Kingsley. Tom wondered who else it could have been, unless she had given the keys to half the city.

He heard the sound of packages being set down nearby – results of her foray to the shops, no doubt. He heard the sound of clothing being removed, and felt a stab of alarm. Was he on again so soon? Her hands were on him, removing the condom and giving his cock a playful squeeze in passing, as if to reassure herself that no harm had come to it in her absence. Despite being tired, he felt himself respond to her. There's life in the old man yet, he thought wryly. He was becoming a sexual athlete.

'Did you enjoy the surprise?' Harriet asked brightly. 'Of course you did,' she continued. 'There's no one I know who wouldn't enjoy a day with her. Except perhaps the sexually constipated – of whom there are not a few about. I've known her for a long time.' Harriet was removing the gag and blindfold as she spoke.

162

The sudden light dazzled Tom's eyes. When they had adjusted, he saw that it was late afternoon. Harriet's watch said 4:47. So he had been there for almost seven hours. He felt stiff and cramped and was glad relief was at hand.

'I don't suppose she said anything to you. That was part of our arrangement. And of course you have no idea what she looks like. Would you like to see a photo? I have one somewhere about . . . Yes, I can see you would. Just give me a moment to get you untied and I'll show you.' Harriet was working on his legs. She spoke in her usual headlong manner. When he was free she brought the leg-irons and locked them onto his ankles. 'There,' she said, 'now you'll be more comfortable.'

She finished untying him and he stood up. He was stiff, and moved about slowly as the muscles unknotted themselves. Harriet pulled the plug from his anus and set it aside fastidiously.

'You'll have to wash that off in a moment. And empty the bucket. You can walk about a bit to get the circulation going while I get the cutters for that tie wrap.' Harriet went into the kitchen. In a moment she came back with the cutters and removed the plastic strap from his balls. She also laid a photo on the table.

The woman was a brunette. Beautiful was the first word that came to Tom's mind. Something told him not to say it. 'Nice. Very nice,' he amended hastily. Even so, Harriet frowned slightly. The woman in the photo was wearing a leather outfit not unlike Harriet's. Apparently it was a popular garment in the B&D trade.

'Her name is Helen,' Harriet said.

'Of Troy?' Tom asked.

163

'Of Earl's Court, actually.' Harriet's tone caused Tom to look sharply at her.

In an attempt to relieve the tension, Tom said jokingly, 'Then she'd have nothing contagious, would she?'

'Nothing but her cunt,' was Harriet's acid reply.

Could she be jealous, Tom wondered? Yes, he thought so. But she had been the one to set up the encounter. Now, it seemed, she regretted it. That remark about Helen of Troy must have done it. Tom was glad to learn that the woman he had thought of as aloof and cool, who insisted he call her Mistress, could feel jealousy. He would have to remember that in future. He shrugged and turned away to go to the bathroom, picking up the bucket and plug as he went. In the mirror he noticed a long red hair entangled in his own chest hair. He plucked it off and studied it. His visitor had had brunette hair in the photo. But there were such things as hair rinses.

When he came back Harriet was still putting the shopping away. She looked grim and Tom concluded she was still upset by his remark. He shrugged again. No accounting for her moods. Nothing to do but wait for them to change. If he had learned anything about women, Tom knew that anything he might say now would only make matters worse. Best keep quiet and out of the way. Wait for the weather to clear. There was no telling when that might happen. Another imponderable. And there was the rest of the day to get through and tomorrow as well.

So he said nothing and went to make a cup of tea. Usually he would have made coffee, but tea seemed more appropriate at this moment. When the ship goes down, when your cat gets run over, when your mother is murdered, a cup of tea is the universal remedy. So it ought to work when your Mistress is angry.

He turned on the TV without being asked and they

164

sat drinking the tea. Harriet seemed pleased by his manner and by the service, which he had performed in silence. It took an hour or so for the first smile to appear, ostensibly at something on the box. Tom reckoned he was halfway home. The first word required another hour.

'Did you really find Helen attractive?' Harriet asked.

Tom thought it best not to tell the obvious lie. 'From her picture, yes. But you have to remember that I had no idea what she looked like until you showed it to me. And, before you ask, I enjoyed the surprise very much. I liked the idea of being helpless while someone else – a complete stranger in this case – did everything. Wasn't that the idea? He turned the conversation around to what Harriet had done, rather than dwelling on Helen's part in it. It seemed both safer and more effective in restoring the normal atmosphere. He relaxed when Harriet's rueful grin told him she was getting over her fit of pique.

The rest of the evening passed in desultory but relaxed conversation that cleared the remnants of the tension from the air. When it was time for bed Harriet led him to the basement cell with her old manner and air of cheerful good humour. She locked him inside with a cheery good night. Even though this was apparently not going to be the night he got promoted to one or other of the upstairs bedrooms, Tom went to sleep with a feeling of relief and satisfaction.

In the morning Harriet came to unlock the cell door. Tom was pleased to see that she was wearing a dominatrix costume once again. It was not the one she had worn up till now. This time she wore a leather harness including a brief uplift bra that emphasised her breasts (needlessly, Tom thought, but he liked the

165

effect). Below the tit level a strap ran vertically down-
ward to a wide belt that nipped her in at the waist and
gave her a pronounced hourglass shape. A further
strap descended from this and passed between her
legs, where it widened slightly to cover her mons
veneris. When she turned to lead the way out of the
cell, he saw that this strap continued up her back,
dividing her generous bottom most provocatively. It
led up to a collar at her neck and was pulled tight with
a buckle. Suspenders from the waist belt held up a pair
of glossy grey stockings. This morning Harriet wore a
pair of knee-length laced boots with stiletto heels. She
was a most agreeable sight. Quite daunting, in fact.

Instead of going upstairs, Harriet turned towards
the back end of the basement where the rest of her
gear was stored. It began to look as if she intended
to settle the account she had told Tom she was
keeping. As he followed her Tom felt the first stirring
of the mingled desire and apprehension he associated
with his sexual arousal since meeting Harriet.

She led him to one of the cabinets at the side of the
room. Inside there was a step ladder. 'Carry that over
to the post there,' she commanded tersely, pointing to
one of the pillars that supported the ceiling and the
floor above. 'Lean it against the post and wait there.'
She moved to another cabinet to collect some other
gear.

The pillar she had indicated was obviously meant
to serve as a whipping post. There were several hooks
set into it at various heights, all of them above head
level for the average person. As he stood where she
had directed, Tom watched her open the cabinet and
extract a quantity of rope and a riding crop. He
watched in a detached fashion as she came back to
him, admiring the way she moved and the way the

leather harness defined her body, underlining her eroticism. He found the sight of her more absorbing than the thought of what she was about to do to him.

Harriet wasn't interested in his admiration just then. There was something more pressing on her mind. She climbed the step ladder and beckoned Tom forward. Without being told, he brought his arms around the post and waited while Harriet tied his wrists together. She hoisted his arms up until he was stretched and tied the rope off to a hook near the ceiling. This left Tom standing against the post with his arms high over his head. Harriet climbed down and moved the ladder out of the area of operations. She picked up the riding crop and showed it to him. 'This will hurt you a good deal more than it hurts me,' she told him jovially.

He smiled stiffly in spite of the tightness in his scrotum and belly. He was struck by her indefatigable humour.

Then Harriet stepped behind him, out of his view, and he was struck by something more weighty. The first blow landed on his bottom – the obvious target. It stung more than anything else. He thought it wouldn't be so bad if that was the best she could manage, but it wasn't the best, as the next blow told him. Harriet didn't pull her punches this time. The blow drove the breath from his lungs in a surprised snort. It too landed on his bottom, but it felt more like someone had laid a line of fire across it. Harriet didn't pause for effect. She continued to lay into him, criss-crossing the blows up his back and over his bottom and down the backs of his legs. Tom didn't dare turn around to see when the next one was coming for fear of bringing other, more essential parts of him into range.

Harriet changed the target often enough to avoid drawing blood, but Tom felt as if his entire rear elevation was on fire before she had finished. He was biting his lips to stop himself crying out. He thought that would be too undignified. Begging her to stop seemed equally undignified, and he didn't think she would. He held as still as possible.

When she finally paused she was breathing heavily. Tom could hear the rasp of her breath as she stood behind him. She came closer and pressed herself against his back. A nice sensation, that, he thought. Harriet took his prick in hand. 'I don't want you to get the idea that it's all suffering here, even when we settle up for your lapses. I want you to begin associating pleasure with pain. You have to know about that so you can help me teach it to others. So, are we having fun yet? Yes, I can see that we are,' Harriet said, using the editorial, the royal and nurses' 'we'.

'Umm,' said Tom. This really was quite agreeable. He was stiffening beneath her hand. The memory of the lashing was fading as Harriet continued to fondle him. He could see how her method worked. First the whip, and then the hand that had wielded it bringing pleasure. Keep it up long enough and your subject would soon be thinking of them as cause and effect. It was one of the few times when even a logician might not object to the *post hoc* fallacy.

Long before he lost control she stopped. Harriet got the ladder and untied him. He rubbed his wrists but deliberately didn't rub the other parts. He might as well have saved himself the trouble. She was paying no attention to what he was or wasn't doing. Tom wondered if her lack of attention was intended to underline another point, that bondage and sex were no big thing, just part of the day's activities. If she was she gave no sign of that either. She was her usual matter-of-fact self. That saved him from having to remark on what they had done, which was just as well, because he had no comments ready. In any case Harriet was already moving towards the stairs, and he didn't fancy commenting to her retreating back. Instead he followed her upstairs, admiring the way her bottom was divided by the leather thong.

Chapter Six

Up until now Tom had been forbidden to call Harriet or communicate with her during the week. As it had with Beth, the week became a period he had to get through in order to enjoy the weekends with his Mistress. Nor had she ever attempted to communicate with him during the time he spent living the other half of his life. Therefore he was surprised to get a letter from her. It was waiting for him when he came home on Wednesday evening. The handwriting was strange to him at first. He didn't connect it with Harriet because of her weekends-only rule.

When he did eventually make the connection, he hastily tore the envelope open half fearing it was her notice to him that he was not to come back. Such things happen even with people in Harriet's line of business. Maybe he had not measured up to her standard and she was going to look for another assistant. Tom realised with a start how much he would miss the tantalising sessions with her. She had become a part of his life in the short time he had known her, as Beth had, and she had gone abruptly.

Before you come on Friday evening, I want you to do several things, the letter read. Tom felt a huge sense of relief. It wasn't the dismissal he had feared. *First, you will have to buy some lingerie to go with the maid's outfit I have for you. Get a panty-corselet and several pairs of the firmest support tights you can find, in case we ladder one pair*. That sounded vaguely ominous. Tom thought of the riding crop again.

He also thought of the embarrassment he would feel buying the things she specified. He remembered the first time he had bought a peignoir for his first serious lover. It had taken several days to screw up the courage and the saleswoman had looked at him rather queerly. She had added to the embarrassment by holding the chosen garment up for him (and everyone else in the vicinity) to view. He had wanted to shout at her, 'Put it away! Hide it!' But in the end he had fled from the store with what he wanted. The orders from Harriet condemned him to another such scene. This time it would be complicated by the knowledge that the lingerie was for him and not for a lover. But Harriet had spoken. Nor had she finished:

Second, you will need to borrow or hire a closed van or an auto with tinted windows. We have to pick someone up at the airport and I do not want people on the street to be able to see what we are doing. That was both mysterious and intriguing enough to distract his attention from the first part of the letter. It was no use asking Harriet for further details. If she had wanted him to know more, she would have told him. And in any case he was still bound by the no-calls rule. If she decided to break the rule by writing to him, that was up to her. She gave the orders. The letter concluded: *We need to be at Terminal Two at Heathrow by 1900 hours, so make your plans accordingly.*

The 1900 hours sounded military, and was just the sort of touch Harriet would relish. He didn't have much time to get things done, and failure to do what she wanted was not something he wanted to contemplate.

On the next evening, after work, Tom bought the corselet and tights. It was almost as embarrassing as he had feared, and he guessed that Harriet had taken that into consideration when she had told him to get the things. She could have got everything as easily as not, so she had probably wanted to humiliate or, at least, intimidate him. Part of the treatment. At home he had wrapped the lingerie in plain paper and put it into an anonymous plastic carrier bag.

The next day he had phoned a car-hire firm and rented a Rover with tinted glass. He assumed Harriet wanted something large and impressive, but not as memorable as a Rolls-Royce. When he arrived at Harriet's place with the car, he found her ready to go. She looked approvingly at the car, and only then gave him a quick hello and a smile. She stood expectantly at the passenger door, waiting. Only at the last moment did Tom realise she was waiting for him to open the door for her. He hoped his hesitation would not be noticeable to passers-by, but he guessed that Harriet had noted the lapse and would add it to the next lashing she decided to give him.

She directed him to drive to Heathrow. The evening rush was beginning to thin out, and he made good time to the M25. When they arrived, she directed him to the Terminal Two car park, and waited again while he came around to help her out. Perhaps she let her skirt ride up deliberately to reward him for his diligence. Or maybe it was accidental. But in either case Tom admired the view of her legs as he got out. Harriet had not been schooled in the ladylike method of getting in and out of cars and she didn't seem to care.

All during the drive Tom had wondered who they were meeting, but Harriet had not enlightened him. There was also the question of how greatly this mysterious party would disrupt the weekend with Harriet. He didn't fancy sharing her time with anyone else, and was prepared to resent whoever it was. It did no good to tell himself not to be so proprietary, but he had the wit not to mention these sentiments to Harriet. He knew she would regard them as trivial or irrelevant when set beside whatever she had decided to do.

Inside the terminal Harriet checked the flight arrivals as, if daring the board to show a delay. Tom went to get coffee for them and a table at the restaurant. She joined him, looking satisfied. Tom wondered if she had ordered the airline people to make sure the plane arrived on time. He waited for her to supply further information. She continued not to. The public address system said something incomprehensible, but Harriet looked up at the sound and checked one of the ubiquitous TV monitors displaying arrivals and departures. She must have seen what she was expecting, for she finished her coffee quickly and got up, motioning for Tom to follow her.

There was the usual steady stream of people emerging from the customs area into the arrivals hall, looking bewildered or anxious or tired, or all three. They would look around until they caught sight of a familiar face, or gratefully make for someone holding a cardboard sign with their names on it. Since Harriet had no such sign, Tom assumed that she would recognise the person or people she was looking for. Or vice versa. Presently she did, stepping forward as a couple emerged from the doorway. Harriet waved cheerily, and they came over to her.

The man was tall and fair, with lots of blond hair brushed carelessly back from his forehead. His wife, or at any rate the woman with him, looked apprehensively at Harriet as she approached. She too was blonde and somewhat younger than the man, or at any rate better kept, though with the increasing popularity of cosmetic surgery it was getting harder than ever to tell someone's age.

Harriet went directly to the couple, embracing the man and giving him an affectionate peck on the cheek. The woman watched silently, as if sizing up a possible rival. Harriet and the man began to speak simultaneously, but Harriet prevailed after a moment. She usually did. Tom couldn't catch what they were saying. He was trailing in Harriet's wake without any clear idea of what he was supposed to do. Obviously Harriet knew the man well, because they were talking animatedly in what sounded like Dutch while the woman listened anxiously.

Like most Englishmen, Tom knew no foreign languages and could only surmise they were catching up on news. He had no idea that Harriet could speak Dutch, and he wondered what other surprises she had to reveal. She had already revealed quite a few. Presumably she would introduce the others when she was ready.

In the meantime Tom studied the woman. She appeared to be Dutch as well, though there was no way to be sure of that. About twenty-eight, he guessed. Certainly no more than thirty. Very pretty. Nice figure. Her breasts seemed slightly out of proportion to the rest of her, larger and heavier than her frame called for. He instinctively looked down at her legs, always the leg man. He expected her to have the slender, not to say skinny legs of the large-breasted woman. Dolly Parton was the image that occurred to him. But no. She had full legs. Nicely shaped, according to Tom's personal preferences, and she was

174

apparently not ashamed to show them off. He noted approvingly that she was not wearing a long skirt and he liked her choice of tights or was it stockings and suspenders? It couldn't be, with a skirt that short, unless she was also an exhibitionist, which was a not unpleasant prospect in itself.

During a lull in the conversation she looked up and noticed Tom's scrutiny. She smiled nervously, glancing at Harriet and the man she was with. To hell with it, Tom decided recklessly. He didn't like feeling left out until called for. He moved over to her and held out his hand. 'I'm Tom. Sorry I don't speak Dutch.' He didn't know how else to introduce himself. He was with Harriet but she had apparently not said in what capacity.

'Katrina,' she said quietly. 'Katrina Roos,' she added, with a glance at the man. He and Harriet were still deep in their conversation. 'I can speak English. It's nice to meet you.'

Tom liked her voice. Soft and well-modulated. Apparently an educated woman. He felt foolish about his lack of skill with another language. There could have been an awkward silence, but Tom decided to plunge ahead. 'I'm pleased to meet you too. Did you have a good trip?' He smiled at her and at the triteness of the opening.

Katrina smiled back and asked him if he was with Harriet. The question was direct and it steered the conversation away from the banality in which it could have foundered. She had noticed the offhand way Harriet had treated them both in her absorption with the man.

Before Tom could outline his somewhat ambiguous relationship with Harriet, he became aware that she had noticed his overtures to Katrina. Remembering her reaction to his admiration of Helen, Tom expected a frosty remark. But Harriet merely turned the conversation to English to include him and Katrina. Maybe she was saving her disapproval for later, starting another account which would have to be settled in the basement. The last one had been enjoyable enough, so that wasn't a real worry for him.

'Adriaan – Tom.'

She performed the introductions offhandedly, then turning to Katrina, she introduced herself. 'I see you two already know each other,' she said to Tom and Katrina. Harriet said nothing about what he was doing at the airport with her. Perhaps she had already covered that topic in her conversation with Adriaan. In any event he was too polite to ask the same question Katrina had.

Tom found himself shaking hands with the tall man and exchanging polite conversation. He missed the directness Katrina had exhibited. In fact, he realised, Beth and Harriet had a similar openness in speech and action. He had responded to their overt approaches by beginning relationships which were at once bizarre and satisfying. He wondered if his relationship with Katrina would be equally satisfying.

He brought himself back from these reflections and tried to keep up his end of the conversation. He succeeded mainly because neither of them was paying attention to the words. They were merely going through polite form, on autopilot, as it were. Tom was grateful for that as well. It gave each of them time to form an impression and respond to the other.

'Ari,' the man was saying. 'The other name is too long. Are you working with Harriet now?'

The question seemed to imply that there had been others working with Harriet at some remote time and that still others would do so in the future. Tom didn't know how to reply. He also noted Katrina listening intently. It was the same question she had asked before Harriet had included them in the conversation.

Harriet unexpectedly came to his rescue this time. 'Tom is my assistant. I wanted him to meet both of you with me. Among other things he's a more than adequate chauffeur and can negotiate the traffic around here.'

Harriet didn't say what else he might be. Presumably they would all find that out later. 'Ari's not going to stay with us this time,' she explained to Tom. 'He's dropping Katrina off before flying to Singapore and Hong Kong. Business,' she ended vaguely. 'Katrina will be staying until he gets back and we will be looking after her.' Harriet let the ambiguous statement stand without further explanation.

Tom noticed that Katrina had gone red and swallowed nervously. She looked confused but said no more. Either she had agreed to the sojourn or was well-schooled in doing what Ari asked her to do. She and Harriet should get on famously. Tom was surprised and pleased, though he said nothing, at his battlefield promotion from nonentity to Harriet's assistant. He wondered if it would stand when there was no one around to notice. Time to find out later.

Ari was looking at his watch and mumbling something about tight schedule. He bent to kiss Katrina on the lips and to whisper something that made her smile. With a final, 'Be good, darling' to her he moved away, leaving Katrina standing awkwardly between Harriet and Tom.

Harriet turned to Katrina and assumed her no-nonsense air. Pleasantries over, it was time to get down to business.

177

'I guess Ari has told you why you're here.'

It was more of a statement than a question. That was Harriet's characteristic approach to her business, and Tom was watching closely to see how she applied it to someone else. Katrina went red once again at Harriet's directness, but she nodded once mutely. Tom wondered if the flush extended further down to the more interesting bits. It might be nice to find out.

'Tom, go get the car now. Meet us out front in,' glancing at her watch, 'ten minutes. Take Katrina's bag with you if you don't mind.'

Once again it was more a command than a request. Back to nonentity, Tom thought ruefully, but Harriet gave him a small smile that took some of the sting from her words. A complex woman, he thought, not for the first time. As he turned away with Katrina's flight bag – really no more than an overnight bag – he noted it was quite light. Nothing like the department store most women insisted on dragging along with them, so either her stay was going to be short, or she wouldn't need many clothes. Tom found the latter possibility distinctly promising, though he wondered if Harriet would leave them on their own for any length of time.

Tom honked the horn and watched Katrina and Harriet detach themselves from the small crowd by the terminal doors. Harriet gave the impression of frogmarching the younger woman towards the car.

Katrina was looking dubious again. Tom got out and opened the rear door for them and Harriet gave him another of her small smiles, mouthing the words, 'You're learning' to him as she got in beside Katrina.

He closed the door behind them and went around to the driver's side. As he drove away he heard Harriet saying cheerfully, 'You'll be much more com-

178

fortable in these thumbcuffs, Katrina. If you'll just hold your hands out, and give us a big thumbs-up. That's right,' Harriet said encouragingly. Tom heard the distinctive click as Harriet closed the cuffs on Katrina's thumbs, and the soft snap as she double-locked them. In the rear-view mirror he caught sight of Harriet putting the keys into her handbag. Katrina sat beside her with her thumbs cuffed in front of her. She still looked dubious, but it was too late to protest. Unable to use her hands, Katrina tended to slide on the seat whenever the car took a turn.

Harriet noticed Katrina's doubtful expression, and tried to cheer her up with small talk. She rattled on like a tour guide as they drove back through town, pointing out the more familiar landmarks. 'Is this your first visit to London?' she asked.

Katrina replied, 'Yes,' in a small voice. She shifted awkwardly in the seat as she tried to find a comfortable position for her hands.

Harriet continued the travelogue as they drove through the darkening streets towards her house, and by the time they drew up outside, Katrina was relaxed enough to remark on how nice it looked. Trite as the remark was, it showed that she was getting accustomed to the situation.

As he listened to Harriet talking Katrina round, Tom reflected on how different her approach was from Beth's. Beth had been intense, determined to impart an air of the outré to their meetings. She had largely succeeded in this – not that Tom thought any the less of her for it. Harriet, on the other hand, tried to bring the air of the everyday to her bizarre dealings with others. Both women, he thought, had succeeded in their own ways. Almost idly, he wondered where Beth was, and what she was doing (and with whom).

She had managed to ease the pangs of separation by the timely introduction to Harriet. This compact, sturdy woman had taken her place at the centre of his activities.

Harriet broke into this train of thought. 'I'll get Katrina settled in for the night. I want you to return the car and come back in the morning. Around ten will do. No point in getting up too early. The old saw about the early bird and the worm merely proves that it's unhealthy to get up with the lark.'

Tom got out to open the door for them. Harriet stepped out confidently and turned to help Katrina as she slid awkwardly across the seat. Harriet draped her coat over the younger woman's hands, concealing her thumbcuffs. She took the small bag with one hand and with the other she steered Katrina firmly by the elbow across the pavement and up the front steps. Harriet set the case down and fumbled the keys from her handbag, never letting go of Katrina. Tom wondered if she was afraid the blonde girl would bolt if left alone. Cuffed as she was, running would be awkward.

Harriet got the door open and pushed Katrina inside. Then she said something to her and came back to the car. She dug into her handbag and came up with an envelope. She handed it to Tom. 'Almost forgot this shopping list. Would you be good enough to pick them up before you come round. It doesn't matter if you're a bit late. We won't be going out.' When he got home Tom made himself something to eat and went through Harriet's list as he watched TV. She asked him to buy some food for the three of them at the supermarket. Her list specified what he was to get. She ended by reminding him that this was to be the TV weekend she had mentioned. She told him to be sure to bring the things he had bought when he came the next day. Harriet added that she would have the rest of his costume waiting at her house.

His dreams that night were disturbed by images of him dressed as a French maid, waiting on Harriet and Katrina. He felt uneasy about having a stranger present, and wished Harriet had chosen a different time to begin her newest game. But then she had probably taken Katrina's presence into account when devising his debut as a ladies' maid. This probably came under the heading of embarrassment for him – a salutary lesson in submission from Harriet's point of view. It was what the B&D groupies would call humiliation.

The next morning Tom arrived at Harriet's place to find she was out. He was disappointed. Surprisingly so. He also felt silly carrying the things he had bought around with him, even though no one could tell the package contained women's clothing. Then he noticed a piece of paper sticking out of the letter box. Hopefully he drew it out, and yes, it was addressed to him. Or it was in a manner of speaking. It said: *Go to No. 37 across the road and ask for Pamela. She has a key and will admit all eligible persons in my absence.* Tom wondered what she meant by all eligible persons, and how many there might be on that list, but speculation was fruitless. Either Harriet would tell him, or she wouldn't. He already knew that she had clients for her services, and supposed he came under that heading. Not surprisingly she had made no secret of her business, nor any apology for it. He would have to take her as he found her. She had at least made that much clear.

He went across to number 37 and rang the bell. The door was opened by a woman who looked familiar, even though Tom had never been in there before. She was dressed smartly in a green dress with a pearl choker at her throat. 'Yes?' she said.

'Pamela?'

'No. I'm the maid. She's out just now. What can I do for you?'

Tom handed her the note from Harriet. He didn't comment on the incongruity between her dress and her title. He knew enough about prostitutes to understand what 'maid' meant in this context. From the maid's dress, he gathered that Pamela must be something more than a casual prostitute. Not the type who felt it necessary to advertise by leaving hastily scrawled cards in the local newsagent's shop window.

She read the note and then invited him inside. Apparently satisfied with his bona fides, she said, 'I'm Helen. Just a moment while I get the key.' Tom looked more closely at her when he heard her name. He was almost certain this was the woman whose photograph Harriet had shown him when she came back from her shopping trip. But she said nothing about that visit, and gave no sign of recognition. Tom wanted to ask her, but hesitated. What if she weren't the same person? It wouldn't do to be blurting out to just anyone what he and Harriet were doing across the road. He remembered the red hair he had found. Helen's hair was brown.

Helen came back with a key which she gave to him. Still she gave no sign of recognition. Tom thanked her and went back to Harriet's house, where he let himself into the hallway. He was careful to lock the door behind himself. Harriet's habits were rubbing off on him. As he closed the door he felt the silence of an empty house. It was different from a house in which someone was merely sleeping. Hard to say what the difference was, but it was there. A certain quality of silence which said empty.

He went through into the front room. True to her word, Harriet had left the French maid's costume ready for him. She had also left a note. It said: *Called out unexpectedly. Wait until I get back before you try this on. I imagine you'll need help the first few times anyway. While you're waiting go to the cellar and look in on our guest. I think that will pass the time agreeably enough until I get back.* It was signed simply, H.

Tom put the note back on the settee and inspected what she had left for him. There was a black satin dress with a short skirt; a lacy apron; a silky black lady's slip; and a pair of black high-heeled shoes with ankle straps. There was also a pair of breast-shaped foam rubber pads whose use he could readily imagine. When he saw these things, he was glad he had chosen a black corselet and tights. At least everything would match. He also found a long brown wig which she had left for him.

It all seemed straightforward enough. He thought he could manage to dress himself, but he knew better than to disregard Harriet's clear instructions. Besides, there was something else he had to do. A decidedly pleasant something else. He brushed the silky material of the dress with the back of one hand, imagining how it would feel against his skin.

The key was hanging in its usual place. He opened the door quietly and went down the steep wooden steps. The door to one of the cells was ajar, and he concluded that Katrina was in the opposite one. On the locked door there was a notice: *Katrina Roos. Stay indefinite. Nil by mouth.*

It was exactly the sort of notice one saw so often in hospitals. Tom remembered that Harriet had trained as a nurse. He wondered how strictly the nil by mouth part of the note was to be taken.

The key to Katrina's cell was hanging on a hook nearby. When he opened the door and looked in he saw the reason for Harriet's instructions. Katrina was gagged, though he couldn't think why that should be necessary. Harriet had said often enough that the walls were soundproof. Perhaps Harriet had simply decided that the gag was something Katrina needed to experience.

Katrina had heard the key turn in the lock. She turned to look directly at him as he entered her cell. She was nude and wore an iron collar about her neck. A chain led from her collar to a ring in the wall. She also wore her thumbcuffs and a light rosy flush from head to toe. It was probably from embarrassment, but it could have been due to anticipation. Beautiful blonde women do not ordinarily sit starkers, in a locked cell with their hands cuffed behind them so that they can be found by passing strangers. More's the pity, Tom thought.

There was a look of alarm on her face: eyes wide and nostrils flaring as she regarded him. Her shoulders moved convulsively as he entered. Probably she was instinctively trying to cover herself, but her hands were held behind her.

Katrina relaxed somewhat when she recognised him, but he could clearly see that she wasn't totally at ease. Harriet might have asked, 'Why ever not?' But Harriet was a naked (or at any rate a partially clothed) singularity. Tom decided on the Mary Kingsley approach. 'It's only me,' he said, as reassuringly as he could manage. It couldn't have been all that reassuring in these circumstances. Nevertheless the words had a soothing effect. Katrina relaxed visibly

184

but still kept her eyes on him. Tom produced the note which Harriet had left on the door. 'She says "nil by mouth",' he explained. Otherwise I'd take your gag off. But it's best to follow Harriet's rules in her own house.'

As he spoke Tom noticed another note above Katrina's bed. It too was in Harriet's distinctive handwriting and said simply *Take me.* It reminded Tom of the label on the bottle Alice was adjured to drink. Katrina must have seen and understood the note already, so she knew what to expect. When Tom looked back at her she looked either alarmed or anticipatory, it was hard to be sure which.

Tom took the time to admire her heavy breasts and her legs. Seen for the first time, they fulfilled the promise he had noted at the airport. He was glad she didn't have skinny legs, as so many large breasted women did. When he looked at her stomach, he noticed stretch marks. Apparently she was a mother, and a recent one at that. He glanced back at her face to see how she was taking this scrutiny. Katrina seemed calmer, with just a hint of suppressed excitement. She held his gaze for a moment then she trembled slightly and looked down at her breasts. Following her glance, Tom noticed that one of them was leaking. There was a wet trail from the nipple and down the underside of the breast, continuing down her ribcage. Katrina was still lactating, which explained the extra weight of her tits. She seemed embarrassed by her condition. Tom felt excited. He had never known a woman who was still giving milk.

But he realised it was impolite to stand fully clothed before a woman who was nude and unable to cover herself. So Tom, always the gentleman, as he told himself repeatedly, took off his own clothes before moving to sit on the bed beside Katrina. He couldn't help his fascination with her breasts. When he cupped them he was impresed by their weight and tautness. They were obviously full of milk. He squeezed her nipples and she leaked over his hands. Katrina gave a low moan which wasn't a sign of pain. She seemed to be enjoying this tentative foreplay.

Tom had heard that nursing mothers were stimulated by the act of giving suck. It was supposed to be one of the fringe benefits of breast-feeding. He had never, until now, been in a position to verify the information. He knelt quickly on the floor, urging Katrina to spread her legs so he could get closer to her tits. He took one long nipple in his mouth and began to tease it with his tongue. When she leaked again he swallowed the milk. With his free hand Tom cupped her other breast and squeezed the nipple. At this Katrina gave a loud moan and leaned forward to offer herself more fully to his hands and tongue. It looked as if the tales were true. He continued to arouse her, swallowing the milk from one breast and letting the outflow from the other run down his hand and arm.

Tom moved his free hand down between her legs and gently parted the labia with his fingers. She was warm and wet, so that was all right. When his finger slid inside her Katrina gave a loud snort behind her gag. Her hips began to jerk spasmodically almost at once. She was obviously on the verge of orgasm. Tom continued working on her breasts and her sex, encouraged by the muffled sounds of pleasure Katrina was making through her nose and deep in her throat, and by the thrusting of her pelvis against his hand. The simultaneous stimulation of all her erogenous zones was driving her wild. Katrina was now leaking milk copiously. It was dripping down his arm and onto the floor between her feet.

Katrina spread her thighs even further without any urging from Tom, trying to allow him access to all of her. She was making loud continuous moaning sounds through her gag, and her nostrils were flaring as she drew breath in great shuddery gasps. Her nose had to do all the work since the gag prevented her from breathing through her mouth. A long drawn-out groan seemed to signal her orgasm.

But she didn't pause there, going straight on to the next, and the next. Tom was doing his best to keep up, fighting his own rising excitement. He was stiffly erect himself, and wanted nothing more than to plunge into her open sex. But to do that he would have had to change position, and he knew Katrina wanted him to continue with what he was doing. So he resigned himself to waiting a bit longer. Katrina was responding like someone who hadn't had sex in a long time, and Tom wondered fleetingly if she had been abstaining because of the baby. But there was no time for further speculation.

In one of the short pauses between orgasms Tom stood up. Katrina opened her eyes and looked up at him questioningly and a little desperately. The gag prevented her from saying anything beyond an inter-rogative grunt. Tom drew her to her feet and quickly lay down on the bed. He helped Katrina to kneel astride him and guided her down onto his erection. She gave a small gasp as she settled down onto him. The chain from her collar hung down between her breasts, making a disturbing contrast with her flushed skin.

Katrina shifted slightly and then settled. Tom reached up and began to tease both her nipples with his fingers. The combination of the penetration and the continued stimulation of her sensitive breasts set

Katrina off on another series of wild orgasms. She was lunging up and down, almost losing him on the up stroke, then sliding down to take him fully with a moan of pleasure. Tom meanwhile was having some difficulty holding onto her breasts, so violent was her motion. During it all Katrina continued to leak milk in spurts. It ran down her ribcage and into her pubic hair. Tom could feel the warm fluid dripping onto him as he lay beneath her.

Katrina's eyes were closed and her face contorted. She was having her orgasms one after another, with almost no pauses. Under these conditions it wasn't long before Tom felt himself losing control. He thrust himself deeply inside and came, holding her against him by pulling down on her breasts. Not that Katrina was making much effort to escape. When they were both spent she collapsed slowly onto his chest. He could feel her heart pounding as she struggled to catch her breath.

Gradually they both subsided. Tom put his arms around her and they both dozed, oblivious to the damp patches of milk and the sweat drying on their bodies.

Tom was pleasantly surprised when he woke up to find himself still inside Katrina, and becoming erect again. Never one to examine gifts too closely, Tom began to stroke her bottom and the backs of her thighs, which were all he could reach from his position. He shifted himself and felt the liquid sliding of his cock inside her. Katrina said, 'Ummmm,' and opened her eyes. She smiled directly down at him and nodded her head vigorously. Clearly it was time for the next exercise.

Katrina began by sliding herself up and down his body, her breasts rubbing against the rough hair on his chest and her nipples stiffening as she moved. Abruptly she leaked again, the warm milk acting now as a lubricant between their bodies. That seemed to drive her frantic, for she began to move much more quickly and violently, at one point almost sliding off. Tom had to catch her quickly to hold her in place on top of him. He almost wished her hands were free so she could do the holding and he could use his own on the rest of her body, notably on those amazingly full breasts.

Katrina must have had something similar in mind. Tom could feel her struggling to sit up. He helped her by pushing up on her shoulders until she was once more astride him with her breasts jutting out proudly, if a bit damply, within easy reach of his hands. Tom thought briefly of homing pigeons as he reached up to touch both of them. Once more he teased her nipples and Katrina gasped with pleasure as he extracted her milk. Tom felt her vaginal muscles tighten in rhythmic spasms around his cock as he manipulated her breasts.

Tom saw that her eyes were closed. Katrina was apparently enjoying the ride. She stiffened abruptly and he almost lost control himself as she came. The orgasm was accompanied by an explosive whinnying noise through her nose. When she stopped shuddering Katrina opened her eyes and looked questioningly down at Tom. Did she expect him to stop there? When it became apparent that he intended to continue Katrina looked alarmed and tried to shift off him. Once again Tom held onto her to keep her in place. She made muffled noises of protest but he paid no attention. As he moved inside her Tom felt her tighten once more around him and knew she was still capable of yet another orgasm. For a moment she seemed inclined to fight it, but as he watched her face he saw the tension go out of it. Her nipples leaked again as the wave of excitement swept over her.

He felt the stiffness leave her body as she settled onto him. This time he had to work a little harder to bring her to climax, and it seemed to be weaker than the last. Perhaps she was tiring. Tom relaxed as her vaginal muscles contracted warmly around his shaft, and he let himself come with her. When she was spent Katrina once more collapsed against his chest and lay recovering. She made small contented sounds from time to time.

This time they both slept, Tom holding Katrina atop him to keep her from sliding to the floor. The next sound he heard was Harriet's footsteps coming closer. He was beginning to recognise her character-istic decisive tread. And of course it could hardly be anyone else. She was wearing high heels, Tom could tell from the sound. At first he was alarmed at the idea of Harriet finding him and Katrina in flagrante delicto, but he remembered her instructions. If no-thing else, he had looked after their guest.

Harriet strode into the cell as if she owned the place, as of course she did, and everyone there (still a matter for debate). Harriet wasn't interested in legal debate just then. She asked unceremoniously, 'Every-thing all right, then?'

Tom nodded and indicated Katrina, who slept the sleep of the sexually exhausted, if not exactly that of the just.

Harriet lowered her voice and added, 'When you can disentangle yourself, lock her in here and come upstairs.'

She left the room and Tom could hear her foot-steps receding up the stairs. Harriet had set no time limit on the disentangling process, but he knew enough of her by now to realise that she didn't mean hours later. There was no way to predict how long Katrina might sleep, and he didn't want Harriet to get impatient. There were other reasons urging prompt compliance as well. He had to go to the toilet rather urgently, as he frequently had to do after sex. And there was the matter of the French maid's uniform waiting for him upstairs, about which he felt a strange mixture of curiosity and nervous anticipation. He shifted slightly and began to ease himself from beneath the fragrant weight of the Dutch girl who had almost literally dropped from the heavens into his life. Katrina sighed but slept on.

Tom let himself out carefully and locked the door behind him. He hoped the sleeping woman would understand the reason for his unceremonious exit. A few days with Harriet would teach her the rules of the house she found herself in. Harriet was waiting for him upstairs. She was still wearing her street clothes, which Tom found disappointing. He had imagined her striding around in her leather dominatrix outfit. Whenever he thought of his new mistress he imagined her in the outfit which was one of his favourites. He liked the way it defined and outlined her body. Indeed much of his own excitement about the French maid's uniform was based on the idea of wearing such a form-fitting garment himself, even if only as underwear. And Harriet was certain to have other and more interesting ideas in mind.

Tom had taken his clothing from Katrina's cell but had not bothered to put it on. He knew Harriet wouldn't be offended by nudity so long as it was him without clothes. He reflected that he had never seen her in the nude. Nearly nude, in her dominatrix outfit, but still covered where society said it mattered. Of course her outfit was more provocative, to Tom at least, than total nudity would have been. A fact as well known to designers of lingerie as to novice B&D assistants.

Characteristically, it was Harriet who got in the first word:

'How is she doing?'

'All right,' Tom replied. He hoped his face didn't betray too much satisfaction over what he considered a job well done. He remembered Harriet's angry reaction to his remark about Helen. 'Why is she here?' He realised it was a daring question even as he asked it. Indeed, almost any question could be daring around this house, but he hoped his audacity would distract Harriet and allow him to conceal his own feelings. In any case, she might well ignore the question.

Surprisingly, Harriet answered. 'She's gone off sex, Ari says. Ever since the baby she's been avoiding it, saying it's too soon, that she'd like to recover. He thought a visit to my place might change her mind.'

Privately, Tom thought that Katrina might have gone off Ari, because she gave no sign of avoiding sex. But it might not be wise to say that just now. Instead, he asked, 'What do you intend to do about the problem?'

'Expose her to you, just as I've already done. Tell me how she reacted.'

That sounded like an order to Tom. Harriet's orders brooked no evasion. So he recounted for her the interlude with the blonde Dutch girl. Harriet showed keen interest in Katrina's reaction to the manipulation of her breasts. 'What did the milk taste like?' she asked.

Tom paused to gather his thoughts. At the time, he hadn't been particularly interested in the taste. 'Well, a bit like warm evaporated milk, only sweeter,' was his reply. He wondered if Harriet really didn't know what mother's milk tasted like. Or were there subtle variations in flavour he wasn't aware of? Now that he thought of it, he didn't know of anyone else who had discussed the matter. Perhaps Harriet was really in the dark, though it was difficult to imagine her admitting ignorance about anything. 'And it was thinner. Thinner than the stuff in tins. More runny. Not bad, though,' he added.

The answer seemed to satisfy Harriet. She nodded and changed the subject abruptly, as was her wont. 'So you'd say she was going to respond?'

Tom nodded wordlessly.

Harriet sighed. 'It looks as if the problem is Ari, not Katrina. I was afraid that was the case, but he's not going to admit it readily. Just like a man – always thinks it's the woman's fault. I can see why the feminists sometimes lose patience with the male of the species. He's the one who should be here,' Harriet added darkly.

Tom wondered what she would do with him if he were here. His own experience with Harriet suggested that she would certainly try to change Ari's point of view, much as she was doing with him. Would she try to train Ari with the carrot or the stick? If the former, would she play the part of the vegetable, something she had so far not done with him? Tom reflected that he had known Harriet for a fair time, but so far he hadn't got between her legs with anything but his mouth. And even that had been on her own terms. He felt a momentary flash of envy for Ari.

But Harriet gave him no time to brood. She turned

to the package Tom had brought. 'Let's see what you've brought for the evening's fancy-dress party,' she said brightly as she dumped the corselet and tights out of the bag. 'Black,' she sighed exaggeratedly. 'Men are so predictable. Still, the colour will go with the rest of the outfit. Go have a wash and we'll get started.'

Tom went into the bathroom to shower off the traces of his session with Katrina. As he washed he felt his heart thudding against his ribcage with a sudden excitement. He hadn't realised just how eagerly he had been looking forward to this. Beth had never suggested anything so bizarre, even though she had been aware of his interest in female underclothes. She had dressed to please him on every possible occasion. Now he was going to get into the same sort of clothing which excited him so much when women wore it.

Harriet was waiting for him in the living room. She handed him the corselet and a pair of tights. 'Get on with it, then,' she said.

With fingers that shook slightly he peeled the cellophane wrapping from a pair of tights.

Harriet noticed the barely suppressed excitement but said only, 'Go on then.' She smiled slightly to encourage him when he looked up.

Tom sat on the settee and began to put the tights on. Harriet watched critically as he got his feet into them and began to pull them up his legs. The smooth nylon felt cool on his skin. When he stood up to tug the top part of the tights into place, Harriet moved closer and helped him with the unfamiliar task. When the panty part was in place she reached into the front of the tights to move his cock and balls so that they lay against his lower stomach and not between his legs.

194

'They'll be less pinched that way,' she explained. 'And handier,' she added. She handed him the black corselet with a sign that he was to put it on. When he had got the garment up as far as the waist she once more stepped in to help with the final fitting. She pulled it up until the gusset was tight against his scrotum, smoothing out the wrinkles and pulling the shoulder straps into place for him.

'Thanks,' he said briefly. 'I don't think I could have managed it on my own.' Was there the slightest tremor in his voice? He didn't trust himself to speak further just then. He was excited by the constriction of his legs and torso. Wordlessly he accepted the two contoured-foam rubber pads from her hand and fitted them into the brassière part of the corselet.

'Instant tits,' Harriet observed. 'Don't want to make them too big or the rest of us girls will get jealous.' She indicated a smooth black slip lying on top of the maid's dress. When he had put that on she helped him into the dress itself. It consisted of a short black skirt with a short-sleeved top. There was a long zipper up the back of the outfit. 'Step into the skirt first,' Harriet instructed. When he had done so she smoothed down the skirt and then helped him get his arms into the sleeves. Then she zipped him up. 'I didn't think you'd be able to manage a back zipper just yet. It takes even us real girls some time to get the knack. But you'll learn with practice.'

There was a frilly white apron which Harriet tied around his waist. She handed him the long brown wig next, adding a white lacy cap as a final touch. 'Next time I'll give you some tips on make-up, but you'll do for now,' she pronounced.

Tom felt his heart lurch with excitement at the mention of the make-up and the next time. Evidently there was more to come. He moved over to the mirror so that he could see himself as Harriet saw him. The familiar face stared back from a figure that was far from familiar. There was a definite pinching-in of the waist which gave him more pronounced hips. Not exactly the hourglass effect so admired in women of the last century, but definitely more hip than he normally had. And the tight garments made themselves felt all over his body. He felt himself getting hard inside the corselet.

Harriet came to look also. 'Don't stand too long in front of the mirror. Remember Narcissus.' She handed him a pair of black high-heeled shoes. 'Put these on and do a practice walk. It isn't as easy as we women make it look. It's another of the awkward things we do to please men,' she finished in a much-put-upon tone of voice.

Tom stepped into the shoes and fastened the ankle straps. He took a few tentative steps. It *wasn't* as easy as it looked. He had a sudden new appreciation of walking. He had to be careful not to trip and to remember that his heels would be touching the floor a lot more quickly, and he had to balance more than he was accustomed to. As he passed the mirror he caught another glimpse of himself. His calf muscles were much more prominent, the effect of wearing the shoes. He understood now how women produced the effect he admired so much, and which was described by the phrase, a well-turned leg.

'When you can walk again – and if you can stop admiring yourself – you can go get something for us all to eat. That's what maids are for, you know.' Harriet's words broke the mood like a shower of icy water. 'And put these on before you start.' She held out his leg-irons. 'Be careful not to ladder your tights with them.'

Tom took the chains and locked them around his ankles. Harriet knelt to double-lock them and then made a dismissive motion with her hand. He went to prepare coffee and sandwiches, reminding himself not to trip and spill anything onto the outfit which he was beginning to think of as his. As he worked he wondered how many other men Harriet treated this way. It was one of the questions he wanted to ask, but he didn't really want to know the answer. In her line of business Harriet doubtless did this many times. He had caught sight of several other outfits in the cupboards downstairs.

This maid's outfit looked and smelled new, as if she had recently purchased it for him. The unworn soles of the shoes told much the same story, as did the tightness common to all new shoes. She must have put some thought into this latest game. He was pleased by that. And by the way his erection rubbed against the smooth tight material of the corselet and tights. He pressed his stomach against the counter top as he prepared the sandwiches, making himself more excited by the moment. Careful, he warned himself. Don't want to spill anything on the outside or the inside of the uniform just now.

'Enjoying yourself in there?' Harriet called out, as if she had guesed what he was doing. 'Hurry up. People are starving all around the world – not to mention right out here.' To his consternation he could hear Harriet speaking to someone else. It could only be Katrina, unless she had sent out invitations to the world and his wife to come view her new maid. He realised with a flush of embarrassment that he was going to have to appear before his erstwhile sex partner in the maid's uniform. He was extremely reluctant to do so. All his previous excitement vanished in a moment and he could feel the erection disappearing just as quickly.

Harriet must have removed Katrina's gag. How else could she eat? And they were holding a conversation while they waited for him to appear. Tom cast about desperately for a way out of this predicament, but there was none. Running out of the house, even if the back door might be unlocked, which he doubted, wasn't on. Nor was disobeying Harriet. He was trapped.

Grasping the nettle, and also the tea tray, Tom went through into the front room. Katrina was too surprised, or too well-bred to say anything so Harriet once again got in the first word. 'I think you know one another by now. Tom, you'll have to help Katrina to eat.

Despite his own embarrassment Tom noticed that Katrina was ill at ease too. She was wearing nothing but her thumbcuffs and the rosy flush he had noticed when he entered her cell earlier. He set the tray down and attempted a smile which, he hoped, concealed his own discomfiture. He helped Katrina to seat herself comfortably on the settee while Harriet took the armchair opposite, intending no doubt to observe her two charges. There was nothing for it, but to go on. Tom sat down next to Katrina and held a sandwich for her to eat.

It was like hand-feeding an animal, and was doubtless one of Harriet's rituals designed to show who was in charge here. Katrina nevertheless gave him a small, self-deprecating smile as she ate from his hand. Tom wiped her mouth with a serviette and offered her coffee. She swallowed a mouthful and ate another sandwich. She must have felt awkward, because she avoided looking directly at anyone whenever she could. Tom knew exactly how she felt.

198

It was Harriet who filled the awkward silence, sounding not the least abashed herself. 'Cat got your tongues? I thought two people who had just made mad passionate love to one another would have more to say. Never mind,' she went on, not giving either of them a chance to frame a reply. 'Katrina, Tom tells me you enjoyed it immensely when he milked your breasts. Do tell me all about it.'

Tom thought of bulls at large in china shops as Katrina blushed an even deeper shade of red and almost choked on the food. Tom patted her back and helped her to recover. He was forgetting all about his own awkwardness in the face of Harriet's gaucherie.

Katrina looked accusingly at Tom, as if to rebuke him for revealing what had passed between them.

Harriet intercepted the look and said, 'No need for false modesty, Katrina. Tom says you are a real artiste, and that you put a lot of effort into the gentle sport. He meant it as a compliment. And besides, there are no secrets in this house, especially not from me. I don't allow any, so you'd better get used to that. I ordered Tom to tell me all about it, and he knows better than to disobey me. Something you'll do well to learn,' she ended ominously.

Katrina looked alarmed at her tone of voice, but she could only sit helplessly and wait for developments. Tom wanted to reassure her, but he knew that anything along those lines would be added to his account later, and maybe to Katrina's as well. He gave the Dutch woman a brief, guarded smile, trying to tell her not to worry.

When Harriet resumed, she adopted a more kindly tone. 'Relax and try to enjoy the time here. No one suffers permanent harm from me so long as they do as I ask. And I don't ask the impossible. Only the very difficult, sometimes,' she added with a smile. 'Tom is doing what he is doing because I want him to. This is his first outing – if that's the word – as a transvestite. I know he feels awkward. It will all pass.'

This last was probably intended to make Tom feel easier as well. Or at any rate he took it as such. Be grateful for small mercies, he told himself.

Harriet continued, 'You needn't worry about me being jealous over what happens between you and Tom. That's why you are both here. He is my assistant and everything he does is with my approval. I hope you can relax and enjoy your stay with us.'

Katrina asked, 'Why am I here, then? Ari didn't say very much about that. And who are you? To Ari, I mean.'

Harriet said, 'You're here because Ari said you were avoiding sex after the baby came – using that as an excuse.' She held up her hand to forestall Katrina's response. 'I already know from what Tom has told me that you're not avoiding sex. The reverse, rather. So I guess you're avoiding Ari. Why?'

Katrina made no immediate reply. She seemed to be considering what to say.

Harriet continued, 'You don't have to answer right now, but you'll have to think about the answer before he comes back for you. Unless you're not planning to go back.' Harriet let the implication dangle.

Katrina seemed upset by the suggestion. 'Oh, no. I can't leave the baby,' she burst out. And then was silent once more.

Tom and Harriet looked at one another. The choice of words was revealing.

In the silence Harriet asked, 'Then you *are* thinking of leaving Ari?'

Tom could see Katrina's confusion clearly in her

continued silence. He guessed the trouble had only come to a head with the arrival of the baby. It must have started much earlier. Marriages seldom go bad overnight.

Katrina's shoulders began to shake, and when she looked at them there were tears running down her cheeks. Tom put his arm around her, acutely aware of her warmth and softness through the material of the maid's outfit he wore. Harriet came from the other side to add what comfort she could.

'I don't know what to do,' she said shakily, when she had regained some measure of control. 'When we got married I thought Ari was going to exercise more control over things. Over me, too. You know, keep me in line. I never had any real discipline from my parents. No guidance. They were both easy-going people and I married another one just like them. I guess we're all doomed to repeat our parents' mistakes. Ari lets me do pretty much what I like. I wish he'd be firmer with me, take more responsibility. Something like that.'

'Firmer in what way?' Harriet asked.

'I don't know. I found some books in the attic at home, when I was in my teens. They were probably my father's, but he never said anything about them. They were all about women who liked to be ... locked up. Or chained or tied up. I'd never thought about that before, but I went all hot and cold as I looked at the pictures and read the stories. It was like discovering something you really want. I don't know why I'm fascinated by the idea, but I am. That's what I want Ari to do. But he's so easy-going and I'm afraid to ask him. He might think I'm crazy.'

Harriet nodded knowingly. Tom thought this was a case of the right person finding the right person.

'*I'll* tell him,' Harriet said. 'And we'll show him. You describe what you want to me and I'll make sure Ari gets the message, just as soon as he gets back. I'll explain to him how you feel and I don't think he'll believe you're crazy. After all, he knew something about my methods before he sent you here. Maybe he's afraid to ask you about bondage for the same reason you're afraid to speak out.'

Katrina looked at her in alarm. 'But you can't just . . . tell him . . . that.'

'Why not?' Harriet asked. 'Don't worry. I won't hang out a banner in the street with "Katrina is a B&D groupie" printed on it. But I'll make sure he knows what you want. Or rather, we will.'

Tom was grateful for the 'we'. It seemed to ratify his status as Harriet's confidant and assistant, as well as giving him another chance at Katrina with Harriet's approval and collusion.

Harriet broke into these pleasant thoughts with an abrupt order to Tom. 'Take Katrina into the bathroom and wash her. She's all sweaty and sticky from the milk. She needs a long bath.' To Katrina she said, 'We'll have a good long talk later on. I want you to tell me what you want Ari to do and I'll make sure he understands.'

Katrina looked slightly ressured by Harriet's manner. Tom rose and led her away as directed. Since Harriet had not removed her thumbcuffs, nor given Tom the key, he concluded he was really supposed to wash her. Maid's work, he told himself as he drew the bath water for Katrina. As he did so he was conscious of her gaze on him. She wanted to say something that was clear. But she was probably too shy, and probably well out of her depth.

Tom decided to speak first. He was feeling uncomfortable at his transformation from sexual partner to lady's maid. Talking about it would make them both feel easier, or so he hoped. 'I've been taken in hand by Harriet, just like you. I've found it easier to go along with her whims, and so far it's been enjoyable. Even this.' Tom indicated the maid's costume. 'I don't know what she's planning – why she wanted me to dress like this – but I don't mind. This is the first time for me. Call it a voyage of discovery. I'm interested to see how it turns out.'

'For me as well,' Katrina said softly. 'These cuffs, and the gag, and being locked up. And, what you . . . did to me earlier . . . milking me, I mean, and making love to me while you did it. I was close to fainting from the pleasure. Did you guess? It's what I want Ari to do.'

The exchange of confidences had made Tom feel easier. He hoped she did as well. As he helped Katrina sit down in the tub he could smell the lingering aroma of their earlier lovemaking. A pity to wash it away, he thought. She made a pretty picture as she sat in the waist-high water. Because of the thumbcuffs Katrina couldn't lean back against the end of the tub. She was forced to sit upright, which made her breasts stand out proudly. Tom admired them as he washed her.

Katrina made small sounds of pleasure as he soaped her breasts and stomach. He could feel her stomach muscles clench as he washed her there. Katrina was becoming pink all over, a dead giveaway to her arousal. When he reached the area between her thighs she went a deeper shade of rose and parted her legs invitingly. Tom slid a finger inside her open sex and probed until he found her clitoris. With his thumb and forefinger he kneaded it gently until

203

Katrina was breathing in gasps and making a steady low moaning sound. He could tell she was trying to keep herself from making too much of a row, but at the same time it was clear that she wanted him to continue. He did, and she came. She bent forward at the waist and drew her knees up, opening herself wider and shuddering as the orgasm took her.

Inside the tight-fitting corselet Tom felt himself growing hard as Katrina became more and more aroused. He was glad Harriet had taken the trouble to arrange him inside the garment. But he knew she wouldn't like it if he got undressed and joined Katrina in her bath. As in the kitchen, he could only press himself against whatever was in front of him. The side of the tub, in this case. But even so, he knew he didn't dare come. Harriet hadn't given him permission. It was going to be an exciting but ultimately frustrating affair for him until Harriet changed the rules. But he could at least enjoy Katrina's pleasure, and she was having a lot of it, if the noises she made were any indication.

Speaking of the devil, or in this case thinking of her, had the usual effect. Harriet poked her head around the door to discover the source of the noises. Tom didn't notice her – he was facing the wrong direction and was preoccupied with matters nearer to hand. His first inkling was the way Katrina stiffened under his touch. She jerked her head to indicate the new arrival. The expression of dismay and embarrassment on her face caused Tom to look around. When he saw Harriet he too felt a stab of embarrassment mixed with apprehension: caught playing doctors and nurses by the real thing.

But Harriet seemed more interested and amused than angry. 'I thought I heard some peculiar noises from the bathroom. I'm glad to see you're entertaining our guest, Tom. So carry on. There's nothing worse than coitus interruptus, even if only one of you is getting the benefit of the activity.'

Tom was relieved by her words. He resumed his interrupted labour with Katrina. She was not so accustomed to having a witness to her intimate experiments, and took somewhat longer to return to the boil. While Tom was working on her, Harriet came into the room to observe more closely. She knelt beside Tom and he could smell her perfume, and something else that definitely didn't come in perfume bottles. It appeared that Harriet was aroused too, though she had managed to control every sign except the aroma. She must have been watching for some time before her presence was noticed.

As she slipped to the floor beside Tom she rubbed her hand over the front of his skirt. 'I thought I saw a bump there when I came in. Be careful not to lose it or you'll have some washing to do, and I wouldn't like that.' Though her tone was light, there was an undertone of warning which those in the know couldn't miss. As she spoke she continued to rub his erection, making it harder for him to heed her warning.

Luckily for his self-control and for his new outfit, Harriet left off rubbing just short of the critical point. She had almost infallible judgement in these matters. She turned her attention to Katrina, who reddened with embarrassment and lost her concentration once more beneath this close scrutiny. Tom could feel her tenseness under his hands.

Harriet concentrated on Katrina's breasts, leaving the other areas to Tom. This evidence of her approval finally convinced the Dutch girl that there was no strong resentment. She relaxed and began to respond to their joint manipulation of her body. Her breasts leaked a few drops as Harriet fondled them, but she had not yet replenished her supply of milk after the earlier encounter with Tom. Nevertheless, she seemed to appreciate the attention her breasts were receiving under Harriet's skilled hands, and Tom felt Katrina's vaginal muscles tightening around his fingers as she prepared to come again. When she did, she squealed with pleasure and release, no longer trying to hold herself in check.

In the midst of Katrina's throes Harriet observed clinically, 'You were right, Tom. She's definitely still interested in sex – at least with perfect strangers. We'll have to see if we can't get her and Ari onto the right track.'

Tom thought she could have waited until Katrina was finished before rendering her opinion, but the Dutch girl either didn't hear the remark (being to busy with internal matters) or she didn't mind being discussed and observed. When Katrina seemed to have finished Harriet withdrew and left Tom to get her onto her feet and out of the bath. This wasn't an easy matter. Her legs didn't want to support her, and her eyes were slightly glazed. Clearly she had had a busy day. Tom pulled the plug and set about drying Katrina. He powdered her unresisting body, having a dim memory of seeing his mother doing that after her own bath, in those days before he was too big to be allowed to watch her. Katrina seemed grateful for the service. Harriet was waiting for them in the living room. She handed Katrina's gag to Tom and directed him to return her to the cell. Tom led the unprotesting woman away. Before he locked the door he gagged Katrina. She submitted tamely. Tom left her lying on her bed as he went upstairs to rejoin Harriet. He presumed that he would now find out what she had in mind for him. Harriet wasn't in the room, but the handcuffs were. There was a note as well. It said tersely: *Put these to good use.*

Remembering the previous evenings chez Harriet, Tom thought he knew what she meant. He brought his hands behind his back and locked the cuffs on his wrists. A glance in the mirror showed someone who looked like a woman in handcuffs and leg-irons. He sat down on the settee to wait for Harriet. As he did so, the skirt of the maid's uniform rode up his thighs, but he couldn't do anything about that. There were noises from upstairs that suggested Harriet was making her toilette before dealing with him.

Tom felt the tight, smooth material against his cock and marvelled that women wore such clothing constantly without the slightest tremor. He was aroused by them when they wore it, and was now aroused by it when he was the one on the inside. Of course, from a woman's viewpoint, this was water to a fish, but in his case, to continue the piscatorial metaphor, he was a fish newly introduced to the ocean. He had never thought of himself as a transvestite until Harriet suggested it. After she had sown the seeds, he had thought of this moment off and on with a shiver of anticipation. She had added another new experience to the list of novelties that had begun on the day he spoke to Beth in the open-air market. It was too soon to know if the excitement from this newest game would last but he was still surprised at his readiness to try it.

Tom didn't know any transvestites personally. Like most of his contemporaries, he had tended to snigger at the idea of wearing the clothing of the opposite sex.

If he had thought of the men who did so regularly, and he knew from the adverts in the daily papers that there were many, it had always been with some small doubts about their masculinity. He had always professed tolerance for them, but had never been able to eradicate the doubts. Now he was wearing the maid's outfit with something like equanimity, Tom realised that merely wearing women's clothing had not changed his sexual orientation. Until now he had thought that transvestites were the same as gays. Now he knew that these beliefs were simplistic, if not downright erroneous. He still desired Katrina and looked forward to the next encounter. Moreover, Harriet was still the long-term object of his sexual designs too. But at the same time he was excited by the feel of the tight corselet on his body, and the smooth feel of the tights on his legs. He told himself that part of the excitement was due to the anticipation of yet another sexual game of Harriet's devising, with unknown but almost certainly pleasurable results. Yet that was only part of the excitement: another part of it was the discovery of yet another facet of his sexual nature – amazing how a little personal experience changed one's viewpoint.

The fact that the family jewels were safely tucked away inside the tight undergarments presented a problem so far as sex was concerned. He imagined that Harriet had another evening of what she earlier called blue balls in mind. She would dress provocatively in something tight and revealing. Then she would sit and watch TV, ignoring the effect that she and her own garb were having on him. Afterwards there would be another night in the closet or in the cell. If she put him downstairs, there would be the added excitement of Katrina's proximity, locked away from him as well.

Harriet was piling frustration on frustration. He knew she was trying to discover his tolerance level, but he didn't know what she'd do when she discovered it. Probably just go on and exceed it. Or try to increase it by the addition of other mild torments. In any case he could only go along with the game. Tom was reminded again that he had submitted himself to her will completely. Curious how long it had taken for him to understand the nature of their relationship. She called him her assistant and he was happy at the promotion, thinking himself on a firmer footing with Harriet. And so he was, but that was definitely a subordinate position. Tom couldn't imagine Harriet ever letting him take the lead. So long as he stayed with her, and he was already finding the opposite idea painful to contemplate, she would lead and he would follow. There would be rewards, of course. He considered Helen and Katrina, not to mention the ultimate prize, Harriet herself. No relationship, however servile, could exist without them. But they would be chosen and doled out by Harriet.

Tom was aware of a paradoxical freedom he had not felt with Beth. In the relationship between mistress and slave the latter had no freedom save what she allowed. On the other hand he had no responsibility, and with the absence of responsibility came a certain peace: no need to make difficult choices. Perhaps that was what Beth had felt during the long weekend he had left her bound and gagged. She had certainly reacted more explosively to the sexual interludes during that weekend. It may well have been the immobility and the helplessness, the utter dependence on him, that had caused this reaction. She must have known that already, but he had only just made the same discovery for himself. Beth had been the necessary prelude to Harriet.

The sound of high heels on the staircase alerted him to Harriet's imminent arrival. She came from behind him as he sat waiting, so he was unable to see immediately what she was wearing. Harriet paused to inspect the handcuffs, and to double-lock them as she always did. This small act probably meant he would be wearing them for some time. When she moved into his range of vision, he was pleased to see that she was wearing her leather dominatrix costume with the dark tights – his favourite outfit. But it looked like another evening of passive watching. He was safely tucked away inside his corselet, and she in hers. All the interesting bits were out of reach. But she did look stunning. Tom was once more aware of an erection inside the tight confining garments he wore as she sat down opposite him.

Harriet used the remote control to turn on the TV, while the other TV on the settee was being turned on by her remoteness. She was indeed remote, yet tantalisingly close. And disturbingly desirable, the more so because of her inaccessibility and his helplessness.

But this time Harriet seemed unable to settle. She shifted her position several times, crossing and uncrossing her legs with an exciting whisper of nylon on nylon. She showed little interest in the programmes, flipping from one channel to the other, channel surfing, as it was called. Tom thought she looked abstracted. Even disturbed, if such a self-contained and self-sufficient a woman as Harriet could fall prey to such feelings. He wondered if she would talk to him, or if her agitation had anything to do with him. In the past she had kept her own counsel – part of her remoteness and authority.

With characteristic suddenness Harriet seemed to reach a decision. She turned the set off and looked directly at Tom. Luckily she caught him in a moment when he was admiring her appearance. He had been looking at the TV in a desultory manner, as people do when the set is turned on, but he had been alternating between the TV and her. He didn't like to think what she would have thought if she had caught him absorbed in the programme at just that moment. Always afterwards he thought of that as one of the crucial moments in their relationship.

Without preamble she asked, 'Do you like what you see?' As she spoke she sat up straighter in the chair and thrust out her breasts. The leather corselet creaked disturbingly as she shifted her weight. Harriet parted her legs slightly and Tom could see how the crotch of her outfit outlined her sex while denying access to it. 'I mean,' she continued with a slight flush and an air of specious casualness, 'does the old bod make you go as hard as it did before?'

Tom's attention woke up with a jerk. The words 'old' and 'before' set alarm bells ringing. This was a serious question beneath its air of apparent offhandedness. How he answered might well have the profoundest effect on their relationship. Fortunately he didn't have to invent an answer, he *had* been absorbed in watching her as she sat across the room. He had been, as she said, admiring the 'old bod'.

'It's not old,' he replied, the correct answer in several senses. It appeared that even Harriet had her moments of uncertainty, few though they might be.

Harriet permitted herself the ghost of a smile. Was there the faintest touch of relief in it?

Heartened by the initial success, Tom hurried on to answer the rest of the question. 'If you mean before Helen and Katrina, remember Shakespeare's remark about Cleopatra: "Where others satiate she but

211

makes more hungry."' As he said this, Tom recalled saying much the same thing to Beth. Shakespeare could always be mined for useful nuggets. 'If you'd care to come over here you could feel the hard evidence yourself.'

That brought a full smile to Harriet's face. But she said, 'I'll bet you say that to all the girls. The conventional disclaimer of flattery however sincerely it may be meant.'

'No,' Tom denied, 'just to those who handcuff me and make me wear outfits like this. And who wear outfits like yours. There aren't too many of those about. But if you'd care to allow nearer access to the "old bod", as you put it, I could be a bit more convincing.'

'You just want to get into my pants,' Harriet said. 'But it won't be that easy.' She was smiling more openly now and seemed reassured by the declaration. She got up and crossed over to the settee. 'You'll have to earn the "access", as *you* put it, by more hard work.'

The moment of tension had passed. Tom could see the change in her mood, and he relaxed with her. Harriet sat beside him on the sofa and ran her hand up under the skirt of his maid's outfit. She caressed his thighs through the tights, much as he would have liked to caress hers. She moved her hand up to his crotch until she could feel the stiffness in his cock. Tom clamped down just in time to avoid a gasp as she continued to rub it through the tight elastic material that covered it.

Harriet was observing him closely. She grinned. 'Yes, I'd say you've got the hard evidence you claimed. And that's the best testimonial a man could give a girl. Keep it up and you'll get your access card.'

As she continued to rub and fondle, Tom found

that not all responsibility had been taken from him. He had to make a hard decision just then. 'Harriet,' he began, but hastily corrected himslf when he caught her warning look, 'Mistress, if you keep that up I'm going to have an accident in the nice new outfit you bought me. You warned me to be careful about that.'

The reminder didn't sit too well with Harriet. 'I make the rules around here,' she told him with a touch of asperity. 'And I decide when to break them. I do what I like. You do as you're told.' With a sudden mischievous smile she continued, 'I thought I'd give you something to remind you what us older women can do, and it just might lessen your ardour for our guest during the night.'

Tom closed his eyes and surrendered to her decision. Not that surrender came all that hard, though he came rather hard not so long afterward. Harriet removed her hand when he stopped shuddering and made a show of wiping it on her handkerchief. She made a *moue* of distaste and moved away. She gave no sign of letting him undress and clean himself. Tom lay back and closed his eyes.

He did not, however, think of England. Nor did he think immediately of Harriet, though she was sitting most provocatively just across the room from him. His thoughts were on cleaning his outfit. Harriet's training was beginning to sink in. She, however, didn't seem too worried about his needs, and he didn't want to say anything about them himself. He remembered her sharp retort when he had ventured to remind her earlier. He resigned himself to the inevitable, and there was something obscurely exciting about being unable to clean himself or prevent her from doing whatever she wanted with him. He was back in the realm of the irresponsible.

Tom heard her stand up. He opened his eyes as Harriet motioned for him to get onto his feet as well. He struggled to stand and she helped him up. Then she led the way to the cellar door. For the first time since she had gone to work on him he thought of Katrina locked in her cell. Was Harriet taking him to join her?

No. She led Tom to the other oell, obviously intending to keep them apart for a time at least. Maybe she wasn't wholly reassured by his earlier declaration. But Harriet said nothing beyond a terse order to sit down on the bed. She left him there and headed toward the back part of the cellar where she kept the bondage gear. Tom admired the receding rear view as she moved. Presently she came back with several tie wraps, longer and stronger than the one she had used on his balls before Helen's visit.

Wordlessly Harriet knelt and unlocked his legirons. Putting them to one side, she drew Tom's legs together and secured them with a tie wrap around the ankles. She drew it tight and clipped off the end. Next she secured his knees in the same way, grunting slightly as she drew the plastic band tight.

'Lie face down on the bed,' she commanded.

It was more of a struggle than Tom thought it would be. With his legs bound tightly together, he couldn't get much leverage. Harriet once again helped him, this time by lifting his feet and tipping him over backwards. She rolled him over onto his stomach, and as she did Tom felt the wetness from his earlier orgasm. The tight corselet pressed it against him. Only now it was clammy rather than warm.

Harriet removed the handcuffs, crossed his wrists behind his back and secured them with yet another tie wrap. There was no slack in it when he tested it. Next

214

she fitted a tie wrap around each arm above the elbow. She fitted a long wrap between these, drawing his elbows closer together behind his back. Always thorough, Harriet paused to clip the ends of the plastic straps and to test each one for tension. 'I do so like a neat package,' she commented half to herself. 'Now a gag, I think. I wouldn't like the love birds calling to one another while I'm away.' Harriet produced a rubber pear-shaped object which she inserted in Tom's mouth. She secured it with a strap that buckled behind his neck, pulling it tightly into the long brown wig he wore.

'I'm off now,' she said unnecessarily. 'I've got another appointment but I won't be long. And,' she continued as an afterthought, 'I'll be wearing my leather costume as underwear in case the thought excites you. Don't want to make things unnecessarily dull for you.'

With that she was gone. Tom heard the key turn in the lock and her footsteps receding up the stairs. There was the sound of another door closing, and then the lights went out. It was pitch dark in the cellar. Since there was no sound from Katrina's cell, he guessed that she was likewise still gagged. The thought of her lying so close to him, helpless like himself, made Tom go hard inside the damp corselet. Part of his excitment came from his own predicament. As he shifted in the bed he felt his cock slide against the elastic that imprisoned it. The friction on his legs where the tights rubbed together sent electric shivers through him, and at that moment Harriet's parting words came back to him. He imagined her going about her business – the mysterious appointment she had mentioned – in her tight leather corselet and black tights. She would have put a dress on over it, but he imagined her body moving against the leather as she walked the streets.

He pulled against the tie wraps, but there was no give in them. Harriet had left him lying face down on the bed when she had finished tying him. That position became uncomfortable, and he tried to turn onto his side. It was a struggle without the use of his arms and legs, as doubtless Harriet had foreseen. She appeared to know everything there was to know about bondage. In his efforts to turn over he could feel the silky slip sliding against his skirt, and the tight corselet against his body. Experimentally he moved his hips and felt his cock push against the tight material. That felt promising. He kept moving, and soon realised he was going to come if he didn't stop. He didn't stop. There was no reason to. The damage (if that was the right word) was already done, and after the first orgasm upstairs Harriet would never know if he induced another. In for a penny, in for a pound, he reasoned.

This was another new idea to him. Previously, when Harriet had left him tied up he had merely sat waiting for her to release him. Now he was trying to bring himself to orgasm while tied and gagged. He imagined he was a woman who had been abducted and left bound in a deserted house. The maid's outfit, and the way it hugged his body, helped the fantasy. Was this what Beth had fantasised about when he had left her tied up in her house? Quite possibly, Tom thought, before he stopped thinking and concentrated on the rush of feeling as he came again inside the corselet and tights.

When he had finished Tom managed to heave himself over onto his side. He could tell from the cool air on his legs that the skirt had ridden up during his struggles. There was nothing to be done about that. In the dark, and with no clock to remind him of the passage of time, Tom couldn't tell how long Harriet had been gone. Nor would that have helped, because he had no idea how long she intended to be away.

Tom dozed, and woke, and dozed again. Noises upstairs woke him some indeterminate time later. Harriet had evidently returned, but she didn't appear ready to come downstairs to see how he and Katrina were faring. She gave the impression of having forgotten about them. It must be a calculated effect, he told himself. Harriet wasn't the absent-minded sort.

Eventually the lights came on, and he heard her familiar tread on the stairs. A few moments later the door opened and Harriet stepped into his cell. She still wore her leather outfit. She moved to the bed and helped Tom to sit up by lifting his legs. The skirt and slip rode up his thighs, and Harriet looked briefly at him before turning abruptly away.

'Some people have no modesty,' she said over her shoulder. 'Wait there. I'll be right back.'

Her last remark was wholly superfluous, but Tom was in no position to reply. Presently she returned with several lengths of rope. Harriet rolled him out of the bed and had him kneel on the floor near one of the legs. With the rope she lashed his knees to the leg of the bed so that he couldn't get up or move away. Next she tied a length of rope around his neck and fastened it to the opposite side of the bed, so that he was kneeling over it with his bottom in the air. Once more she strode purposefully from the room, and he heard her rummaging amongst her storage cabinets.

It was all terribly reminiscent of his school days, when he was made to bend over prior to a caning. He didn't have too much trouble guessing what Harriet was going to do next. Tom felt himself getting hard again – something he didn't remember from his school days.

And indeed when she returned Harriet carried a riding crop. She lifted the skirt and slip up so that there was nothing between him and the leather but the corselet and tights. Wordlessly she began to lash him about the bottom and the backs of his thighs. She was putting considerable effort into each blow, as Tom could tell from the effect at his end. He bent all his efforts to keep from crying out, merely grunting occasionally into the gag, but he did squirm against the bed as she lashed him, liking the feel of his cock rubbing against the tight damp corselet as he moved. He knew he was going to come again unless she stopped soon. Or maybe even if she stopped immediately.

The combination of the tight clothing and the dampness and the pain was driving him toward the brink once more. New things kept happening to him. Tom remembered the earlier lashing, after which Harriet had stopped to fondle him, driving him just to the edge of orgasm before leaving him hanging. It looked as if she intended to drive him over the edge this time.

The next moment she did. Tom wasn't able to conceal his orgasm and he ground his cock against the side of the bed and groaned as he came. Harriet kept on lashing him until he stopped moving, spent. Did she know what she had done? Tom guessed she knew very well. When she put down the crop he could hear her breathing heavily from her exertions. He couldn't turn to look at her, but he could imagine her sturdy compact body heaving inside the leather outfit.

'Disgraceful!' was all she said, not very convincingly, then turned and left the room again, the sound of her high heels receding.

He imagined it was now Katrina's turn to feel the lash, and indeed in a few moments he heard the hearty smack of leather meeting flesh as Harriet whipped her. There were choked-back cries after each blow. Evidently Katrina wasn't as concerned to conceal the pain as he had been. Tom wondered what reason Harriet had for using the crop on Katrina. The programme called for her to discuss her needs with Harriet and to find some way to acquaint Ari with them. Was Harriet maybe not so disinterested in what had passed between Tom and the young Dutch woman as she professed to be? There had been earlier signs of jealousy which Harriet had not been able to hide completely. She might well be working it off by lashing both of them now.

After so much sexual activity Tom felt a pleasant lassitude. And now there was no urgency to do anything at all. Still he wondered when Harriet would get around to untying him so he could get out of the soiled maid's outfit. No doubt he would have to wash it out before bed time. Otherwise the new outfit would begin to look old before its time. He found himself reluctant to let that happen, on his account, wholly apart from Harriet's wishes. He thought of it now as his outfit, even though he didn't know when Harriet might want him to wear it again.

Presently the sounds from the other cell stopped. Tom guessed that Katrina had been lashed as soundly as he had. Harriet came back to free him. She untied the ropes that held him to the bed and then cut away the tie wraps that bound him. As she did so she explained to him the necessity of cutting them from the sliding end, as near to the locking head as possible.

In that way, she explained pedantically, they could be used again. Of course on a smaller person. She hoped to get at least two uses out of each one before they had to be thrown away because they were too short. 'Waste not, want not,' she explained to him, exactly as if she had just coined the cliche.

'You'll have to get out of those clothes now, and wash them out.' As she once more helped him with the back zipper, Harriet remarked that he really should continue to wear the maid's outfit because she wanted him to wash Katrina and get her ready for bed. 'But you've spoiled all that now by losing control. We'll have to get you a more extensive wardrobe so the problem doesn't arise in future.'

Tom forbore to remark on her own contribution to the spoiling of the outfit. Somehow he knew she wouldn't appreciate comment along those lines. She might even regard them as an attempt to shift the blame, and add this to the account she was surely keeping. Her remark about a more extensive wardrobe he filed away for future consideration. Evidently there was more of this to come. Tom stripped off the slip, the corselet and the tights.

He crossed to Katrina's cell and looked in. The Dutch girl was still wearing her thumbcuffs and gag. When she stood up awkwardly he saw that she was also wearing a suit of red stripes on her bottom and the backs of her legs. He imagined it matched his own pretty closely, since both had come from the same source. She was as sweaty and damp as he was. He gave her an encouraging smile which she returned wanly. She appeared to be having second thoughts about what was happening to her, but she said nothing. Tom led Katrina up the stairs, walking behind her in case she stumbled.

Harriet was waiting for them in the living room. 'About time,' she said to them when they emerged from the cellar. 'I was just about to come see what was taking you so long. There'll be no hanky-panky in this house.' Considering the source, this was more than a little ironic. Katrina blushed at the words. Harriet noticed, but she only smiled. She removed Katrina's gag. 'Off with you now and get clean. You both smell like you were on the receiving end of a golden shower.'

Katrina looked puzzled at the expression.

'One of our quaint English idioms,' Harriet explained. 'It means having someone piss on you, usually for a fee.'

This explanation puzzled Katrina even more. She blushed and asked, 'But why would anyone pay for that?'

'Another innocent,' Harriet remarked. 'There are all sorts of variations in the sexual game, my dear,' she said in her best didactic tone. 'Your wish to be tied up and used sexually is one of them. The golden shower is another. I don't have time to go into all of them now, but there are many more that are stranger than anything you can imagine. Off you go now, and be sure to wash behind the ears. And the other places.' She turned away and seemed to forget them.

Tom led Katrina into the bathroom. 'One of the nice things about nudity,' he remarked as he adjusted the water temperature, 'is that you don't have to take your clothes off. There are one or two other things as well. I'm looking at two of them just now.' She registered puzzlement once again. He continued: 'That was meant as a compliment to present company. And to these,' he added as he teased her nipples.

Katrina flushed and she leaked a few drops of milk.

But she didn't pull away. 'You ... like them?' she asked shyly.

'Yes. And the rest of you,' Tom replied.

'But what about Harriet? I thought you were ... lovers. That is the word, no?'

'Yes, and no. She is the boss – the Mistress to use the title she prefers. I am her assistant. Maybe we'll become lovers. I don't know. That's for her to decide. I'm waiting to see what she will do.'

'So. You have not ... slept together?'

'No,' Tom admitted. 'As I said, I'm waiting for her to decide.'

'It is a, how do you say, a queer relationship, is it not?'

Tom shrugged. 'We're working on it. It's too early to say how things will go.' As he said these words Tom wished he felt as nonchalant as that.

'But she does not mind that we ... before? And maybe again?'

There was a shy eagerness in her manner that made Tom wish he hadn't spent himself so thoroughly earlier. 'I don't think she minds,' he said, hoping he was right. 'Not now. We've talked about it and she knows what we – you and I – are doing. It's our problem, not yours. If it is a problem ... In you go,' Tom said, ending an awkward conversation before he had to say too much. He helped Katrina into the shower, making sure she didn't slip while unable to use her hands.

The warm water ran over both of them, washing away the smells that had accumulated during the last few hours. Tom began by soaping Katrina's rear elevation. As he did so, she leaned suggestively against his hands. 'Like that, do you?' he remarked. 'Wait until I get to the more exciting bits.' He soaped her back thoroughly and rinsed her before reaching around to do her front.

When he touched her, Katrina said, 'Would you do what you did before? To my . . . tits? That's the word, isn't it? No one has ever done that to me. I really liked it.'

'Yes, that's the word. And yes to your request as well,' Tom replied as he soaped her breasts and began to tease her nipples from behind with both hands.

As her nipples erected she leaned back against him and moaned softly. Abruptly she leaked a few drops, and at that she let out a low growl of pleasure. Katrina was using her hands awkwardly to fondle his cock as it pressed against her bottom. Her thumbcuffs were pressing against the top of his shaft as she caressed him.

Tom didn't think he could come again so soon after the last time, but he had no objection whatever to what she was doing to him. He thought her gesture showed at least a generous nature.

He felt her shudder as she had a small orgasm. He continued to squeeze her breasts and Katrina moaned her approval. She laid her head back against his chest and he could see her eyes were closed. Gradually she became more frenzied and he could feel the tension in her body as she lay against him. Tom transferred one hand down between Katrina's parted thighs. When he found her clitoris she let out a loud 'Oooooohhhhh' of pleasure.

Tom had a fleeting thought for Harriet. If Katrina got any more demonstrative, she was sure to know what they were doing – if she hadn't guessed already. The shower was taking an inordinately long time by anyone's standards. But he was too deeply into what they were doing to stop. He supposed that he should have the courage of his convictions and let Harriet think whatever she liked. The trouble was, Harriet tended to do a lot of her thinking with a riding crop. But he went on. Katrina was having a wonderful time if her shudders and moans were any indication. And she hadn't forgotten about him. Her hands were busy on his cock.

This time he knew he was going to be a gentleman and make sure his partner came. It looked as if Katrina hadn't come earlier when Harriet was lashing her, and was now ready for her rewards. He made a mental note to ask her how she reacted to the whipping when there was more time. All in the interests of establishing her limits, of course. No idle, prurient curiosity on his part. But now he had his hands full of nubile woman in full cry. Katrina seemed determined to make up for any lack of sexual opportunity.

Tom alternated between her breasts, trying to make sure each got equal attention. Katrina was leaking milk almost every time he squeezed her, and she was very warm and wet between the legs. Harriet must have heard what was happening, but still she made no appearance. Katrina shuddered and bucked against him as she came again. Suddenly she went limp and her knees gave way. Tom found himself supporting her as she threatened to fall.

It was then that Harriet chose to make her appearance, first as a shadow on the shower curtain like the knife-wielding killer in *Psycho*, and next (as she pulled the curtain back) as the leather-clad dominatrix surprising her charges in a compromising situation. Tom was relieved to see that she was wearing an indulgent smile as well as her severe outfit.

Katrina suddenly became aware that they were not alone. She struggled to get her feet under her and break away from Tom's embrace. Not that that would have prevented Harriet from drawing the obvious conclusion. She started to speak but Harriet stopped her.

'No need to stop just for me,' she said. 'I just came to see if you were both all right. You were taking a long time, and making such a great deal of noise, that I feared the worst. You might even have needed some help from me. But I see you didn't.'

Katrina blushed again (it seemed to be a speciality of hers), but she said nothing.

Tom turned the water off and accepted the towel Harriet held out to him. As he dried Katrina he managed to catch her eye. He gave her an encouraging wink. She responded with another of her wan smiles, unsure of the etiquette that governed such ambiguous situations as this. Nor was Tom, but he was playing it by ear and hoping for the best. At least Harriet didn't look angry.

Harriet took charge again as soon as Katrina was dry. 'Time for bed. It's been a busy day.' She led an unprotesting and rather tired-looking Katrina upstairs to the guest bedroom.

Tom watched with a certain regret. He had hoped this would be the day he got promoted to the guest room. If nothing else, it was bound to be more comfortable than the closet, which now looked like being his resting place for the night. He dried himself and went into the living room to wait for Harriet. She had left his handcuffs and leg-irons lying prominently on the coffee table. Tom got into them and sat down, waiting for his Mistress to check and double-lock them. She was taking her time with Katrina.

Idly, Tom wondered whether the Dutch girl would be spending the night with her hands behind her back in those thumbcuffs. She had been wearing them for some time now. Her shoulders must be aching from

225

being held for so long in that unnatural position. Tom knew about that. He guessed his own shoulders would be aching by morning but that was Harriet's rule for sleeping. She was the only one who got to spend the nights free.

When Harriet came down she said nothing about Katrina. She automatically checked and double-locked Tom's manacles. She gave a grunt of what he hoped was approval when she was done. He wondered if she was going to take him to task for the latest romp with Katrina, but she merely went to sit opposite him in her usual look-but-don't-touch pose, crossing her legs with that exciting whisper of taut nylon. She appeared pensive rather than angry.

'Ari's coming for Katrina on Tuesday,' she said without preamble. 'We'll need to get her ideas down tomorrow so we can make a video for Ari on Monday. Good job it's a Bank Holiday. We'll need the extra time. I thought a video would be the best way to show him what she likes. What do you think?'

Tom was pleased that she was asking his advice. Up until now she would have just gone on and done whatever she wished, consulting no one. He wondered at the same time if he would be playing opposite Katrina in the projected video, although maybe Ari wouldn't like seeing his pretty wife being rogered by someone else who amounted to little more than an errand boy. He must have suspected what Harriet was going to do when he left Katrina in her charge, but that wasn't the same thing as actually seeing what was being done to her.

But Tom said only: 'That sounds like a good idea. Have you asked her what she thinks?'

'Yes. She'll go along with it. She's been missing the sex for a long time and wants to get things moving again.' Changing the subject abruptly, Harriet asked, 'What do you think of her?'

This was the question he had expected and dreaded. He alluded to his earlier reply, 'Where others satiate . . .' That seemed the safest thing to say.

'Yes, yes, I know all that,' Harriet, said crossly, but she looked pleased none the less. 'Really?' she asked finally.

'Madam, your chains are like Wonder Woman's magic lariat. I cannot tell a lie while wearing them.' Curiously enough he was telling the truth. But that may have been only because he hadn't yet got into Harriet's pants, he told himself. When he compared her with Beth, his late lover suffered in the process. Where Beth had been serious and, towards the end, almost completely passive, Harriet tried to lighten the atmosphere with her banter. And she was most definitely not passive. She drove him to lengths he had never thought of.

'Well, anyway,' Harriet said, returning to the previous subject, 'do you think we can do it by Monday evening? Katrina is willing to do whatever is necessary.'

Once again Tom agreed. Harriet wasn't the sort of woman one said no to very easily, and in any case he approved of the idea, both for aesthetic and selfish reasons. This might be his best chance to have another go at Katrina. So long as Harriet held herself aloof, he had to make do with whatever else was available. So far, that hadn't been too bad.

'Bedtime,' said Harriet abruptly. She stood up and waited while Tom struggled to his feet. 'Think about some scenes for the video before you go to sleep,' she said as she led him to the closet. As she had done before, Harriet had placed the bucket within Tom's reach. She fastened the short chain to his leg-irons and left him tethered to the floor.

The door closed and Tom heard the key turn in the lock. Then the light went out and he was alone for the night. He tried to think of scenes for Katrina's demo tape, but instead found himself thinking of Katrina herself. Was she likewise thinking of him as she lay in her solitary bed? Or had Harriet decided that she shouldn't sleep alone? Tom didn't know if Harriet was that way inclined, but suspected that there were very few things she ruled out. With that thought something else came up to disturb his concentration. Too bad he couldn't get his hands on it. In her thoroughness Harriet had seen to that.

Chapter Seven

Harriet opened the door in the morning. Katrina stood close by, peering in at him. Her hands were still cuffed behind her, and she was still nude. 'Did you spend the whole night in there?' she asked. She sounded sympathetic, and Harriet glanced at her sharply. She didn't say anything more, but gave Tom a smile of commiseration when Harriet turned her back to unlock him.

He was stiff after the night's confinement and Harriet had to take his arm to help him stand. Tom wondered if there weren't a certain possessiveness in the gesture. Was this show for Katrina's benefit? He hoped they had laid that particular ghost to rest the previous night, but he was still not sure. Jealousy is not easily forgotten. As he stretched his cramped shoulders Tom glanced surreptitiously at Katrina. She shrugged her own shoulders as if to say that she'd like to stretch too. Harriet gave no sign she had noticed this by-play.

Without waiting for orders Tom went into the kitchen to prepare breakfast for the three of them. He served Harriet and then turned to feed Katrina, who of course couldn't feed herself. His own stomach felt empty, but he said nothing, concentrating on the scenery as the Dutch girl ate from his hand. Katrina seemed less embarrassed than she had been. She was getting used to the regime, Tom thought. Ari didn't know what he had missed by ignoring his wife's predilection for B&D.

'If you can tear your thoughts away from our guest,' Harriet said acidly, 'perhaps you can outline your ideas for the video.'

Tom came back to reality abruptly. The ground was still dangerous. Ad-libbing furiously, he said, 'We should dress her provocatively – something like you wore last night would do. Let's show her figure off for Ari, in case he's forgotten what she's got. We can always invent some poses to show her off when she's tied up – again as provocatively as possible. As you said a neat package always looks more seductive.'

He hoped the oblique compliments to Harriet's appearance and her ideas would turn aside the gathering storm. Apparently the remarks passed muster and Harriet gave a grunt which was more approving than otherwise.

In order to forestall any further questions, Tom concentrated on feeding Katrina, who looked apprehensively from one to the other of them as she sensed the tension in the air. Harriet finished eating first and announced that she was going upstairs to dress for the occasion. Tom took the breakfast things into the kitchen to wash up. Katrina followed him. She appeared to want company so Tom pulled out a chair so she could sit down and got on with the washing up.

Katrina asked abruptly: 'Will she use the riding crop on me again? That was painful.'

'I'm not sure,' Tom replied, 'but if you really object you can always tell her so.'

'I wouldn't like to cross her when she's in this

mood,' Katrina said. 'The beating hurt. I mean,' she said confusedly, 'it hurt but at the same time I found it exciting to be naked and helpless. But it's more important to be tied up and . . . how do you say . . . used? Sexually.'

'Yes, that's close enough. I understand what you want. So does Harriet. After all, her whole business is built on people like you and me. I don't think you have to be afraid to say what you want. In the first place, I think she's on your side and wants to help you with Ari. And secondly you're more a guest than I am. I'm her assistant, not much more than an employee now. You're more in the position of a customer who has come to her for help in solving a problem. She'll listen to you.' And, he added silently, she'll be glad to get the job done and you safely out of here. Tom had thought Harriet was going to overcome her jealousy, but maybe he had overestimated her capacity for accommodation. The fact that Katrina was younger didn't help.

Harriet came down shortly thereafter, wearing, Tom was glad to see, her leather dominatrix outfit. He thought she looked both lovely and menacing, but he said nothing. He had made his point earlier, and there was nothing to be gained by fawning. She beckoned to Katrina to follow her. To Tom she said: 'Join us downstairs when you finish here.'

Tom was looking forward to the video session, but he took his time in order to give Harriet the opportunity to make her preparations. He guessed that Harriet had given more thought to the operation than he had. He planned to follow her scenario, since he had none of his own. Give her time to get moving and it would be easier to play along.

When Tom got to the cellar things were well

231

underway. Katrina was strung up by her wrists to an overhead hook. Her legs were spread and her ankles tied to ring bolts set into the floor. She looked appealingly helpless and evidently excited. Her face was flushed and her heavy breasts were rising and falling quickly in time with her rapid and shallow breathing. This was different from merely wearing thumbcuffs as she had done since her arrival. Now she was spread out, on display, open to anyone who happened by. The fact that only Harriet and Tom were there made no difference to her.

Harriet was busy setting up the lights for the video camera when Tom came down. He thought she looked equally appealing in her snug leather outfit and tights. The pair of them made a nice contrast; the one helpless and naked; the other encased by what was in effect armour. Harriet's cheerful efficiency and bustle were set off by Katrina's enforced immobility. Tom wondered how Harriet would look strung up in Katrina's place and what it would take to get her there.

He was relegated to running the video camera while Harriet moved and posed Katrina. Harriet was having all the fun while he did the dull bits – a not uncommon situation for an assistant. And there were many times when he wished he could get closer to Katrina, whose ordeal had got him very excited. But Harriet ignored him for what seemed hours as she tied and untied Katrina and moved her from place to place.

Finally Harriet called a halt. She untied Katrina from the chair to which the Dutch girl had been tied for the last sequence and while she stretched her cramped limbs, Harriet collected the camera. 'I'll have to edit this so Ari gets the best shots. Amateur

232

films and video tapes usually need a lot of cutting.'
She managed to imply that the cuts would be primarily due to his ineptitude with the camera.

From the cabinet where she stored her bondage gear Harriet selected a pair of handcuffs. With these she fastened Tom's wrists together behind his back. She gagged him, and then told Katrina, 'Amuse yourself with him while I'm working on the tape. If you manage to amuse him at the same time I won't mind.'

Katrina looked dubiously at Harriet. She seemed to have no idea what to do next, but Harriet swept from the room without another word. When she was gone, Katrina looked somewhat relieved but still at a loss. She looked to Tom for some hint.

Although he couldn't say anything, he managed to convey the idea by semaphore.

Katrina noticed the erection and moved in his direction, an interesting look on her lovely face. She seemed to have got over her initial puzzlement and shyness. The time with Harriet had done her some good.

Somewhat to his surprise, Tom was elected – ordered would not be too strong a word – to drive Katrina back to the airport to meet Ari for the flight home. When he arrived at Harriet's place she was ready to go. He found both women sitting demurely in the living room. Katrina was wearing the dress she had arrived in, and her legs in the dark tights looked every bit as good as they ever had. Harriet too was dressed to go out. If he had had to choose between them at that moment the choice would have been hard one. Perhaps it was just as well Katrina was going.

Harriet saw them to the door, where she kissed Katrina goodbye. 'You've got the parcel for Ari, haven't you?'

Katrina nodded as she hugged Harriet. 'Thank you so much for everything. I hope I can come back soon to see you.'

Tom hoped the same but tried not to show too much obvious interest.

'Goodbye then. And good luck,' Harriet said. To Tom she went on, 'I'd like you to come back tomorrow evening, please. I'll be busy this evening and tomorrow but I'll need you in later.' She spoke exactly as if she were giving the maid some time off – which in a manner of speaking she was. She waved as Tom helped Katrina into the car and drove off.

Tom was struck by a sudden thought: this was the first time Harriet had asked him to come in during the week. Maybe this was going to be another turning point in their relationship. She hadn't asked him to turn over the key he had got from Helen. That looked like a good sign.

Katrina was smiling in reminiscence when he glanced at her. The smile grew shy dimples when she turned to look at him. 'I'd like to thank you too,' she said. 'I didn't want to say anything in front of Harriet, but you helped make this weekend unforgettable. So I want you to have this.' She dug into her handbag and came up with a scrap of paper: her address and telephone number. 'If you're in Holland and at a loose end, call me. Maybe we can meet.'

Tom took the paper and put it into his coat pocket. 'Yes, I'd like that very much.'

But Katrina wasn't done. 'Can you find a place to stop?'

Tom knew there was a lay-by about half a mile further along, and he kept his eyes open for it. When he stopped the car Katrina dug into her handbag and came up with the thumbcuffs she had worn most of the time at Harriet's house.

234

'A parting gift from Harriet,' she said with a smile. 'Something to help us start our own collection. Would you put them on me, please? I think it would be exciting to be driven to meet Ari like that. And maybe it will give me the luck I need to start again.'

Tom took the cuffs from her and Katrina held her hands out with the thumbs close together. 'Do you have the key? It wouldn't do to forget that.'

Silently she handed the keys to him.

When he was sure there were no other cars or people nearby, Tom locked the cuffs around her thumbs, double-locking them as Harriet always did. He put the keys into his pocket and came out with a small parcel in his turn. 'I had intended to give you this at the airport – a little gift from me. But I think you'd enjoy it more now.' He unwrapped a pair of handcuffs and leg-irons and showed them to Katrina. 'Something to help you sleep more securely at night. Think of me when you wear them. Harriet won't miss them, and I'll replace them before I go back there. In case you want anything else along those lines, the maker's name is on the box.'

Katrina sat very still as he cuffed her wrists together. When he bent down to lock the leg-irons around her ankles, she gave a small shiver of excitement. 'Tighter, Tom. Could you make them just a little tighter? Please?'

Tom closed the irons two or three more notches and double-locked them. He did the same to her handcuffs.

'Oh, Tom. Thank you so much.' She reached over with her manacled hands and pulled his face closer. She opened her mouth and kissed him long and deeply, her tongue sliding warmly into his own mouth. Suddenly she said, 'Oh!' and gave a small shudder.

Helplessly she stared down at two small damp patches on the front of her dress. 'I . . . I came. Just a little. And I leaked again,' she confessed. 'This makes me so excited.'

'I'm glad,' Tom replied. 'I hope your nipples stay that sensitive after you've finished giving milk.' He reached out to touch her nipples. They were stiff under the material of her dress. Then he twitched her skirt above her knees, admiring once again the firmness of her thighs under the glossy nylon. 'If you'll stay that way until we reach Heathrow, I'll be excited too,' he said with a smile.

'You really like to see my legs?' Katrina asked.

'And the rest of you,' Tom replied. 'Too bad this isn't the best place for it.' He started the car and pulled out into the stream of traffic. As he did so he caught a sudden movement out of the corner of his eye. When he could spare a glance at Katrina she was struggling with her manacled hands to raise her skirt still higher. Finally she had it up around her hips and her legs were on display from her crotch down to the leg-irons on her ankles.

'It's the least I can do for you,' she said with a smile. She turned in the seat so that her legs were as close to him as she could manage.

Tom shifted into top gear and then rested his hand on her thigh, feeling the warmth of her flesh through the smooth material of her tights. 'Just like being fifteen years old again,' he joked. 'But I never thought of using handcuffs to excite my girl friends.'

In the tunnel they were halted briefly alongside a lorry. There was a loud whistle of the sort every woman loves to hear but some profess to hate. They looked up to see the driver looking down at the display Katrina made.

She smiled at him and he gave her the thumbs-up sign. With a giggle she said to Tom, 'I don't suppose I should give him the same. Do you?'

'I suppose you'd better not.'

The traffic inched forward and eventually they were entering the car park at the terminal. Tom took the ticket from the machine and began to look for a place to park. He found one on the second level and took one final look at her legs. With a sigh he dug the keys out of his pocket.

Katrina noticed the bulge in his trousers. She asked mischievously, 'Is that for me, or were you planning to erect a tent and camp out?' Quickly she shifted in the seat and used both her hands to unzip Tom's trousers. The thumbcuffs made it awkward, but she managed in the end.

When his erection was in full view she bent down and took him into her mouth. Her tongue felt delicious as it circled the head of his cock. She sucked gently at it, tightening her lips around the head as she felt him stir with excitement. With her manacled hands she cupped his balls. Tom felt the thumbcuffs bite into the underside of his cock as she used her thumbs to stroke its base.

Tom gave a sigh of satisfaction as her hands and her busy tongue found the sensitive spots. He reached down to tease her nipples – the only part of her he could reach from his position. At once Katrina jumped, and she clamped down on his cock with her lips.

She moaned in pleasure as he continued to fondle her, and Tom knew they were both going to come soon. He tried to time things so that they both could finish at the same time, but Katrina beat him to the wire. She could manage only a choked-back

'Mmmmmmmnnnnhhh' because her mouth was full of him, but he felt the dampness as her nipples leaked again. She bit down on him as she came. Then he exploded too, and Katrina had to swallow quickly to avoid making a mess of them both.

Afterwards they sank back into the seats to recover. Katrina made a small sound of dismay as she saw the front of her dress, but her smile belied it.

Tom reached once more for the keys and this time he got Katrina unlocked. He zipped up his trousers and got her bag out of the boot. He stowed the handcuffs, leg-irons and thumbcuffs in her overnight bag. Airport security might wonder why she chose to carry such things in her baggage, but there would not be any awkward questions so long as they were not in her cabin baggage. Tom carried her bag to the terminal for her.

Inside, Katrina made a dash for the toilets and emerged looking less like someone who had leaked milk from her breasts as she gave a man a blow job in the front seat of the car, and more like a very attractive woman who had had an unfortunate accident with her coffee. If anyone noticed the faint red marks on her wrists and ankles and at the base of her thumbs, they couldn't connect them with what had actually happened.

When Ari came in a few minutes later Tom saw them off. He didn't ask any questions about the weekend, and Tom was glad for that. He and Katrina could discuss it in their own time. As she went into the departure lounge, Katrina looked back once more and mouthed, 'Remember the address.' Tom nodded and waved goodbye.

Chapter Eight

As it always did, the time during which he was away from Harriet's place dragged by. So it was with a great sense of relief that Tom left work and drove to her house at the appointed time. She let him in with a brief smile of welcome. To Tom she looked preoccupied. He wondered if he had caught her at a bad moment, but she said nothing. She was wearing a housecoat and looked as if she was in the midst of getting dressed for some occasion. If it had been anyone but Harriet, Tom would have said something was worrying her. The Harriet he knew was not the sort to let things get to her. She went out and dealt with them instead. Or defeated them the moment they came to her door.

His leg-irons were already laid out on the coffee table, so he knew he was expected. Without any further instructions he took off his clothes. As usual, Harriet double-locked the manacles when he had put them on.

'Have you eaten yet?' she asked. Tom said he hadn't.

'Good. You go through and fix something while I get dressed for the occasion. We have to have a talk this evening.' Harriet smiled when she said this, making the pronouncement less ominous. She went upstairs as Tom turned away to fix supper.

239

Harriet seemed to have something important in mind, so Tom decided to make something more substantial than the coffee and sandwiches he had been doing. A bottle of wine might not go amiss either, he thought as he selected one and put it into the fridge. Harriet was taking her time, so Tom was able to prepare pasta and salad before he heard her familiar footsteps descending the stairs.

She looked into the kitchen to see how he was doing, and Tom was surprised to see her wearing, not the leather outfit he liked so much, but something altogether softer. Harriet wore a filmy negligee in black (and she had said that men were predictable!) and her hair was carefully brushed so as to frame her face and to take away the severe look she usually had. Yes, something was definitely in the air and it didn't look like another lashing, unless Harriet had deliberately dressed so as to disarm him.

They ate in companionable silence. Tom wondered if this was the evening he would have his a chance with Harriet. It certainly felt that way. Halfway through the meal the door bell sounded. Tom was surprised, but Harriet looked downright annoyed. Clearly she hadn't planned on any interruptions.

Hurriedly she donned her housecoat and went to answer the door, ready to summarily dismiss whoever it was. Tom was surprised when she took her time about returning and when she did, he was even more surprised to see Beth come with her. Beth looked much as he had remembered her, perhaps even more attractive after her protracted absence. She smiled uncertainly at Tom and he found himself recalllng their time together. He hoped Harriet didn't notice his sudden erection.

Harriet looked distinctly less pleased. Nevertheless

240

she offered their visitor a seat and asked her if she was hungry. Beth ignored the strained atmosphere as she sat down in the vacant chair. She declined food but poured herself a glass of wine. She said nothing about Tom's nudity or his leg-irons. Nor did she comment on Harriet's seductive apparel, though she had to be aware that she had interrupted a cozy evening at home for the other two. Compared with them she was vastly overdressed, but she ignored that as well.

Tom had a hundred questions to ask her, and he momentarily forgot Harriet as he asked where she had been. As Beth was framing an adequate reply – she couldn't merely give the name of the last place she had arrived from – Harriet broke in.

'Wherever she's been, she's back now.' There was a strained smile on her face as she delivered this conversation stopper. The air in the room was distinctly chillier, even though Harriet and Beth were supposed to be friends. Harriet was becoming possessive.

Beth spoke into the silence, 'I've come to beg bed and bondage until I get sorted out with a place of my own.' She looked at Tom as she said this, rather than at Harriet. It was a challenge: Tom knew he was being invited to choose between them. It wasn't fair. Beth had gone off with no promises and no commitment. She had left Tom to Harriet, and now she was back and looked like reasserting her claim on him.

Harriet said nothing but she couldn't miss the challenge. Nor did Tom miss the hardening in her expression. He was in a very awkward situation. Beth had been a completely different lover from any he had ever known, but so had Harriet. And he had since discovered that he had a taste for the games she had played with him. He preferred to be the assistant.

241

The freedom from responsibility he had felt when Harriet was in control was more satisfying than the sense of being in charge he felt with Beth. She was the passive one, though she had more experience with B&D than he had.

Harriet broke the impasse by action, as she usually did. She ordered Tom to stand up. He was still erect, though it was impossible to say who the erection was in honour of. But as is the case with women, both would think it was for the other, and be angry with him. She beckoned both of them to follow her to the cellar, with the air of one who plans to settle things in short order.

Tom let Beth go first, then went down behind her. Whatever Harriet had planned to do or say that evening was on hold. Tom was disappointed, but there was no point in trying to restore the cozy atmosphere that had prevailed before Beth's dramatic reappearance. Harriet herself appeared to be at a momentary loss, and Tom guessed that she was going to leave them both downstairs while she decided what to do. He had become accustomed to doing what Harriet told him, and he knew that Beth too was inclined to be submissive. He felt a momentary regret that he had not been more dominant with her, but knew he too preferred the opposite role.

Harriet led him to the cell on the left-hand side of the passageway. When he went inside she locked the door and turned to Beth. She didn't close the spy hole so Tom could see Beth being hustled into the other cell. She didn't seem to be making any protest. And she had begged bed and bondage earlier. She was now getting it. Not long afterwards the lights went out, but Tom could hear Harriet moving about long after that. It was too early for bed and she probably had quite a bit on her mind. Tom certainly had much to think of.

In the morning Tom heard Harriet coming down the stairs. Her footsteps sounded normal, no hesitation, so he guessed she had decided what to do about the awkward situation. Tom didn't think she intended to throw in the towel and let Beth walk away with the prize. Hey! That's me! Tom thought. It might be interesting to be fought over by two women. Pleasing to the ego! But somehow he knew it wouldn't turn out that way. Harriet wasn't the sort to lose a fight and Beth was just submissive enough to let her have her way. She might even leave again for good after Harriet was done with her. Tom felt ambivalent.

Harriet went to Beth's cell first. She was a long time there. So long that Tom was beginning to think she had forgotten him. When she came for him she unlocked his leg-irons. He followed her out into the cellar, where he saw at once the result of Harriet's overnight thoughts. Beth was waiting for them. She was naked apart from a belt of light chain which circled her waist. From that another length of the same chain ran tautly between her legs and joined the waist belt at the back, where they were all secured with a single padlock.

Harriet allowed Tom to look at Beth until he took in the significance of her chains.

'A chastity belt?' he asked, even though he had guessed what Harriet had done.

'With a difference,' Harriet replied. 'The ones they used in the Middle Ages tended to be heavy and cumbersome. Although they might have served their purpose, they must have been very uncomfortable to wear, but the feminists didn't have much influence then. There have been improvements. I might even claim a modest amount of credit for re-inventing the device, but the Patent Office would just get stuffy and refuse to acknowledge the inventions.'

Harriet moved over to where Beth stood and Tom followed. Harriet continued: 'The joy of this little beauty is that it absolutely prevents penetration, something the earlier models didn't always do. It relies on the well-known fact that two objects can't occupy the same space simultaneously.' She thrust her hand between Beth's legs and showed Tom a ring which encircled the chain and slid over its links. 'On the other, or Beth end of this, is a rather large dildo which fills the relevant space. There's another one in the other place and neither one can be taken out without first unlocking the waist belt. There's not enough slack to slip the plugs out unless you have the key – which I will keep safely.'

Harriet motioned for Beth to turn round. She obeyed wordlessly reminding Tom of her earlier behaviour.

Harriet continued her description as if she were introducing the latest fashions at a show. 'It's light and comfortable, even airy. I've been told by others that one can wear it all day without trouble.' It sounded as if Harriet had already made that test – no doubt with one or another of her clients. It was hardly the kind of thing the general public would go in for. 'And it can be worn under clothes in public – which is what Beth will do today when she goes out with me,' she added. 'She will wear it for as long as it takes us to work out a *modus vivendi*, especially when it is necessary to leave you two here alone. You can think about that all day at work. Speaking of which,' she said with a glance at her wristwatch, 'you'd best be on your way. I'll have Beth do the cooking. I'll let you know when I want you to come back.'

Dismissed, Tom went upstairs and got dressed. There would just be time to have a shower and shave at his place before he had to get to work. Good job Harriet was an early riser. He wondered how long his exile would last, and he found himself resenting Beth for coming back just when she had. Harriet, he felt, had been on the verge of taking him more fully into her confidence, and doubtless into her 'old bod', as she described it, the ultimate prize in their game. Now all that was on hold, and he himself was banished to outer darkness for an indefinite period while Harriet dealt with the new ingredient in the relationship. Tom had no doubt that she would deal with Beth, and come to some resolution, Harriet being Harriet. But the shape of the resolution was worrying and he knew he had to have a talk with Beth as well, for his own peace of mind if for nothing else.

Work went as work had gone since he had first met Beth: an interminable period in which he did necessary but savourless things until he could escape into the weekends. Harriet had continued the same pattern. Now Tom wondered if he was spoiled for work. Only the diversions of the weekends had any meaning and now he was cut off even from that until Harriet relented. And Beth was just as inaccessible.

Tom went through the motions successfully enough to fool others and conceal his growing edginess as the days went by and there was no word from either Harriet or Beth. The days of uncertainty passed as slowly as the time had gone when Beth left. Valerie began to show signs of interest. She took to lingering in his office longer than was strictly necessary, or finding an excuse to come and talk to him. Several times she had dropped things, apparently by accident, and in stooping to recover them had allowed more of her undeniably attractive legs to show than was usual among bending women. Once Tom had even been able to tell that she was wearing stockings and suspenders during a particularly deep bend. He had even speculated about the presence, or the absence, of pants as she bent down. It was a pleasant enough fancy, but he had never gone further than that, even in the short but bleak period between the disappearance of Beth and the advent of Harriet.

Even now Valerie seemed undaunted by his lack of response. During the present dry spell he had been granted several glimpses down her cleavage as she bent over his desk to hand him a document, taking, as with the stooping, more time than was called for. She would make someone a compliant girlfriend or wife, if she didn't turn off the taps after the relationship became more stable, as so often happened. Too bad, he thought, that such invitations and opportunities hadn't come to him sooner. Now he was effectively immune to them. Vaccinated against the more conventional liaisons by the stronger medicine of the two women who were even now working out their, and his, future. He didn't think of being faithful to either of them. He knew rather that he had found his niche in their bizarre games, and that nothing less would satisfy.

When the recall finally reached him, it was in the form of a note from Harriet. It said nothing about what may have passed between her and Beth – only that he was to present himself at Harriet's place on the coming Friday after leaving work. It was a typical Harriet touch: she liked the slight air of combined mystery and menace such terse notes engendered, and

246

suggested that it was she (and not Beth) who was giving the orders. Tom had never considered that she would give way to Beth. It had always been up to Harriet to work things out. Apparently she had, and he was now to see what form the resolution had taken.

There was no one at Harriet's when he arrived. Tom was beginning to recognise this as another of her ploys. She was putting him on his honour to do whatever she had told him to do, and not to snoop into things that were not his business, in her absence. Of course her trust was backed up by the threat of her displeasure should he fail to do her bidding but he had to have a talk with Beth, and would have to risk Harriet's wrath to do it. Tom hurried down to the cellar, but it was empty. Quickly he searched the rest of the house, listening for the sound of footsteps outside. There was no one in the house, though he caught the lingering traces of Harriet's perfume as he looked into her room. Disappointed and oddly relieved, Tom went back downstairs into the safe part of the house.

And then he found the note in the kitchen that would have made his furtive movements unnecessary. It was lying next to his chains on the work top. Like the other note which had summoned him here, this one was cryptic – pure Harriet: *Back later. Watch the tape in the video player. It should be interesting.*

She didn't need to tell him what to do with the handcuffs and leg irons. Their proximity to the note made directions unnecessary. Tom went into the front room with the manacles. He switched the TV and video on and took his clothes off. He locked the leg-irons around his ankles and sat down on the settee. With some awkwardness he locked his hands behind his back, then settled back to watch the tape.

As he had expected, it was a home video of the same type he and Harriet had made with Katrina. Only this time Beth was the subject of it. As usual, Harriet took the active role. From the camera angles Tom knew that the camera had not been simply set on a tripod. It was being operated by a third party who never appeared in shot. He wondered who it was but knew he'd never ask Harriet.

She appeared briefly, facing the camera and speaking to the viewer. She wore her number one dominatrix outfit and in the background Beth appeared. She was not in focus, but Tom could see that she was spread-eagled against the wall behind the raised dais at the back of the room. Harriet said, 'Welcome to Harriet country. If one picture is worth a thousand words, I hope you will enjoy the book you're about to see. Sit back, take firm hold of your partner, or yourself if you're flying solo, and explore the ins and outs of B&D.' Tom knew now why she had directed him to put the handcuffs on. Harriet made a sweeping gesture with her arm to indicate Beth, and the camera zoomed in on her. Beth was nude – the approved uniform for erotic bondage – and was doing her impression of a starfish, her wrists and ankles tied to rings set into the brickwork.

The camera traced the rope from Beth's wrist to the ring in the wall, with a close up shot showing the rope biting into the flesh and holding her tautly upright. She smiled apprehensively.

Harriet came into shot, moving towards Beth but with her back to the camera. She inspected the ropes holding Beth against the wall, and the camera followed her. Beth was standing with her weight on her feet, but her arms and legs were stretched tautly apart. Her nipples were erect, stiff with anticipation.

Tom reminded himself that she had always seemed happiest when most helpless. She was breathing shallowly, her breasts rising and falling rapidly. The camera focused on them, then moved down her body until her flat stomach and rounded sex were revealed. Tom had forgotten the difference in the shade of her pubic hair. It was lighter than her more public hair.

Harriet's hand came into view, moving toward Beth's crotch. With her finger she stroked the pubic hair and slid her finger inside the open sex. Beth jumped at the touch, and drew her breath in sharply. The camera zoomed out until Tom could see her face. Beth's eyes were closed and her mouth was open. Clearly she was enjoying Harriet's exploration. Harriet withdrew her finger. It glistened wetly in the bright artificial light. Beth gave a little whimper of dismay and tried to thrust herself back into range.

Harriet withdrew still further but murmured, 'Be patient. I'll be right back.' There was no other sound but Beth's rapid and ragged breathing. In a moment Harriet was back, this time reaching for Beth's heaving breasts. She daubed rouge on the erect nipples, causing Beth to catch her breath sharply again. 'Gilding the lily,' Harriet remarked to no one in particular. Beth moaned softly in pleasure as Harriet began to fondle her breasts, teasing the nipples until they stood out red and swollen. Beth's hips were making slow circles and little thrusts as if she were seeking for something to rub her sex against.

Harriet supplied the something: with her hand she covered Beth's mons veneris and began to massage it gently, up and down and then round and round. Beth strained against the hand, moving as far as the ropes allowed and making small, satisfied sounds. Suddenly Harriet darted a finger into her sex and Beth sighed

249

deeply. With her other hand Harriet continued to tease Beth's nipples. Between the thrusting and the massage and the teasing Beth became gradually more aroused. Before long she was frantic, jerking against the ropes and moaning deeply in her throat, as she came.

When the shudders stopped Beth opened her eyes and looked at Harriet. She smiled languorously, and Tom was reminded of a cat being stroked; the only thing missing was the purr. Harriet paid no attention. She continued her two-handed massage of her victim and Beth looked startled, as if she had expected things to stop. She relaxed quickly then she saw that there was going to be an encore. Her eyes closed and she leaned against Harriet's hands, offering herself again to the pleasure. Tom recognised the moment when his erstwhile lover surrendered again to his Mistress. Her muscles became taut as the next orgasm washed through her. She shuddered and jerked against the ropes, crying out as the spasms took her. When she was done this time her knees sagged and she hung from her wrists.

Harriet moved back and the camera panned over Beth as she sagged in her bonds. Sweat glistened on her body and her long red hair – the first thing that had attracted Tom – lay damply across her half-averted face. Small shudders like the aftershocks of an earthquake rippled through her body. Her rouged nipples softened. The scene faded to dark and Tom sat on the settee at the back end of an erection he couldn't do anything about. He hadn't realised how much the return of Beth had affected him, or maybe it was only the scene he had just witnessed. Or both. In any case, there was a tautness in his belly and the unmistakable approval from slightly further down. Harriet had doubtless foreseen this.

But there was more on the tape. When the TV screen came to life again Tom realised that during much of the time he had been howling in outer darkness, Harriet and Beth had been making this tape. Like the one he and Harriet had made of Katrina, this one had probably been edited. She and Beth were working things out, Harriet would have said, though there didn't seem to be much talk involved, unless the talking was all in the action captured on tape. Harriet had called the tape a book.

Beth was once more tied against the wall. Perhaps she had never been untied as there was no way to tell how much time had passed between the first scene and this one. Tom recalled that Beth had wanted him to leave her tied up over the weekend; maybe this was more of the same. Harriet, however, was dressed differently. In fact not dressed at all unless one counted the leather harness she wore. A rather large dildo stood out in front, and Beth was gazing fixedly at it. As it was aimed in her direction, there was no doubt about who it was intended for. This was another experience for Tom. He had read of women using dildoes on one another, but never thought he'd ever see it.

As she had done earlier, Harriet began by teasing Beth's nipples until they stood out stiffly and she began to breathe rapidly. But instead of going directly on to her open sex, Harriet drew back and out of view. Beth groaned in dismay and Harriet smiled. Evidently she was enjoying the sport. Tom thought back to the case of blue balls to which Harriet had treated him at their first encounter. This was the female equivalent, with Beth in the role of victim. Tom settled back to watch, not that there was much else he could do.

Harriet came back into shot. She carried her riding crop. Tom remembered how he had briefly considered using something similar on Beth but had not done so. It looked as if he was now going to learn what her reaction to pain was. Harriet stood to one side so that Beth was in plain view.

She brought the crop down with a sharp crack across Beth's stomach. Beth's eyes flew wide open and she whuffed in pain and surprise. Harriet struck again, this time with an upward swing that caught the under slopes of Beth's breasts. They bounced wildly and Beth let out a shriek. She was going red in the face and was jerking ineffectually at the ropes that held her. Her fingernails were biting into the flesh of her clenched hands. Harriet struck her again across her belly, perilously close to her spot – as the Victorians had coyly called it. Beth shrieked again and tried to twist away. The dildo Harriet wore was waving about in a most alarming manner as she laid into Beth with the riding crop. Harriet must have lubricated it because the bright lights picked out highlights. The effect was apparent to Tom as a spectator, but was lost on Beth, who had other things on her mind.

Harriet then dropped the crop and resumed her arousal of Beth by more orthodox means. Once more her nipples were teased until they stood up alertly until Beth was getting into the swing of things nicely. First the pleasure, then the pain, then the renewed arousal. It was the same routine Harriet had used on Tom, and he found himself with another erection he couldn't do anything about as he watched the application of the same technique to someone else. Beth seemed to react well to both sorts of stimuli. Tom filed that fact away in case he got another chance with Beth in the future. At the moment he didn't know if Harriet had done all this in order to drive Beth away and so get rid of a problem, or if she was merely putting Beth through her paces so that he would know the full range of her talents. Tom hoped it was the latter, but he'd have to wait and see.

Beth was breathing heavily again as Harriet continued to arouse her. Harriet had reverted to the two-handed approach that had been so successful on the previous occasion. Beth was thrusting herself backwards and forwards as far as the ropes permitted while Harriet's finger moved in and out of her sex. The dildo, which appeared to be made of hard rubber, waggled about suggestively as Harriet worked on Beth. Tom was interested in seeing how she was going to use the instrument in anger, as it were.

Harriet must have reached the same conclusion at that point. She substituted the dildo for the finger she had been using inside Beth. With one hand – the other one was still busy with Beth's tits – she guided the shaft between Beth's thighs and allowed the head to prod her clitoris gently. Beth looked downwards at the unfamiliar touch and her eyes went very wide. It was hard to tell if she was alarmed, or merely eager. Harriet pushed harder and the shaft slid inside. Beth gasped in delight as it went fully home. Harriet now had both hands free to work on Beth's nipples and breasts. This too had a salutary effect on Beth. Not to put too fine a point on it, she was becoming frantic as the hands on her breasts and the dildo inside her did their work.

Harriet began to pump faster, the wet shaft moving in and out between Beth's straining thighs and Tom noticed something else. Harriet herself was gasping and showing all the classic signs of arousal as she worked over Beth. Amongst the in-and-out motions, Tom thought he detected something dark that showed momentarily between Harriet's thighs. Was she using a double-ended dildo – one for you and one for me? Apparently she was. Or she was showing a remarkable degree of rapport with her victim.

The two of them were galloping towards their separate climaxes, Harriet varying the in-and-out motion with a rocking up-and-down motion which must have had the effect of bringing the dildo up against the clitoris (or clitori?) most decisively, if Tom could judge from the increasingly frantic motions and noises the two women were making. Harriet was grinding her own full breasts against Beth's, using her fingers sometimes on herself, and sometimes on the other woman. Harriet abruptly stopped her play with breasts and nipples to put her arms around Beth, between her and the wall to which she was fixed. She tightened her embrace, holding them together breast-to-breast as the orgasms took them together and separately.

At last it was over, and Harriet withdrew, the dark shaft seeming to take an eternity to come all the way out. Beth hung from from her bound wrists, and Harriet sat down on the floor at her feet, the hard black shaft standing up incongruously between her thighs. She made no move to take it off. Like Beth, she was covered in a light sheen of perspiration, and her breathing was rapid. Tom had another sympathetic, and inaccessible, erection which showed no signs of going away. He wondered why he couldn't keep it up so well in straight intercourse – not that he had had much of that lately. Enough of the other sort, though. This time Tom was able to spot the point where the tape had been cut and rejoined. There was a bright flash of light before the screen settled down to show the next scene. Again there was no indication of the passage of time between the different scenes. Apparently Harriet had turned off the time and date functions of the video camera. It might have been the same day, or the next, in the scene Tom saw. In any case, Beth had been taken down and rearranged. Now she was bent over a frame that resembled a bench in that it had four legs. Two of the legs though were shorter than the others, so that with her wrists tied to the bottom of the shorter legs, Beth's bottom was thrust up invitingly into the air. Moreover, her ankles were tied to ringbolts in the floor so that her legs were spread widely and Tom could see her labia and the tight pink flower of her arsehole. She was blindfolded this time.

In the background Harriet was getting into the harness she had worn in the previous scene. It was more obviously now a double one. Tom watched as she slid the dildo into her sex and buckled the straps around her waist. Harriet was not the selfless dominatrix she sometimes purported to be. She obviously intended to get as good as she gave. The size of the thing Harriet was stuffing into herself gave Tom an instant feeling of inadequacy. That would be a hard act to follow – in several senses – if he ever got the chance.

Harriet approached Beth with the riding crop again. This time she was more invitingly presented, and Tom imagined himself in Harriet's place, with Beth helpless under the lash. He wondered again just how strong was his own desire to inflict pain. Beth must have heard her approaching because she turned her head from side to side as if she were trying to guess Harriet's intention by hearing alone. Harriet said nothing as she took up position behind Beth, between her legs and with all the exciting bits well within range. The exposed end of the dildo bobbed interestingly.

With the handle of the crop Harriet stroked and prodded Beth's labia and arsehole. It wasn't long before the instrument began to look wet, evidence of Beth's arousal. Beth herself was moving her hips and bottom as if seeking contact with the instrument. Harriet spread Beth's labia with her fingers and slid the crop slowly inside her sex. Beth sighed softly as she was penetrated. Harriet drew back and allowed the camera to record the sight of Beth with the riding crop thrust up her cunt. The shot was a lingering one, as if the camera, or its operator, more likely, was reluctant to move on.

It was Harriet who broke the tableau and once more Tom thought of bulls in china shops. She pulled the crop out abruptly and reversed it. With a wide swing she brought it down across Beth's bottom. Beth yipped and jumped but the ropes held her. Harriet waited until she was still before striking her again, this time vertically, on the arsehole. Beth shrieked this time and Tom winced in sympathy but didn't take his eyes off the screen. Harriet continued to strike Beth on her bottom, which began to take on a striped appearance. She landed the occasional stroke on Beth's arsehole, for variety's sake. Beth occasionally screamed, but she made no attempt to plead with Harriet to stop until it was becoming clear that she enjoyed what was being done to her.

As she had before, Harriet stopped lashing Beth and used her hands to arouse her, only this time she took the trouble to shove the handle of the riding crop up the Khyber Pass. Beth looked comical with the thing sticking out behind her like a tail, but there was nothing comical about her response to Harriet's sexual foreplay. She was taking it very seriously indeed and enjoying it immensely. The sounds she was making left no doubt about that. Beth shuddered as Harriet's fingers found her clitoris and rubbed it gently.

Harriet must have thought things had gone far enough and she withdrew the crop from its socket and struck Beth across the backs of her thighs. Beth let out a yelp now and again but she did not leap about. Tom guessed that Harriet was merely warming her up as he knew that Harriet could hit quite hard when she wanted to. Abruptly she stopped. She knelt between Beth's legs and grasped the dildo, guiding it into the open cunt. Tom could see the labia being pressed inward; then they suddenly gave way and the rubber cock slid inside. Beth moaned as she felt herself penetrated. Harriet then hunched herself against Beth's bottom and began a steady in-and-out motion. She grasped Beth by the waist to hold her steady.

Beth was thrusting backwards as far as the ropes allowed to meet Harriet's counterthrusts. Both women were breathing heavily and Tom was sure he saw Harriet come. He couldn't see her face clearly but she slowed suddenly and moaned softly and then, after a few moments, she resumed her thrusting. Beth was moaning almost continually, the louder sounds probably signalling her own orgasms. There certainly seemed to be a lot of them.

Harriet drew back and the dildo slipped out of Beth. She made a dismayed sound but could do nothing, tied as she was. Harriet, however, had no intention of stopping there. She grasped the tool, now showing glistening highlights from Beth's own juices, and guided it into Beth's arsehole.

Beth raised her head and shook it violently from side to side. 'No! Not there, please! It hurts!' She jerked convulsively against the ropes on her wrists but couldn't get free.

Harriet paid no attention. She continued to press in, but slowly, letting the lubrication ease the passage. With one hand she reached between their bodies and found Beth's clitoris. Tom thought that perhaps this had a lot to do with the sudden cessation of protests from the underdog. Harriet moved gently, more a round and round motion than in and out, letting Beth get used to the full feeling. Beth's clenched fists relaxed and she stopped straining against the ropes. She began to moan softly again as Harriet continued her arousal. Tom remembered suddenly the time when he had done much the same thing with Beth but it seemed like a long time ago as he watched the two women enjoying each other. Beth let out a guttural sound and collapsed against Harriet. She lay unmoving for what seemed like hours as the camera recorded the scene. They were still locked together as the scene faded to dark.

Tom managed to switch the video off. He sat in the darkening room trying to put his thoughts in order. The tape had shown him how attractive Beth was, and how appealingly submissive she could be, but he had formed a strong attachment to Harriet in her absence. Now it looked as if he was going to have to choose between them and it wouldn't be an easy choice. Beth might not be jealous, but Harriet had shown definite signs of it with Katrina and later with Beth.

There was the sound of a key in the door. Harriet called, 'Tom, are you there?' as she came in.

He replied, 'In here.'

Harriet turned on the lights. She smiled at him as she drew the curtains. 'No reason to let the neighbours see what we're doing here,' she said in her usual brisk voice. She seemed to be her normal self.

Tom was relieved. At the same time he wondered what had become of Beth. Harriet seemed to read his mind.

'I left Beth in a safe place,' Harriet said. 'She'll be along later. But now I'll just slip into something provocative so you'll not be able to think straight. Back in a tick.'

Harriet went upstairs and Tom could hear the sound of running water and of drawers opening and closing. The brisk tattoo of Harriet's steps could be heard as she moved about. Presently she came down. Tom turned to look at her and gave a low whistle of appreciation. She wore the same transparent nightgown she had worn on the previous occasion. Maybe Harriet thought of these as her 'talking' clothes.

Harriet turned on the table lamp, giving the room a soft intimate glow. Tom didn't miss the significance of that. In the soft lighting Harriet looked more desirable than ever. He waited for her to begin.

She did. 'Beth and I have been trying to work out a way for us three to live together without going for one another's throats. Between us we've come to an arrangement, but now you and I have to see if it will work for the three of us. In what follows you can assume that I speak for Beth as well as myself. We want you to stay here with us.'

Tom looked up sharply. Did that mean he wasn't going to have to choose?

Seemingly it did. Harriet went on, 'I think it's a good idea. And I think we can avoid rows if I establish a pecking order from the start. I intend to be in

259

charge in my own house. I will tell you both what to do and when. In other words, I will have two servants – or assistants, if you prefer – instead of just you. If nothing else, that will make for lighter work for you both, and a cosier group for evenings at the fireside. As between me and you two, I'll be the boss. But as between Beth and you, you'll be the one who sets the rules. I can override either of you at any time, of course, but I'll try not to interfere in everyday life below stairs too often.'

Tom thought the arrangement would suit the submissive in Beth, as well as the same streak in him. It might work, if Harriet could manage her jealousy. But there was no way to tell beforehand if she would be able to. And so long as her displeasure didn't extend to throwing one or both of them out, they could probably survive the occasional lashing with the riding crop that would come their way.

But Harriet wasn't finished. 'I will decide who sleeps with whom, and when. And I will sleep with either – or both of you whenever I wish.'

Better and better, thought Tom. He had never been part of a *ménage à trois*, but if the French had taken the trouble to invent the phrase for three in a bed, it must be worth the effort. He found himself nodding in agreement, even before he had thought out the implications.

Harriet noticed, and smiled at him. 'I'm glad you agree. I've grown rather fond of you in the time you've been here. It would be a shame to have to break things off. And,' she continued with a mock serious look, 'getting good servants these days is always a problem. A person needs to hang onto those she's got. I'm sure we can work out the day-to-day routine as we go along. I just wanted to have general agreement on the broad principles. I think that closes the business meeting. I vote we adjourn to the directors' suite upstairs for the business of pleasure. I think I'll make it mutual.'

Harriet led Tom up the stairs. It looked as if school was over. It was now prize-giving day. She led the way to her bedroom, Tom following more slowly in his leg-irons. Harriet turned on the bedside lamp and gestured for Tom to lie down on the bed.

He lay on his side watching Harriet draw the curtains and then brushing out her brown hair. In the lamplight it shone with highlights as she counted out the strokes.

'We girls were taught at school always to brush our hair two hundred strokes every night. It was supposed to be good for us – a wholesome discipline. And I've learned since that it can be good discipline for assistants who have nothing but sweaty sex in mind. It does them good to wait. They didn't tell us girls about that at sohool. One of the many shortcomings of the education system.'

Tom thought of the way she had teased him the first evening he had spent at her house. She seemed fond of the technique, and he was responding to it.

Harriet laid the hairbrush down and picked up a key from the dressing table. With it she unlocked Tom's handcuffs and told him to lie on his back. When he did so she drew his hands up to the headboard and locked the cuffs again, leaving him chained as Beth had done at their first meeting. And as Beth had done, Harriet stood in full view and slowly removed her nightgown. Her sturdy body glowed softly in the subdued lighting as she knelt over Tom with her open mouth poised over his cock. She straddled him so that her sex was in range of his mouth and said, 'We'll begin together on the count of sixty-nine.' She took his cock in her mouth.

Tom strained upward to reach her cunt, and Harriet sighed in satisfaction as his tongue found her clitoris at the first attempt. He was getting some extremely pleasant reports from further down as well. Harriet's tongue, teeth and lips were teasing and hardening his cock as he aroused her. Tom could smell the odour of her sex as she became moist.

Tom heard the door open and close. Beth called up the stairs, 'Harriet? Tom?'

Harriet replied, 'Up here. Come into my bedroom.'

Tom was chagrined. It seemed that Beth had come at just the wrong time again. She seemed to have a talent for it. But Harriet wasn't annoyed by the interruption, in fact she paid no further attention to it. She resumed work on him straight away. She seemed to expect him to continue as well, so he did.

Beth didn't come up immediately. She allowed them time to arouse one another more fully, to the point where it would have been difficult to stop, or it may have been that she was simply going to the loo or taking off her clothes. In any case she was wearing nothing but a smile when she finally did come into the room.

Harriet broke off long enough to tell her, 'You've come just in time. Rearrange his leg irons so he can't move around quite so vigorously.' She returned to the task in hand – and mouth.

Beth studied the tableau for a moment as if making up her mind what to do. Tom glanced at her when she came into view. Beth used the key to unlock one of the irons on his ankles, then Tom felt her spread his legs slightly, and heard her threading the chain through the footboard of the bed. When she refastened the iron on his ankle he found he couldn't move his legs.

Beth came nearer to the head of the bed where he could get a better look at her. Her nipples were erect and crinkly and she was breathing rapidly. In the soft diffused light her skin glowed as Harriet's had. She seemed to have some definite ideas in mind. Or maybe Harriet the Thorough had briefed her. In any case she placed herself so that Harriet's bottom was within easy reach. Tom was busy at the front door, but the back passage was not in use just then. Beth began by massaging the pink rose of Harriet's arsehole. Harriet responded with a little gasp and a renewed zeal in dealing with Tom's cock. When the finger went in Harriet bit down on him sharply.

Tom let out a yip of pain and alarm.

Harriet broke off long enough to say a hurried 'sorry,' then Beth moved her finger in and out slowly. Tom was fascinated by the way the surrounding flesh changed from concave to convex and back again. Harriet seemed to be fascinated by the internal effects, if what she was doing to Tom's cock was any indication. Between times she found time to breathe heavily and groan every so often, and exhibited other signs of enjoying the experience.

Tom began making similar noises. He was approaching the crisis point, driven by Harriet's attention to his cock and the sight of what Beth was doing to Harriet's arsehole.

Just at the right moment Harriet broke off and shifted so that she could kneel astride Tom with her cunt just above his stiff cock. She delayed the penetration until Beth could shift also.

Beth never took her finger from Harriet's arsehole, so there was a slow-motion quality to their movements,

Harriet turning and Beth moving down toward the foot of the bed to stay in touch. It was Beth who guided him into Harriet as she sank down onto the shaft, and Tom could feel her finger moving teasingly inside Harriet through the thin wall that separated her anus and vagina. Presumably Beth could feel his cock in the same way. That mutuality of touch was setting up disturbing currents among the three players.

Harriet placed her hands on Tom's shoulders and began a slow rise and fall, braced on her knees and her arms and centred on the shaft inside her. Her breasts rose and fell rhythmically right before Tom's eyes. He wanted to reach up and touch them, tease her erect nipples and cup her tits in his palms. But the handcuffs held him firm.

As Harriet moved up and down, so Beth moved her finger in and out to the same rhythm. Harriet gave a shudder as she came, tightening her vaginal muscles around Tom's cock. He had to clamp down hard to avoid losing it at the same time. Even more than he had with Beth, Tom felt he wanted to give this self-sufficient woman the best he could, make (or let) her have as many orgasms as he could before he lost control. And he now found himself being helped unexpectedly by the training she had given him in waiting. Maybe that was why she had held back, kept herself out of his reach, until he was ready.

Tom was jerked from the realm of speculation as Harriet shuddered again, more strongly this time. She closed her eyes and groaned softly. Then she resumed her steady up and down movement. Tom glanced down to where his cock disappeared inside her. He could see it sliding in and out as she rose and fell, and he could feel the sliding and the squeezing as she tightened herself around him. And there was Beth's finger, keeping time with both of them.

Harriet seemed to be holding back as well, as if reluctant to surrender to the pleasure that was building up. Or maybe that was how she reached her own peak. Her whole approach seemed to be based on holding back until it was no longer possible to do so. She was breathing rapidly and shallowly now, and there was a faint sheen of perspiration on her body. Now and again a drop of sweat would gather on her nose or her breasts and fall onto Tom as he lay beneath her elastic weight.

Tom shifted his glance from her body to her face just as she opened her eyes wide in surprise. He could feel Harriet bearing down on his cock, and then she came explosively, gasping and shuddering as the waves of pleasure swept over and through her. Her muscles tightened and relaxed, tightened and relaxed and she ground her clitoris against his pubic bone. Tom couldn't hold on any longer. Nor did he want to. It was time for the bed, if not the earth, to move. And it did. Tom could feel himself pulling against the chains that held his hands and feet fast, trying to throw all of himself into the warm tight cave that surrounded him.

When they both subsided, Harriet lowered herself until she was resting on Tom's chest. He could feel the weight of her all along his body. Her breath was loud in his ear as she rested face down on the pillow. Her breasts were crushed beneath her, against his chest. Again he wanted to hold her on top of him as she came down, but his handcuffs prevented him. In the comparative stillness that followed their wild ride he became aware of Beth once more. Her finger was still inside Harriet, and she didn't stop moving it. Tom could feel it against his own cock, and imagined Harriet could feel it just as intensely. But she was not in any condition to respond to it just then.

Beth's moving finger was making Tom hard again. And Harriet was beginning to feel its effects as well. Tom felt her vaginal muscles clench around his cock, and there was an occasional catch to her breathing. He was not averse to another ride like the last one, but Harriet apparently had other ideas.

She raised herself to her hands and knees and glanced down between her thighs to where she was impaled on Tom's cock. With a sigh of regret she slid off him. The air in the room felt cold on his cock after so long in the warmth of her sex. Harriet patted it affectionately as she rose. She said to Beth, 'If you would like to remove that finger from my arsehole, I think we can find a better use for it – and maybe for its sisters.'

Beth withdrew. She didn't resist when Harriet drew her down beside her on the bed. It was a little cramped with Tom occupying the middle, but there was just room enough for Harriet to lie beside him, head to his feet and with her hip fondly touching his. She arranged Beth the opposite way, and the two women fitted themselves to one another so that they could use their mouths to the best effect on each other. Beth straddled Harriet's face and brought her sex down to her mouth. At the same time she lowered her own face between Harriet's open thighs.

Beth's arms were in use supporting her above Harriet, but Harriet's hands were free. She reached out and groped for Tom's cock. When she found it (it wasn't easy to miss), she gave him a firm squeeze and began to fondle his cock and balls as the two women used their mouths on each other. Tom had been thinking he was going to be an idle spectator. He had even begun to feel a bit left out, though he had planned to watch closely what the two women were doing, but with Harriet's hand on him he was brought into their circle. So this was what three people in a bed did. Well, one of the things. If he hadn't been chained hand and foot, he might have taken a more active part, but at least he didn't have to make any decisions. Everything would have to be done to him.

A last observation came to him before he lost interest in everything except what they were doing to one another: Harriet wasn't showing any signs of her previous annoyance.